Mendelssohn is on the Roof

Also by Jiří Weil

Life with a Star

Mendelssohn is on the Roof

JIŘÍ WEIL

Translated from the Czech
MARIE WINN

With a Preface by
PHILIP ROTH

DAUNT BOOKS

This edition first published in 2011 by
Daunt Books
83 Marylebone High Street
London W1U 4QW

1

First published in Great Britain in 1992 by
Flamingo and HarperCollins

Originally published in Czech under the title
Na Strese Je Mendelssohn

A CIP catalogue record for this title is
available from the British Library.

ISBN 978 1 907970 01 6

Typeset by Antony Gray
Printed and bound by
T J International Ltd, Padstow, Cornwall
www.dauntbooks.co.uk

The translator would like to thank Joan Winn for help at every stage of this translation. Acknowledgement is also due to Roslyn Schloss of Farrar, Straus and Giroux, and to Kurt Wehle, Eva Recheigl, Mila Recheigl, and the Reverend Miloslav Baloun.

PREFACE

I first heard Jiří Weil's name in Prague in 1973, where a survivor of a distinguished Jewish literary family told me Weil was one of Czechoslovakia's best writers. When I got back to New York I met a translator who, it turned out, had translated two Weil stories, perhaps the only translations of his work into English. I read them and was stunned, not solely by the horrors they described but by the elemental means that served to communicate Weil's hatred for the Nazis and pity for their victims. They were stories conceived in rage and tears, then told with the matter-of-factness of the journalist and the disarming simplicity of the family anecdotalist. I thought of Isaac Babel. Weil's animating emotions were harsher and less ambiguous than Babel's and, from the evidence of these translations, Weil appeared to have been by nature a colloquial storyteller rather than a relentlessly self-scrutinising stylist of the minimalist persuasion. What he shared with Babel was the ability to write about savagery and pain with a brevity that in itself seems the fiercest commentary that can be made on the worst that life has to offer.

From what I have since learned through various sources about Weil's life and work, there are other resemblances to Babel. The two were born only six years apart, Babel in Odessa in 1894, Weil near Prague in 1900. Both writers were Jews and knew it. Both read Russian and knew Russian literature – in 1928 Weil received his doctorate from Prague's Charles University for a thesis on Gogol and the English novel. Both became literary victims of socialist realism and political victims of Stalinism (and Stalinist anti-Semitism). And each lived through his lonely years as a writer and a man, unpublished, unread, withdrawn and silent – and, by party stricture, unmentionable in literary circles and classrooms.

In the mid-Thirties Weil wrote *From Moscow to the Border*, a polemical novel that partly grew out of what he had observed of Soviet totalitarianism while he was working in Moscow, in the Czech section of the Comintern publishing house, during the early years of the Stalinist terror. A citizen still of the Czech democratic republic, he could not be put to death for his disenchantment, but his comrades' attacks were severe and they were renewed with the post-war publication of *Makana the Father of Miracles*, *The Harpist* and *Life with a Star*. The last was considered by the Communists a 'decadent' example of 'pernicious existentialism'.

In the early Fifties Weil was expelled from the Writers' Union; he had already incurred expulsion from the Party for writing *From Moscow to the Border* (which did not stop him from writing its sequel, *The Wooden Spoon*, a manuscript that remained unpublished for some thirty years before it appeared in 1970 in an Italian translation). In the late Fifties Weil was made director of the Jewish State Museum in Prague – with the thaw, and thanks particularly to the effort of Nobel Prizewinning poet Jaroslav Seifert, he had been readmitted to the Writers' Union – but he is said to have lived a retiring, isolated, unhappy existence until his death from cancer in 1959.

Volume 1 of *The Jews of Czechoslovakia* designates *Life*

with a Star 'the outstanding Czech book published between 1945 and 1948', that is, the brief period of relative freedom between the end of the war and Communist takeover. 'This work,' it continues, 'whose title alludes to the Star of David which the Jews were forced to wear on the street during the Nazi occupation, is the story of the effect of Nazi anti-Semitic measures upon a humble Czech citizen of Prague.' (A similar description might serve to summarise a later Czech novel of some quality, *Mr Theodore Mundstock* by Ladislav Fuks.) When the Nazis entered Prague, Weil pretended to kill himself. Hidden illegally in the city – and believed by the authorities to be dead – he was able to survive the occupation. These harrowing experiences furnished the inspiration and probably much of the story for *Life with a Star*.

His last book, *Mendelssohn is on the Roof*, also deals with Nazis and Jews, and most readers consider it his other major work, after *Life with a Star*. Published posthumously in Czech in 1960, it is reported to have taken Weil fifteen years to write. An SS man has orders to remove the statue of the Jewish composer Mendelssohn from among the statues of musicians that ornament the roof of the Prague Academy of Music. Since he does not know which one is Mendelssohn, he decides to take down the one with the biggest nose. This turns out to be the statue of Wagner. The novel proceeds from there.

PHILIP ROTH

When Zeus heard of the crimes and iniquities mankind had committed, the murders, perjuries, frauds, robberies and acts of incest, he decided to wipe out all forms of life on earth. Explosions destroyed all human habitations, water flooded the countryside, heavy clouds disseminated death. Finally only Deukalion and his wife, Pyrrha, remained on earth. Zeus saved them because they were just. They settled on Mount Parnassus in the land of Phokis. Then the deadly clouds dispersed, the sun came out again, and the skies were blue and shining. Yet Deukalion and Pyrrha wept at being alone in the midst of the wasteland. They built an altar to Themida, the Goddess of Justice, and begged her to teach them how to bring the human generation back to life. For they were old and unable to people the earth. And the Goddess told them to shroud their faces and cast stones behind them. They obeyedthe Goddess. And when a stone fell against the hard ground, a man was born once again.

ONE

ANTONIN BECVAR and Josef Stankovsky were on the roof, walking around the statues. It wasn't a dangerous job – the statues were on a balustrade and the roof was relatively flat. Julius Schlesinger, a Municipal official and a candidate for the SS – not even for the Elite Guard, but just the plain, ordinary SS – was afraid to go out on the roof. Had he had a higher rank, he wouldn't have had to waste time like this here. He might have found more lucrative work with the Gestapo. Still, a job at Municipal was more comfortable. Anyway, how far could he advance as a former locksmith? Unless they sent him to the front, out there in the East, and that would be a bad thing. Until this moment he had been doing pretty well in the Municipal division. But now things were beginning to go wrong.

He didn't want to go out on the roof. Secretly the workmen made fun of him: What a coward! Afraid of climbing up, only shouting orders from the little gate. Of course, you've got to be careful with Germans. They've arrested so many people, or sent them to the Reich for no reason at all, maybe just for not following an order quickly enough.

Schlesinger spoke Czech. He was from Most, where Czech was spoken, and for a time he had worked at the Ringhoffer plant. He had received his commission even before the occupation. He had assumed he'd be better rewarded for his services: why, he'd even had to pretend to be a German Social Democrat in order to get along with the workers. That's how far he was willing to go for the cause. But in spite of everything, they had only made him a Municipal official and a candidate for the SS. It was all because of his name. If only he'd been called Dvorzacek or Nemetschek. That would have been fine. Hundreds of people have names like those and nothing stands in their way. But Schlesinger, and to top it all off, Julius Schlesinger. It sounded like a Jewish name and created doubt everywhere. He always carried his Aryan papers with him, papers going back to his great-great-grandfather and great-great-grandmother. But that seemed a bit suspicious, too, for documents can be falsified. Hadn't he himself been given fake documents by the political boss in Most for the Ringhoffer job?

But nobody could make him go out on the roof. He was afraid of heights and he was afraid of the wrath of God, because as a devout Catholic he had committed a terrible desecration and he knew he shouldn't have done it. Perhaps he could have avoided it. He could have dreamed up some illness. But that probably wouldn't have helped either, for they would have sent him to the front. Possibly to a penal colony. The order for removing the physical remains of the Unknown Soldier had come directly from Frank. Krug had expressly told him so, and Krug had got the order himself from Giesse. So there was nothing left for Schlesinger to do but obey. Besides which, he was a former locksmith. Who was better suited to the task than himself?

This business on the roof was about something else. Here it was a matter of a statue, a Jewish statue. Knocking down a statue of a Jew and, on top of everything, a musical composer, was no sin. A statue can't file a complaint before the heavenly throne. Though who knows the ways of God;

even a statue can bring forth divine retribution; he had once seen an opera about it. But could a statue do it in broad daylight? These are strange times, no rules apply, day can turn into night. For such a grievous sin as his there is no mercy. Who could forgive him the pliers, the screwdrivers, the metal cutters, the hacksaw? There is no absolution for such a sin, except maybe a pilgrimage to Rome, like in the old days, to beg forgiveness directly from the Pope. What would his superiors say to that, that wretch Krug, or fat Dr Buch, who was in cahoots with the Gestapo. Schlesinger had actually been forced to sign a declaration that he'd never reveal anything about it to anybody under penalty of death, not even to his own family. If he were to confess to his priest, the priest might denounce him – after all, the Gestapo had its agents even among priests. But its power didn't extend to the Pope. The question was how to get to the Pope. Maybe he'd find some pretext. Just so he didn't face his judgement before receiving absolution. Then nothing could help him. He'd have to fry in hell for eternity.

The workmen trudged around the balcony listlessly, dragging a thick rope with a noose behind them. There were many statues out here, each one representing a composer. They looked down at the street. Empty. Of course, it's a weekday. Everybody's at work. The universities are closed. Once in a while someone slips into the Museum of Industrial Design. People don't like to walk around here with the SS barracks and the Jewish Bureau nearby. This is the SS zone. What a stupid job this is, walking around on the roof with a rope looking for a statue. Only the Krauts with that efficiency of theirs could think up something like this. And who knows if two people alone can manage such a big statue. Schlesinger doesn't want to bring in more people either. He wants to keep it quiet, so he made the workmen swear secrecy. How stupid, as if people wouldn't notice that a statue is missing. But who can reason with these new bosses. How long do they have to stand around on this stupid roof? Why doesn't Schlesinger come out from behind that gate and tell them what's going on?

'Well, Boss, we're all set, so tell us which statue. Just point to it.' Becvar couldn't stand it any longer.

Schlesinger disliked the word 'boss'. These people didn't even know how to address their superiors. Nobody had ever taught them discipline. Nobody had ever made them go to military drills the way he had had to go. They were just interested in the black market and planting vegetables in their garden plots.

'Walk around the balustrade and look at the plaques until you find the name Mendelssohn. You can read, can't you?' he snapped at them.

'What's that Jew's name?' asked Stankovsky. He held on to his official cap so that it didn't fly away in the wind. He set great store by his cap as a sign of his rank. It had counted for a lot under the Republic. A Municipal worker wasn't any old body, but a city employee, with a pension plan. Except that with those Germans one never knew. Still, a cap was a cap.

'Men-dels-sohn,' Schlesinger said, syllable by syllable.

'Yeah, sure,' said Becvar.

They walked around the balustrade slowly, looking at the pedestals. They knew perfectly well there were no plaques there, but if Schlesinger wanted them to walk around, why shouldn't they oblige him.

'There are no plaques on the pedestals, Boss,' Becvar declared. 'How are we supposed to tell which one is Mendelssohn?'

This was a pretty mess. Nobody had ever told him what the statue of that Jew looked like. And even if they *had* told him, it wouldn't have done any good. The statues all looked alike. He had counted on there being plaques. Such statues usually have plaques. Yet he couldn't and mustn't ask anyone. Probably only the Acting Reich Protector would know what Mendelssohn's statue looked like. Frank wouldn't know, or Giesse, or Krug. Heydrich would know, because he was a musician. But who would dare ask him?

Schlesinger peered out from the gate and looked at the statues, his mind racing. Even if he forced himself to go out on the roof, he wouldn't be able to tell one statue from the other any better than the workmen. They were standing at ease, waiting for his orders. They were probably laughing at him, but they didn't show any signs of it. Their faces were blank, expressionless. They were probably thinking, so what if we have to wait, we're not in any hurry. Meanwhile, he, Schlesinger, had to carry out the order. It came directly from the Acting Reich Protector and he was even more ruthless than Frank. To disobey an order – everybody knew what that meant. Krug had explained it to him that time as they were setting out for the Old Town Square Town Hall: the rules apply just as firmly in the hinterland as they do at the front. The front is everywhere, especially in this country, where their task is to lay down the law for the lowly subjects of the Reich. Military law counts in this country above all. To disobey an order means death. Even if the order is unintelligible.

'Yeah, sure,' said Becvar.

'The rope's not all that strong, it could break on us. We should really test it, but no, everybody's always in such a big hurry,' grumbled Stankovsky. And he wanted to add, 'And now we're wasting time here for no good reason,' but he thought better of it. Schlesinger was steamed up about something. Those Krauts were all crazy. Pretty soon it would be noon. If they didn't get this finished soon they'd miss lunch in the mess hall.

Finally Schlesinger had an idea. 'Go around the statues again and look carefully at their noses. Whichever one has the biggest nose, that's the Jew.'

Schlesinger was taking a course called World View, where they gave lectures on 'racial science' and showed slides. The slides showed a lot of noses, with measurements next to them. Every nose had been carefully measured. It was a very deep and complicated science, but its findings were simple. The upshot was that the biggest noses belonged to the Jews.

The workers walked around the statues. How idiotic to make them look for the statue with the biggest nose. Becvar pulled out a folding wooden ruler he always carried with him. He had studied carpentry before he started working for Municipal. Now he built rabbit hutches after work. He made a good living out of it. People were fighting to get them – rabbits were in fashion.

'Don't be stupid.' Stankovsky shoved him aside. 'We're not going to waste time measuring. Seriously now, we could miss lunch. Come on, we can tell just by looking which one has the biggest nose.'

'Look,' yelled Becvar, 'that one over there with the beret, none of the others has a nose like him. So I'm going to put the rope around his neck, what do you say?'

'Great,' Stankovsky agreed. 'Let's go.'

He began to pull at the rope, and the statue was already beginning to wobble. Schlesinger was peeking out through the gate.

'Jesus Christ! Stop! I'm telling you, stop!'

Becvar and Stankovsky let the rope drop from their hands. That Kraut was carrying on again. Why didn't he look and see for himself which one had the biggest nose? Why didn't he come out from behind that gate?

Schlesinger was sweating with terror. He didn't recognise any of those statues except for this very one. My God, it was Wagner, the greatest German composer: not just an ordinary musician, but one of the greats who had helped build the Third Reich. His portraits and plaster casts hung in every household, and they also lectured about him in those courses.

The workers dropped the rope in confusion. The noose swayed around the neck of Richard Wagner.

Schlesinger thought hard. Then he asked, 'Did that statue really have the biggest nose?'

'You bet, Boss,' said Becvar. 'The other noses were just regular.'

'Pack up your tools,' ordered Schlesinger. 'We're going to the Town Hall.'

Becvar and Stankovsky removed the noose from Wagner's neck and slowly walked to the gate.

Schlesinger didn't look at them. He climbed down the stairs. So the statue had come to deliver judgement on him after all. Not like in the opera, but still, there it was, revenge carried out by a statue. And in broad daylight, what's more.

The time he had committed the mortal sin it had been

night. They had arrived by car at ten o'clock and stopped in front of the Old Town Square Town Hall. There were two Gestapo officers in the car. He had brought the pliers, the screwdriver, the file, the metal cutters, the metal saw. The car drove into the courtyard and they entered the Town Hall by the back door. Krug was waiting for them there. The two Gestapo men were laughing – obviously drunk. But they were relatively quiet about it. They were able to control themselves even when drunk, while he staggered among them with his tools as if he were drunk, too, though he hadn't touched a drop or eaten a bite from the moment Krug had called him in. Krug had told him about the job awaiting him and made him sign the declaration.

They went down into the chapel. The Gestapo men hurried him along, constantly hissing, '*Los*, *los*, *schnell*, *schnell*.' The words seemed automatic. First they took the ribbons off the wreaths. They didn't need him for that, they could manage that themselves. They had boxes all ready. They scowled as they worked and in the dimly illuminated crypt they looked like devils. Yes, devils without names, merely emitting words as if from a phonograph loudspeaker as they stood at his right and left.

And then his work began. He unscrewed the lid of the coffin, stripping the decorations off it and then cutting the coffin up with shears, tearing the metal into several strips. He worked mechanically. Finally he pulled out a wooden crate which held the bones of the Unknown Soldier, and some earth. He carried all that from the crypt to the car. The Gestapo men didn't help him. Krug was waiting for him in the courtyard. He looked at his watch, which had an illuminated dial, the kind they give officers at the front.

He said, 'It's two o'clock. Good, quick work. I'll recommend you for an Iron Cross, second degree. I'll send a report to the mayor, Mr Pfitzner.'

Schlesinger didn't answer, but trudged along with his load. Let them think he was tired. Let them think whatever they wanted. The Gestapo men climbed in the car and sat there without a word. They sat him between them in the back seat and set the load on the front seat next to the driver. Then they drove through the dead, dark city. They crossed the bridge to the other side of the river. Only the river was alive. Only the river was visible in the darkness – you could see its shimmer in the midst of the dark emptiness.

He couldn't figure out where they were going. First he thought they'd go straight to Bredovska, where the Gestapo would receive the remains. But the black limousine was racing along, going somewhere terribly far away. He mumbled prayers under his breath. The Gestapo men were asleep. They crossed yet another bridge. Now Schlesinger recognised where they were – in Rokoska. Could they be taking their cargo all the way to the Reich on the Rumburk Highway? Or might they be going to Panenske Brezany, where Heydrich himself could check the contents of the wooden box? No, they turned off to the left and drove along the Trojsky embankment. The driver was obviously following instructions.

Then the car stopped, right by the river. The Gestapo men woke up and stumbled out of the car along with Schlesinger. The driver pulled a big bag from under his seat. The Gestapo men began to gather stones and quietly gestured to him to do the same. Everything was happening quietly, by the blue light of a few shrouded torches. They stuffed the wooden box, together with the metal and the stones, into the bag. Then they gave it a few swings and heaved it into the water. Only now did one of the Gestapo men speak.

'That's it.'

They dropped him off at the same place they had started from, the Old Town Square, near his apartment in a new house on Dlouha Street. And so ended the night of his mortal sin. Now the ghost was having its revenge. The statue of the Jewish musician was coming to punish him for helping remove the earthly remains of the Unknown Soldier. He had been living in fear from that night on, constantly reminding himself of his terrible crime, the dishonouring and desecration of the dead. But what else could he have done? How could he have got out of it when Krug had threatened him and those two Gestapo men were guarding his every step?

Disobeying an order means death – that's what Krug had said that time. And as long as there was a war on, it still held true, and maybe even after the war.

There was no use tormenting himself with recriminations. Without a word he handed the roof keys to the guard, who didn't ask any questions. He wouldn't have dared.

Schlesinger went out into the street. The workmen didn't dare walk next to him, but glued themselves to his heels, as if they were rejoicing at his bad luck, as if they wanted to wait and see him carried off in the black car to Bredovska.

'What do you want?' he snapped at them.

'Oh, nothing, Boss,' Becvar began mildly. 'We just sort of wanted to go to lunch, if nothing is happening with that statue. We'll be right back after lunch, for sure, just in case something else happens with that statue.'

'Get out!' shouted Schlesinger. 'When I need you I'll find you. At lunch, if need be.'

The workers went into the lunchroom and Schlesinger walked through the door of the Town Hall.

'Yeah, sure,' said Becvar.

'That crazy Kraut, and there's potatoes and gravy again for lunch.' Stankovsky sighed.

Schlesinger didn't even ask if Krug was in his office.

Krug sat at the desk without getting up. He only growled a greeting of sorts. Schlesinger could tell from his face that something was wrong. Krug was sly. Nothing got by him. He knew everything.

'So, has the order been carried out?' Krug asked severely. 'Giesse has already been asking.'

'No,' answered Schlesinger softly.

'What do you mean, no?' Krug screamed. 'Couldn't those two idiots even manage a job like that? I'm going to have their heads. They stuff their bellies here in the Protectorate but they can't knock down an ordinary statue. You should have helped them, Schlesinger, or forced them to do it. This is criminal neglect. There's no other course for you but to work for your Iron Cross at the front.'

Schlesinger stood at attention, shaking. With an effort he stuttered out, 'Those statues have no identifying names. I couldn't tell which one was the Jew.'

Krug barked an obscenity at him. And then he fell silent. They were both silent, Schlesinger with his hands nicely at his hips at attention and Krug at his desk with one leg crossed over the other.

Dear Jesus, dear Mother of God, maybe it won't turn out so badly, since Krug hasn't had him sent away immediately.

He could simply have dialled a number, given the order, and they would have been here in a minute. But Krug is silent. He's in trouble, too. Of course, he's responsible to Giesse, and Giesse to Frank, and Frank to Heydrich, and if the order isn't carried out, Heydrich and Frank will have them all arrested. Well, maybe not Giesse, he'd just get some punishment and stay at liberty, because Heydrich needs Giesse. But Krug would certainly get it. His prewar good deeds won't help him now, or his activities in the Polish campaign.

Finally Krug said mildly, 'The order must be carried out. The General won't stand for any excuses.' (He purposely used Heydrich's military title, to emphasise the meaning of the order.) 'So what do you propose to do now?'

Schlesinger's head was whirling. He had to think up something fast, to gain time. But he couldn't come up with anything. To ask Giesse, the next time he telephoned? That meant admitting that the order hadn't been carried out. And besides, Giesse wouldn't know what the statue looked like anyway. Only Heydrich would know that. In a minute Krug would start screaming again. He was scared, too, and he'd want to save himself at any cost. The telephone was on the table in front of him. In one more minute he'd pick up the receiver.

'I think,' Schlesinger suggested, 'that we should ask for help at the SS barracks. They're near the concert hall. They'll be able to find an expert there. We've got our order directly from the Acting Reich Protector, so they'll have to help us.'

Krug thought it over: Schlesinger was an idiot, but this wasn't such a bad idea. It might be easier to turn to the Gestapo. They had experts on everything there. You could even find musicians. On the other hand, it was always dangerous to get tangled up with the Gestapo. They'd send a report to the Protectorate, and even before the statue went down, Heydrich would hear that Krug had screwed up. And then Krug would never escape punishment, because Heydrich knew no mercy. At the SS, however, they wouldn't make a big deal out of it. They were used to carrying out orders without asking any questions. They wouldn't ask at the Protectorate. It would be enough for them to hear that Krug was a Scharführer and Schlesinger an Anwarter.

'Try it, then,' he said graciously, 'and send me a report.'

The telephone rang. Giesse, thought Schlesinger.

Krug answered. 'Not yet, but definitely today. A small delay, technical problems . . . yes, I understand, an order from the highest level . . . it will be carried out . . . you can rely on me.'

Krug hung up and angrily snapped at Schlesinger, 'Get going, and don't let me see you again until that statue is gone. Do you understand?'

Schlesinger clicked his heels and left with the required salute. Krug didn't bother to respond.

TWO

THE LAST NOTES of the overture to *Don Giovanni* faded away. The hall thundered with applause. It wasn't exactly his kind of music – Mozart was too sweet, too delicate, too restful. But Mozart was connected with Prague, and no other music would do for the opening of the Rudolfinum. Mozart's music had first rung out in this city while it still slept under the chaotic rule of the Austrian Empire. It was sleeping again, this time the sleep of a corpse under the conqueror's heel. But one day it would awaken as a German city, and then a different kind of music would be heard here. Once, in his youth in Halle, he had loved Mozart. Then they played Mozart at home in their household string quartet, and he was assigned second violin. Second fiddle, that would never happen again, he thought with a frown. *Don Giovanni* was also his father's favourite opera. He'd often gone with him to see it as a child. The Commendatore's statue avenged the crime – how ridiculous, how stupid it sounded now, when rivers of blood were flowing: not just the blood of conquered subhumans, but even the best, purest German blood. It remained to be seen, whose blood would flow the most.

The Commendatore's statue wreaking vengeance was only for opera. But Mozart was still German music, even if it was full of Masonry and God knows what else, and this was a German concert hall, after all, where German music would ring out for evermore. Czech politicians would never open their dirty mouths here again. He had accomplished what that cowardly fat puppet Neurath had been too scared to do. The Leader had named Neurath Protector in an effort to gull the outside world. But Neurath had messed things up anyhow. What a lot of filth to get rid of around here – his work was certainly cut out for him. But it had to be done and everybody knew he wouldn't shirk the job. They'd been growing fat as pigs in the muck of this Protectorate. Now he'd teach them to run. But he'd done a good thing with the renovation of the German House of Art. That sort of work had the same value as a sentence of death under martial law. But nobody around here saw that. The Leader would surely understand why this task was his first; the Leader knew the meaning of art in the life of the Reich.

That's what he said to all the people now clapping in the hall as the concert was about to begin. He stood among the musicians at the conductor's podium, feeling strange to be in uniform among people dressed in black tie. They were the only ones in black besides the diplomatic corps, who had been invited purposely to see how the Reich had put an end to the parliament, and to see how the Reich spoke out here in German Prague, not only with artillery, tanks, mine sweepers and aircraft, but also with music, German music. Never again would the works of Jewish composers be heard in this hall. Never again would a Jewish conductor appear at this podium. Race and music, blood and the great German Reich, the Czech and Moravian lands which had returned to it – everything was a holy symbol to endure for the ages.

He also spoke of St Vaclav. He had to mention him because Czechs still lived in this German land. He spoke of the madness of trying to be an independent country – St Vaclav served a useful purpose while a war was going on.

And then he sat down in his seat in the first row, while the audience was still on its feet, hands raised in salute. He sat down heavily at the completion of his difficult performance, because giving speeches tired him out. He didn't like speeches. He preferred the sound of a machine gun. A machine gun was the proper German speech. Every conquered nation understood that sound, from the Pyrenees to Rostov. But he was among his own here and he had to give a speech. He was here representing the Leader and the Reich. He was 'an enemy of all the Reich's enemies', as one of the local newspapers had written. That was a good description.

The orchestra is playing the Prague Symphony. Now he can stretch out his legs comfortably and relax after a tiring day. And he can think about things, make new plans, for he's here only temporarily, after all, until the Leader assigns him another task. He must try hard to carry out his orders here in the shortest possible time – to bring this country to its knees, to terrify its inhabitants so that they become paralysed robots of the Reich, to root out all enemies, to get rid of the Jews. Yes, the Jews, because even that task had been neglected by the indulgent Mr Neurath.

Again he went over the events of the day. He had a bit of time now, while the music was playing. It didn't interfere in any way, though it no longer spoke to him, except to remind him of his childhood.

His day at the castle had begun the usual way. He left by car from Panenske Brezany; he drove past the quiet houses. Now, in the autumn, there was no one to be seen in the streets. This was surely because he had taught the village of Panenske Brezany some discipline: No hanging around in the square. No hens or geese on the streets. No fooling around at fairs or feasts. Quiet after ten o'clock and lights-out until dawn. That's how the village that had the honour of being his residence lived. He would have preferred to have only Germans around, but he couldn't manage that during the war. At least he ordered the farmers to stay in their houses so that he wouldn't have to see their wooden faces or hear their unpleasant voices.

The Mercedes-Benz flew along the highway through the desolate countryside. Not until he neared the city did he pass people on the streets. Even they jumped to the sides of the road as the car with the banners hurtled past them. Even they knew who was driving into the city at this hour. Then, more slowly, the car drove by new villas. Quite a few Czechs still lived there, although some were already flying the flag of his fatherland. The flags rippled in the breeze. They brought him greetings from the Reich. It wouldn't be long before they would line the whole way. But he had to be patient, with a war going on.

As soon as the car drove through the working section of the suburbs, with its shabby little houses and factories, he tightened his mouth and tried not to look out of the window. The air was bad here and it penetrated even the closed windows. Smells of sulphur, smoke and sweat. Right now they needed these subhumans to slave in the factories and breed in their burrows, to provide a greater workforce for the Reich. But some day this, too, would be cleaned out. Great squares would be created here, and tree-lined boulevards. The robots would be herded into reservations behind barbed wire to live in their own dirt under the gaze of guards in towers with machine guns trained on them, to be there for as long as the Reich needed them. And afterwards . . . well, that wouldn't be his concern any longer.

Enough people would be coming back from the wars for that kind of work. He'd have more important tasks assigned him by the Leader.

In town his car no longer attracted attention. Many similar black cars drove through town. But even so, people quickly stepped into doorways and shops, and cars swerved out of his way. They knew that his banner was the symbol of the master of this land.

The car drove into the second courtyard of the castle. He walked briskly up a broad stairway. The officials welcomed him, arms raised in salute as he walked through the office and finally sat down at a long table with several telephones on it. He would have preferred a plainer office, one with bare walls on which would hang only a portrait of the Leader, rather than these tapestries with military and pastoral scenes. But this office had been decorated by its previous owners, who were now begging for help somewhere in London. It seemed to be a legacy that he mustn't give up, because in spite of its annoying tapestries and ridiculous furniture, it, too, had become a symbol of power, now that it had become the property of the conquerors.

There was a purpose to such a luxurious office, he realised today, when Frank brought in a bunch of troglodytes of some sort, devotees of the Reich, dressed in sheepskin coats, embroidered shirts and studded belts. Frank described them as a peasant delegation come to pay tribute to him. They might have been real peasants. On the other hand, Frank might have dressed them up in theatrical costumes. They were sweating in their sheepskins, and a disgusting smell emanated from them. They were confused by the splendour and looked at the naked shepherdesses on the tapestries with horror. It amused him to watch their faces grimacing with fear and amazement. Frank really outdid himself in finding the most thick-headed and dim-witted types.

He spoke to them with the help of an interpreter, because they didn't know German. Frank had taught them the required salutation and they knew how to raise their paws – that was probably all he could expect from them. Frank spoke for them because they weren't able to utter a single word, they were so terrified. He spoke a few words to them, which Frank translated, something about St Vaclav, perhaps the only thing they understood. Then Frank led them away. The office had to be aired out for a long time afterwards. It was quite an agreeable diversion to have cave people suddenly appearing in his office, although it cost him considerable time. Besides, there was the stench to endure. But he was fulfilling his duty as ruler of this land and its protector.

He had already read the newspaper in Panenske Brezany. They brought it to him by motorcycle early in the morning. On the table was a heap of mail that had been sorted by a secretary, and also several envelopes meant for him personally and carefully marked Confidential. He should get started on the sorted mail already initialled and annotated by the secretary, and he should also break the seals and open the confidential dispatches. But first he had to hear from Giesse about his schedule for the day. He pressed a button. Giesse appeared immediately and stood at attention. He ignored Giesse for a long while – an excellent lesson in discipline for secretaries.

Finally he said, 'What work do I have for today? Speak briefly, as if you were giving a military report.'

Giesse blurted out: 'The state secretary's report about

the political and economic situation in the Protectorate, a prearranged conversation with Berlin scheduled for three o'clock, a visit to the military command in connection with the inspection of new weapons manufactured in the Protectorate, a meeting with Reich industrialists who have come to inspect factories that belong to their companies, then a light supper followed by a festive concert. And the poet whose appointment was at ten has been waiting in the reception room for over an hour.'

'What? A poet? Have you lost your mind? Who gave him an appointment? You know how much work I have. I can barely get to the mail by night-time, and you make an appointment for some good-for-nothing poet? Why can't one of the lower officials see him?'

Giesse explained that this was a matter of a prize to be presented by the Protectorate of the Reich on the occasion of the opening of the German House of Art. The Acting Reich Protector himself had suggested that the prize be given not at the celebration but in his own office because it was important to save time under war conditions. The commission had awarded the prize to the poet Mally for his cycle of poems about Prague dedicated to the Leader. The poet was waiting with the rector of the university, two members of the jury, and the state secretary to accept the prize from the hands of the Acting Reich Protector.

'Mally? That's not a German name.'

Giesse answered that the poet came from the Sudetenland, where such names abounded. But the poet had an *Ahnenbrief* proving that he was of pure German origin.

Yes – he grimaced, the Sudetenland, everything was confused up there, a real mess. Czechs had German names and Germans had Czech names. All that would be corrected after the war. But now there was nothing to do but receive the scribbler with the idiotic name.

A uniformed orderly opened the door wide. The secretary, Karl Hermann Frank, in uniform, followed by other men in black suits, walked into the office with slow, grave steps. Heydrich recognised the rector; he had spoken to him once before and his memory was trained for faces. He had called him in that time and told him that the Prague German University, which was supposed to serve this country as a bastion of the Reich, was a regular pigsty. Jews had infiltrated the schools during the Republic. Though the Jews were now gone, their spirit remained. The students only wanted to pursue their studies and evade military exercises. But where was the Reich to find officers? The rector hadn't dared make any objections. He knew well what would happen if he did.

One of the three people standing with the rector had to be the poet. The Acting Reich Protector had learned to read faces in the police service and was pretty sure he could pick out the poet, though it was a little hard, since all three came from the Sudetenland. He would probably be the one with the stupidest face. In any case, Frank took care of everything. He praised the poet, enumerating his achievements as a warrior for the Reich: even as a student he had fought for national rights; during a demonstration against the Jewish rector Steinherz he had pulled off a policeman's helmet, getting beaten up in the process. And during the glorious days before the occupation of the Sudetenland he had fled to the Reich, where he joined the Storm Troopers, in spite of poor health and a heart ailment. Frank spoke about all sorts of things, everything except the content of the poems, though as a bookseller he might have been expected to have read them. But obviously even Frank had no time to read books. In the long run the content of those verses made no difference. The prize had to be given to someone, so it might as well be Mally.

Representing the prize jury, the rector spoke next. He must have actually read some of the Sudetenland scribbler's stuff, because he cited certain verses about a golden city with a hundred towers, about a city whose statues and palaces spoke of its glorious German past, and then verses about the Leader sitting on the seat of Czech kings now belonging to the Reich, whose eagle eyes surveyed the splendour that had returned after thousands of years to the hard but merciful hands of Germany.

He listened to the rector's drivel with half an ear. He wished he could cut him off with an impatient gesture, but one of the duties of the master of the land was to listen to blabbing of this kind. Fortunately, Frank had already tactfully warned the rector to finish his speech quickly. One could count on Frank – a good fellow. Then the rector introduced the poet. He hadn't been mistaken. The poet was the one with the stupidest face. He waved at him to come forward and handed him the envelope with the money and the diploma. Then Heydrich was obliged to say a few words.

'We've been talking about palaces and statues. Yes, statues have always been the faithful shields and sentinels of this German city. The statue of Roland, symbol of the German law that once ruled this country, carries a sword in his hand. We who have come to liberate this city, to reinstate German law and German order, we also hold a sword in our hands, which is a guarantee that no force will ever make us surrender this country. Once it was treacherously snatched away from us, and now we will guard it against all enemies. Wherever we stand, that is Germany. Whatever has been won at the cost of German blood, that will remain in German hands for ever and ever.'

Then Frank escorted the rector, the members of the jury and the poet to the door. The Acting Reich Protector was alone for a few moments. Yes, his words about the statute of Roland and his sword were well said. Too bad he'd wasted his wisdom on nobodies like those Sudetenland bastards. The statue stood above the river with its face turned towards the bridge. The river flowed under the bridge, carrying its waters to the Reich. Formerly the statue had stood alone in the company of twisted and gnarled saints with gaping eyes. Now that tanks and artillery were rumbling over the bridge, now that regiments were marching over it accompanied by the music of fife and drum, the statue was alone no longer, for it was surrounded by all those live beings assigned by Providence to rule in a German land. Didn't Roland's headpiece resemble the steel helmets of the German army that was occupying this city? Didn't the statue hold the coat of arms of the city, its symbol, in its firm hand?

Frank returned and the regular workday began. Frank's report was extensive. Beginning with Protectorate business, he reported on the political situation, on the mood of the inhabitants, on the results of the Red Decrees, which listed those executed. The Acting Reich Protector listened to Frank, but he knew all these things already. They came from various offices and also from the Gestapo. But the Gestapo didn't transmit certain information even to Frank. Only he, the Acting Reich Protector, knew it. Still, on the basis of the information available to him, Frank had given a well organised report. Not a bad job. But nothing new.

And the Jews?

That was his most important task. What Frank didn't know was that he, Reinhard Heydrich, had been commissioned by the Leader himself to oversee the liquidation of the Jewish inhabitants of the entire Reich and subject nations. Even Frank did not know that every office for Jewish Affairs in all of Europe reported directly to him, Reinhard Heydrich. And he also knew nothing about the conference at which the guidelines for the annihilation of the Jews were established, at which deadlines were set and plans made for the construction of gas chambers and crematoria. There was time enough for Frank to find out about it. First he assigned him the task of locating a Czech town where a temporary ghetto could be established. The establishment of a ghetto was also one of the results of the conference. It was to be a trap, a pit. At the same time it would camouflage what was happening from neutral nations.

'Terezin,' said Frank.

Yes, he had seen that town. A sleepy barracks town in the lovely countryside on the very border of the Reich. The inhabitants were Czech, while the German Army lived in the barracks. The Small Fortress contained the auxiliary prison of the Gestapo. All in all, a good neighbourhood, with fortress walls that were easy to guard. It was quite small, but even that was convenient, since it would only be a stop on the way to the 'final solution'. An excellent expression, 'final solution'. A good choice had been made. But it was not necessary to praise Frank. The town had been selected by someone from the Security Police and not by Frank.

'Good. Therefore, it will be possible to begin the transports in the immediate future.'

'Yes.' Frank clicked his heels.

After Frank's departure, he had to move on to the daily schedule Giesse had set up for him – a long, hard workday. Only now, during Mozart's music, could he take a little rest. The music was soothing and relaxing, but still his day was not over. Another tiresome duty awaited him after the concert, a reception for the diplomatic corps at the Cerninsky Palace. He wouldn't make it to Brezany tonight.

The concert ended to thunderous applause, the first concert of German music at the newly restored German House of Art. An orderly was guarding his black limousine at the side entrance, and the chauffeur was already seated at the wheel. But Heydrich had to wait for Giesse, who had remained in the hall to discuss the details of the reception and who'd surely appear in a minute. In the meantime, he could breathe the fresh night air. The sky was clear on this autumn evening and the white light of the moon, the only light in the darkened city, drenched the building, sliding along the statues on the balustrade. They reminded him of the statues at the Leipzig opera, which he had often visited with his father on trips from Halle. Giesse was just coming out of the side door, and he stood at attention before him in order to give his report. Heydrich was still carefully examining the balustrade. Suddenly his face twisted with fury and hatred. What? This was unbelievable! How could he have given a speech in a building with a statue of that disgusting composer on its roof? What a disgrace, how humiliating! Why hadn't someone thought of checking the building before it was dedicated to German art?

'Giesse,' he barked, and pointed at the balustrade. 'See to it that that statue is torn down immediately. Call the Municipal Division this very moment. Somebody must still be on duty there. This is unacceptable. This is outrageous. This is worse than treason – it's incompetence. Mendelssohn is on the roof!'

THREE

THEY LAY in the high grass beside the flowing river, Jan Krulis under the boat and Rudolf Vorlitzer in a sleeping bag. They were tired and silent; they didn't feel like talking after the long trip. Their hands had got used to paddling, to sinking oars into the water – now the absence of movement and the very peace and quiet seemed strange. After supper they rested in the grass on the narrow strip of shore. Though the forest began just behind them, they had no interest in it, except perhaps as a source of the twigs they now gathered to lie on. Their connection was with the river, the river that flowed and flowed around them, that whispered and murmured endlessly, that spilled over the rocks forever.

He lay on a hospital bed in a large room. There was so much pain and suffering all around him that it seemed to rise to the very ceiling of the old building. The disease had struck several years ago and the paralysis was progressive. A slate at the head of the bed bore the name Rudolf Vorlitzer, born March 6, 1904. A clinical chart hung at the foot. But he didn't try to study his chart – he couldn't even stretch his hand towards it. He couldn't make the smallest movement, as all his limbs were dead, petrified. He had an unusual disease, a curious and rare one: all his limbs and organs were gradually turning to stone. Nobody knew how to treat his disease. They brought various foreign visitors to his bedside, professors with famous names, not to help him, because there was no help for him, but to examine a rare case, a unique case. The doctors valued such rare cases in their hospital, and even he shared this pride with his colleagues. His brain was not yet petrified. It functioned, it could think, it could recall the past. His brain hadn't turned to stone and he still had a voice, because the disease had not yet reached his vocal cords. He could still breathe, because his lungs were still working and his heart was still beating. But everything else had turned to stone.

They walked on to the brightly lit terrace of the dance hall, still wearing their sweatsuits. The lights were blazing, the music blaring. They sat down at an outdoor table and ordered black coffee, and its taste overpowered their palates after the awful stuff they'd been guzzling at the river cafés. As they watched the dancing couples whirling around on the concrete circle, they were still on the river, the river was still flowing. Clouds moved above them, the sun stood at a single spot, the waves sparkled over the rapids, the water rumbled at the floodgates. Even the outdoor lights didn't stand in one place; they swayed and circled as if they were dancing on the concrete circle. Finally a sweet fatigue made itself felt through their drunken words, as, their heads bent backward, they looked into the lights falling on the dancers.

The heavy stone weighed down on him. He couldn't make the smallest movement with his hand; nothing in this paralysed body listened to his head. He knew he was sentenced to death. He was a doctor, after all, and he understood all the Latin phrases used by the visiting doctors as they consulted over his bed. They came from far and wide. Some spoke in foreign languages, but even they used the same phrases. He also had ordinary visitors on days they were permitted, but naturally their numbers decreased as times grew worse. All his visitors looked worried, because outside very bad things were happening. But they didn't talk about these things. Rather, they passed along gossip about various acquaintances, and also jokes, which they whispered because these were forbidden jokes. They didn't have to tell him the news; it made the rounds of the hospital in any case. It went from bed to bed and nobody could avoid hearing it. Even as he lay here deprived of movement, knowing he would never leave the sickroom on his own feet, yet he could not avoid the world beyond the doors of the room and beyond the gates of the hospital.

They were paddling in a storm that day. The rain was pouring off their oilskins, filling up the bottom of their boat, coming down in sheets. It was impossible to land; they could only paddle straight ahead. They couldn't even make out the shore, it was so black on the river, only, every so often, the lightning lit up the sky. And not a river café for miles. All they could do was listen to the river and follow its current. Their hands were frozen and their oil-skins soaked through. They took turns bailing. They were alone in the middle of the river, surrounded by darkness. Then, suddenly, the bright lights of a house appeared on the shore. It was the Mandat.

He knew he would die. He was reconciled to it. He had seen so many people die and helped so many people at the hour of death that it held no terror for him. He also knew that he would have been dead long ago had he not been a rare case to show off to visiting doctors. He received a great deal of attention, but he knew the attention wasn't for him, the living person, but only for the case, the rare case that had to be kept alive as long as possible so that it could be studied. His body would end up on the dissecting table, and that was good; he'd serve science even after his death; only science was certain and reliable in this mad world, where some of his friends envied him because he could die in a hospital while they were terrified of dying a violent death.

It's possible to reconcile oneself to death. But even his illness doesn't protect him from what is happening outside. Even the stone can't free him of responsibility. His responsibility is Adela and Greta, his sister's children. They are alone in the world because they've lost both their parents. Now they are tossed about like balls; they stay in this place for a few days, then in that place a few days, living from day to day, always in hiding. He can still help them a little, for he hasn't completely turned to stone. But what will happen to them afterwards? He'll never know the answer.

First they had to pull the boat on to the shore. Then they had to remove the boat bags, turn the boat over so the water could pour out, and place it on the trestle. It was hard and laborious work because they were tired from all their paddling. Their feet were sliding on the muddy ground. But they had to take care of the boat first, before they could settle down in the warm restaurant. They dragged their bags through the hallway, water dripping from them, leaving puddles on the floor. They hung their oilskins in the hall and stood the paddles beside them. Only then did they enter the dining room, fall into chairs and stretch their legs out comfortably. They felt good as they sat at the cloth-covered table and looked forward to warm food and black coffee. Meanwhile, the rain kept falling on the windowpanes. When they had finished eating, they began to doze off. But they forced themselves to stay awake and keep looking out of the window, waiting for the storm to blow over so they could continue their trip. It would soon be mid-morning, and they had a long way to go. Besides, they preferred not to stay at the Mandat because they were running out of money. They'd sleep in a haystack somewhere. Setting up a tent in this sort of weather was out of the question.

He couldn't read, but not because his eyes didn't function. His eyes fulfilled their duties well. They saw everything – the high windows, the white plastered ceiling, the faces of the visitors and doctors. But his hands refused to hold a book and turn the pages. Once in a while his roommate would read to him. Sometimes it was a book that he wouldn't have wanted to read in his former life. Now he was grateful for every word, even of a bad book. His neighbours kept changing. Some were discharged, some died, some were delirious with fever. There was nothing left for him but to look at the ceiling and count the hours and days. They dragged behind him like a chain, all the hours and days, all the years since that long-ago moment when this strange disease had struck, when his legs had buckled and his arms had stopped obeying him. For some time afterwards he remained 'dear colleague', but after a while no one remembered he was a doctor. He had become a rare case and he lived like one. In the end it didn't make any difference, because he had long since ceased to be a living person. And when the bed next to his was empty, or when the patient lying there was unconscious, then there was nothing for him to do but bring up memories, take stock of his life, judge it, assess its fairness, and vainly search for blame. It was hard to figure out why he, of all people, had been struck by this disease that was turning him into a living statue.

They slept in the hayloft. They clambered up the ladder and there they were, high above the river. They slept well, although the dust from the hay got into their nostrils and made them cough. They woke up the next day intoxicated by the scent of hay. The river was already full of sun. They washed and swam in the river and cooked their breakfast on an alcohol burner – it wasn't worth it to make a real fire. They ground the coffee beans in a little mill, tossed some bacon, which Jan sliced on a flat rock, in a pan, some eggs on the frying bacon. They brought out a chunk of bread which hadn't soaked through in the boat bag. They ate heartily that morning, and then rested on the bank for awhile, talking about everything under the sun. They'd have to be careful going through the rapids. They'd have to really knuckle down at the Vranska dam. But once that was behind them they could take it easy.

If the heart stops, if it ceases to beat, if it turns to stone, then all movement ceases. The heart will probably be the last to go, it will probably continue to beat quietly for a while even after the lungs have turned to stone and he has stopped breathing. He'll never see Adela and Greta again. He had promised his sister that he'd take care of them if anything happened to her and Richard. But now he can't keep his promise. He had begged Jan, his last remaining friend, to look after them, though he knew that Jan was working for an underground group and was in constant danger.

Afterwards they floated along slowly on their approach to Prague. It was twilight, and lights were twinkling on the river surface. They found themselves in a caravan of boats, all returning home to boathouses along the river edge. Some were wreathed with flowers and branches, to show they had come from far away. In others people were singing to the accompaniment of a guitar. Flowers and music were floating along the river, as they neared the city. Dance music dropped down from the circle of lights at Barrandov. They lay at the bottom of the boat and rested, letting the current carry them now that there was no need to hurry. Every once in a while, they dipped a paddle in the water just to steer the boat in the right direction or to avoid a steamboat. They bobbed a bit on the water, but they never came really close to one as many others did to show off their bravery. They began to paddle only when they saw the lights. They landed at the little bridge and carried the boat up on shore. They stowed their sweatsuits, sneakers, oilskins and boat bags in a locker, changed into summer clothes, sat down at a table on the veranda, drank milk, and watched the boats landing at the little bridge at the end of their long or short journeys. And then they left, slowly closing the club gates behind them.

Jan Krulis came in, sat on the edge of the bed, leaned towards him, and whispered the news. It was bad news, even worse than the stories making the rounds of the hospital. Transports were leaving for the fortress town, and continuing from there to the East. People were allowed to take up to fifty kilograms of belongings. They were herded into the Radio Mart, where they were picked clean before being crammed into trains and taken away. Numbers were hung around their necks and their apartments and furniture were confiscated.

It didn't depress him to hear this news, though it was dismal. He was able to listen to it because he had settled his accounts with life long ago. He had only one remaining responsibility and it weighed heavily on him all the while his body was turning to stone: Adela and Greta. Jan told him that they were living with friends, that they weren't registered anywhere, that they could never go out. Jan managed to get food for them and went to visit them occasionally late at night. They were being brave – no need to worry about them. He smiled at this, because his face hadn't turned to stone yet. Even his eyes smiled. He was glad that Jan had taken on his responsibility. At the same time, he was sorry that he had to ask him to do it. But he had no alternative.

They strolled about the town square on that summer Sunday evening, taking it all in – music floating from the open cafe windows, reflections of neon lights bathing the cobblestones, newsboys shouting out the headlines, aromas of various dishes from the snack bars wafting over the entire street. They walked slowly, looking quite like other passers-by, but their hands were still throbbing, they could still feel the river flowing through their limbs. They stopped at the lighted shop windows and looked at the displays. After their week on the river, with its floodgates and rapids, its bluffs and sandy banks, its mills, villages and river cafes, everything looked new and strange. Though they weren't hungry they deeply inhaled the delicious food smells. They gazed at the colourful hoardings as if wanting to throw themselves into this different river and float along it forever. They listened to its din rushing through the square from one end to the other, they listened to the laughter, the shouts and the soft whispers. A thousand footsteps accompanied them, a thousand lights assailed their eyes, and the music from the various cafes crisscrossed the squares and streets. They were home at the end of a long journey and for now they were carefree. They parted at the trolley stop.

After Jan left the hospital room, only the ceiling remained, and he gazed at it, trying to concentrate. There was no one to go to for advice. He was helpless. What was happening in the outside world seemed foreign to him, inimical, distant. Even if he had been healthy he wouldn't have known what to do – perhaps try for a personal deferment from the transports. He had to take care of Adela and Greta, after all. But this was all nonsense. Better to suppress such thoughts and find peace before his final days set in, before the stream came to a final stop.

A doctor bent over his bed. 'We must move you out of here, Doctor. Yes, we must, we received orders.'

They hadn't called him 'Doctor' for a long time. Things must really be bad.

FOUR

THE FLAG of the SS Elite Guard fluttered in the wind. The building, formerly the Law School, had been part of the Czech University. As a barracks it had its advantages and disadvantages. The main advantage was central heating. The disadvantage was being located so near the Jewish quarter. It wasn't pleasant to look at Jews. The barracks guards had had enough trouble with them in Poland during the mobilisation, and now they had to deal with them again in Prague. Barracks duty rotated – a tour of duty in the Protectorate was a reward for a tour of duty in the field. Here they could rest and fatten up, here they could bask in the warmth before setting off once again for the Russian freezing cold.

The job was easy, although discipline had to be maintained. The Protectorate had been turned into a non-combat zone. There were no air-raid sirens blaring there. Troop reviews were the most taxing duties.

The telephone rang at the command headquarters. It was Krug, calling from the Municipal Division. Rottenführer Schulze II was on telephone duty. Krug introduced himself as a Scharführer, but that made no impact on the man who answered. Outside the Elite Guard such ranks were bureaucratic, not earned in the field. Just being an SS member was no guarantee of anything. Krug explained that he had an order from the Acting Reich Protector, and that it had to do with some sort of statue. Schulze II was surprised that they'd bother the SS Elite Guard with such a trivial matter. But if Heydrich wanted it done, then it had to be done. But it wouldn't be necessary to disturb the commander about it, Untersturmführer Wancke would do. Schulze II would inform him of the matter, and the gentlemen could visit him at his office.

Krug had been very reluctant to turn to the Elite Guard for help. They'd surely scorn him as a civilian, even if he wore his uniform with the badge from the Polish campaign. He certainly couldn't send Schlesinger alone, they'd throw him out in a flash. Krug ordered a car, though it wasn't far from the New Town Hall to the barracks, because the barracks officers would assume the two of them were mere petitioners if they arrived on foot and then their reception would be even worse. Of course, someone, possibly Dr Buch, might accuse him of wasting valuable petrol at a time when the Reich needed every drop at the front. It was an official car and the driver had to keep a list of every trip. But Krug preferred risking such accusations to going on foot with that idiot Schlesinger. It was an official visit, after all, a matter of an order that had to be carried out quickly.

He settled down in his car, and only then did he have Schlesinger summoned. Let him get a little exercise. Krug had to laugh to see him come running out of the door, all out of breath. Schlesinger was also wearing a uniform. They drove quickly to the barracks without having to avoid any cars. The streets were completely empty and the driver paid absolutely no attention to traffic signals.

They were interrogated by the guard at the entrance for a long time before being admitted to the command headquarters. Everything here was run according to strict military rules.

Untersturmführer Wancke was having a boring day receiving telephone reports and keeping the daily record.

Suddenly his orderly Rottenführer Schulze II burst into the office. Upon giving the proper salute he announced the arrival of two officials from the Municipal Division. What the hell did they think they were doing at the Elite Guard headquarters? Schulze II was going on and on about some Jewish statue and some order from the Acting Reich Protector. He was obviously all mixed up. Schulze II was a former farm boy and didn't even know how to make a decent telephone call. On the other hand, when it came to drill he was always in his place. He was such a good marksman you'd think he'd been in a circus. But that kind of amusement wouldn't do now. Shooting, women, drinking and petty thievery were only for those in the East. Here it was strictly forbidden. The Czech and Moravian Protectorate was part of the Reich. The Reich laws all applied here. There was time enough for fooling around at the front. Once Frank told them that a time might come when their services would be necessary for taking measures against the traitorous Czechs. But that would probably never happen. They had quite a comfortable life in this Protectorate, but it was boring. Wancke would have a bit of fun with these Protectorate loafers. He'd show them what a front-line soldier was made of.

Krug greeted Wancke ceremoniously, right arm outstretched, loudly pronouncing the required greeting. Lamely Schlesinger tried to imitate him. But he didn't dare go too far. He didn't feel sure of himself in the SS barracks. Wancke responded to the greeting in a lackadaisical manner, and inspected his visitors. They looked pretty well fed. It wouldn't harm them to get a little exercise on the front and enjoy the nice Eastern frosts. Krug tried using *Kamerad*, but Wancke cut him off angrily.

'I'm SS Untersturmführer to you.' Obviously Krug's uniform did him no good at all.

He broached the subject of his visit cautiously. They had received an order in the name of the Acting Reich Protector to remove a statue of the Jewish composer Mendelssohn from the balustrade of the Rudolfinum.

'Don't know. Never heard of him,' said Wancke.

'Yes, but the Acting Reich Protector does know this statue and demands that it be removed immediately. He sent SS candidate Schlesinger there with two Czech helpers. But they couldn't find the statue because there are no inscriptions on any of them. They decided to look for help at the SS barracks.'

'I don't understand what you actually want from us. We're not in charge of pursuing Jews here in the Protectorate. There are other bureaus for that, the Gestapo on Bredovska Street and the Security Police in Stresovice. You should try them.'

Krug explained: he couldn't try the Security Police because he wasn't even authorised to speak to them. That was a secret bureau with direct lines to Berlin. And the Gestapo was a little out of the way. He needed help immediately. Giesse from the Reich Protector's office kept calling every minute to see if the statue had been torn down. If the Untersturmführer would be so kind, they could carry out the order immediately.

'What's that? The nerve!' screamed Wancke. 'Are you suggesting that the Elite Guard is here for the purpose of finding the statue of some Jew or other? You can take that job and shove it . . . '

'Oh no,' continued Krug meekly, 'it would be enough for the Untersturmführer to send someone to the Jewish

Community to drag out some learned Jew or other. Then they could take him to the roof and have him identify the statue.'

'Well now,' said Wancke thoughtfully, 'you fellows at Municipal live like pigs in clover. Tit for tat, gentlemen. How about some cigarettes, whisky and chocolate? But it better be first-rate. No imitations.'

Krug began to waffle. He was only a lower official. He lived on rations just like anyone else. If he made a tremendous effort he might scout up something, maybe whisky.

'No excuses,' Wancke interrupted him. 'Either we get what we want or nothing doing. Nothing's free except death. And even that's not always true, because cartridges cost money.'

Finally Krug gave up. There was no sense haggling with Wancke. These people were used to giving orders.

'I'll get you some, Herr Untersturmführer.'

'You'd better,' said Wancke.

Each of them was busy thinking. Krug was planning to wring it all out of Schlesinger, even if that fellow had to give up his pay for the month. The whole thing was his fault, and he should be grateful to him, Krug, for begging at the SS for him. Schlesinger would pay for this humiliating experience.

Wancke decided to send Schulze II. He was an idiot, but he had brains enough to go to the Community to get a Jew. The main thing was that he wouldn't ask any questions and so there'd be no need to share anything with him. At most he'd give him a glass of whisky. Actually, there was very little risk connected with this sort of thing. Of course, the Stresovice people might make trouble. This actually fell under their jurisdiction, because the Jews and their property belonged to them and they didn't intend to share them with anyone. The Security Police wouldn't make trouble. They wouldn't care in the least if he briefly borrowed one of their Jews. Just a small friendly favour – when it was over he'd mention it to the head.

'Very well' – Wancke ended the conversation – 'I'll send Rottenführer Schulze II to do it. He'll bring you your Jew. You'll take him to the roof and then you can let him go. He can get back himself without an escort.'

He called Schulze II in from the adjacent room.

'Go to the Jewish Community. You know, to the main building in Josefovska Street. Tell them to give you a learned Jew and then bring him back here to the barracks. But step on it, step on it . . . '

Schulze II clicked his heels and went out quickly.

People were standing around outside the main building of the Jewish Community on Josefovska Street. They huddled in little knots, whispering together in confusion. There were many little knots going all the way to the Jewish Town Hall. The knots unravelled and then formed again. People ran around from person to person, from someone who thought he knew some bit of alarming news to another who thought he knew some bit of comforting news. Thus they alternated between hope and despair, passing along news to one another. The news travelled back and forth, and sometimes good news collided with terrible news.

Transports.

An ordinary word, one usually associated with furniture moving. But now it had a different meaning. The news, premature disclosure of which had occasioned the shooting of two people, had become a reality. It circulated among the little knots of people. It expanded, and then contracted. 'It won't be so bad, after all. We'll all be together in a work camp.' And then it grabbed the throat and clutched the heart like tidings of death and destruction.

The little knots disintegrated when Rottenführer Schulze II appeared. People ran off in all directions to avoid coming into his view. Here a uniform meant a herald of death.

Schulze II marched along the street as if it were completely empty. He looked neither to the right nor to the left and headed straight for the door. But the whole building knew he was coming; they had seen him from the windows. The whole complex bureaucratic machinery suddenly came to a standstill. The rooms were overflowing with clerks. Before his arrival they had all been furiously working, writing things down, crossing things out, pulling out file folders and then putting them back again, making in-house telephone calls, running from one floor to another. On the top floor they ran across to the adjoining building along a passageway, where other people just as hard-working and just as meticulous sat in offices and did the same unnecessary, mindless work.

Richard Reisinger was on duty at the guardhouse. Formerly only the old and infirm had been appointed to guard duty. It wasn't very taxing to look out of the little window, answer questions, take in the mail, lock up the building and give out the keys. But it turned out to be a painful and difficult job. For the guard was the first person that the new masters, uniformed or not, met up with. He had to endure their slaps and hits, whiplashes, kicks and insults. Because those coming into the building uninvited and unannounced first had to show their power. They had to create fear at the very start, right at the door, so that it would circulate through the whole building, so that everyone sitting in the offices giving out orders, sorting the mail, dictating notes, copying facts on to file cards, would recognise that a representative of power was arriving, one who could make decisions affecting life and death. If such visitors were to encounter an old and infirm person at the guardhouse, it would not be gratifying enough to beat him up – he'd pass out right away. And then they'd get even more enraged. They might actually burst into someone's office to continue their amusement – that was the dangerous possibility. That's why strong people now sat at the guardhouse.

Before he was assigned guard duty, Richard Reisinger had worked on the highway, then in a quarry, and finally as a furniture mover at the Collection Agency. His work at the guardhouse was the worst job he'd ever had. He had liked highway work because he enjoyed being out in the fresh air. The work at the quarry had been hard at first, but once he got used to it, he liked it even better than the highway job, because he worked there with the other quarry workers as an equal, and the quarry workers laughed at all the business with the stars. Working as a furniture mover, one could always swipe a bit of this or that if one looked into a drawer or a pantry . . . Besides which, he received extra tips for heavy labour.

Being a guard, however, meant hearing pleas, cries and sobs every day, because who else were people to complain to as they entered the building? It also meant having to listen to the insults and curses of the Elders, because these were nervous and terrified people who spent their entire days in fear. At least they could vent their anger and powerlessness on the guard.

He had grown used to almost everything by now except the foreign visitors. Beating up people was just a regular thing with them. It could also happen that one of them might have him arrested for no good reason, just for fun. It wouldn't be hard to think up an excuse.

Before the war he'd inherited a little hardware shop on the outskirts of town. It stocked a bit of everything, so people wouldn't have to run into town and buy in the chain stores. He used to sit squeezed between a tub and a balance scale because there was little room in the shop. Nor were there many customers. It was in a sort of half-commercial, half-agricultural suburb. He sold scythes and shovels, and also curtain rods. He led a quiet life on the outskirts of town and got along well with people. His only entertainment was boxing at the workers' club. And now he was sitting in this guardhouse, this wailing wall and entryway to hell. Beasts of prey lurked all around and he could never figure out when they might take it into their heads to organise some amusement at his expense.

Schulze II was in a hurry. Not only because the order came from Wancke, but mainly because he hated this kind of job. There was peace and quiet in the office. Now they wanted him to bring a Jew, but that was demeaning for a member of a military unit. If Wancke had told him to liquidate a Jew, that would have been all right. Too bad conditions were different here in the Protectorate than in the East.

'I need a learned Jew. Call up and get me one here immediately. Or else . . . ' he screamed at Reisinger.

It was clear to Reisinger what that 'or else' signified. If only he could figure out what the SS man meant by the words 'learned Jew'! SS men never said anything properly.

They only barked out orders and expected him to carry them out immediately. The fellow might not even know himself what he wanted but might have simply got an order from his superiors. The trouble was that Schulze II didn't feel like waiting for Reisinger to figure out whom to call. Schulze II started to hit him with his gloved hand. Then, when Reisinger still didn't answer, he struck him in the teeth with his fist and knocked out an incisor. The blood ran down Reisinger's chin. Suddenly it occurred to him that he could get rid of the SS man by sending him to another building. He couldn't think of anything better to do at that moment. He just wanted to get rid of him so he wouldn't beat him to a pulp.

He stammered: 'The Town Hall. Montova Street. That's where the learned Jews are.'

The Elders of the Community, who answered directly to Stresovice, had their headquarters at the Town Hall. That was where orders for all the official activities of the Jewish Community came from. That's where the people responsible for carrying out the orders issued by the higher German authorities were located.

Schulze II screamed, 'Get a move on, you filthy Jew, and show me the way there! Did you think I'd go looking for it myself?'

Reisinger wasn't too worried about leaving the guardhouse: someone could always be found to stand in for him; inside, they'd even be grateful to him for taking the SS man elsewhere. Of course, there'd be a terrible commotion at the Jewish Town Hall when they arrived, even though the people there were fairly safe from arrest, because Stresovice provided them with a certain amount of protection for as long as they worked for them. But not from being beaten up – no one protected them from that.

Reisinger flew out of the guardhouse, the blood dripping from his mouth, the SS man in pursuit. Reisinger kept trying to figure out how to extricate himself from this, but in vain. His head was buzzing from the blows, and his thoughts were confused. He kept repeating the words 'balance scale' as if it were some sort of magic spell. Perhaps he repeated the words because they stood for something ordinary, something familiar to him. As the horror-stricken clerks and secretaries stopped and stared, he led Schulze II directly to the office of the Chief Elder of the Community.

The Chief Elder didn't lose his head. He was experienced in dealing with people from the Security Police. They often called him to Stresovice to receive orders and to listen to abuse for not carrying them out properly. He knew he mustn't show his fear, that he must maintain a military posture, that he mustn't argue, but that he also mustn't whine. He knew his survival depended on acting with complete confidence. But he realised immediately that this SS man did not come from his superiors in Stresovice. He was wearing the uniform of the Elite Guard. The Chief Elder was well versed in these fine distinctions.

When Schulze II began to scream that he wanted a learned Jew, the Chief Elder calmly asked him who had sent him there, since he'd come without an appointment. The other thing he did was to send Reisinger, still bleeding from the mouth, back to the guardhouse on Josefovska Street.

The calm manner of the Chief Elder stopped Schulze II short. He wasn't so stupid as not to know the role Stresovice played. The Elite Guard had nothing in common with the people there, who were neither their superiors nor their inferiors but powerful men who answered directly to Berlin. One had to be very careful with such men. Not even the chief of the SS Elite Guard could stand up to them, to say nothing of Untersturmführer Wancke. Therefore he answered the Chief Elder's questions, even answered them politely, saying that he'd been sent from the SS barracks, that some officials from the Municipal Division needed a learned Jew, and that they had an order for it from the Acting Reich Protector. Nothing bad would happen to the Jew.

The Chief Elder waited until Schulze II finished speaking. 'I'll call in one of our scholarly workers. He'll be here in a second.'

Then he dialled a number on the intercom system.

'Send Dr Rabinovich in at once.'

Schulze II stood and waited. The Chief Elder also stood. He didn't dare sit in the presence of an SS officer.

In a little while an older, stooped man with a small red beard walked in at the door. When he saw Schulze II he turned a deathly white, but he kept silent.

'This is our best scholarly worker, Dr Rabinovich. You can take him with you.'

He turned to Rabinovich. 'The Rottenführer has assured me that nothing bad will happen to you. They seem to need an expert opinion.'

Schulze II left unceremoniously. Dr Rabinovich shuffled along behind him.

When they were gone, the Chief Elder sat down at his desk, picked up the receiver of an official telephone, dialled a number, and reported to his superior's office in Stresovice about Schulze II's visit. No one responded, but the Chief

Elder knew that someone was carefully listening to his report. When he finished he dialled a number on the intercom and gave an order:

'Fire the guard Reisinger immediately for incompetence. Send him to the Work Force Division and let them find him another job.' This time someone answered at the other end, saying that the order would be carried out.

Only now did the Chief Elder begin to feel queasy, only now did he feel weak in the arms and legs. He looked out of the window into the street. There the little knots were forming and re-forming as usual. Someone was unloading some junk from a moving wagon into the warehouse across the street. Suddenly the Chief Elder stopped and stared. They were unloading a wooden statue, a statue of Moses. Moses was wearing a long, flowing robe, his beard was plaited, and in his hand he carried the Ten Commandments. The statue must have come from some Catholic church that had closed its doors for good long ago and from which it had been acquired by some rich Jewish collector. What a lot of junk they kept sending. 'Thou shalt not make graven images . . . ' His religion forbade all representations. But he'd have to take it in. He was forced to take in everything those bandits in Stresovice didn't want and that had been declared Jewish. If he were sent a stuffed crocodile, he'd have to put it away in the warehouse as well.

The Chief Elder stepped away from the window and sat down at his desk.

FIVE

THE VILLA at the edge of town did not stand out in any way. It was spacious, it had a garden and a garage, but there were many such houses in this neighbourhood – by no means a working-class suburb. Still, people seemed to avoid it. They crossed to the other side of the street and averted their eyes to keep from seeing the guard at the entrance or the groups of people standing in orderly lines for hours at a time. These people wore stars with scraggly letters in a foreign language sewn on the left side of their chests. They looked at the ground. They didn't speak at all. They were so quiet they hardly seemed to be breathing.

The villa was the headquarters of the Central Bureau, a division of the Security Police with direct orders from Berlin for the solution of the Jewish question in the Czech and Moravian Protectorate. The 'final solution'.

Death was lurking in hundreds of documents, in file folders, in property deeds, in photographs of houses, villas and factories. It dwelled in signatures and symbols, abbreviations and initials, rubber stamps and graphs. It was neat and orderly, perfectly typed on fine paper, on file cards of various colours. It was everywhere and it filled the house with fear. Over there, where the children's room had once been, where little animal figures could still be seen peeking out of the whitewashed plaster, was the 'Jewish room'. That's what they called it, because Jews were working there, filling out forms, writing names on file cards, dispatching mail. But power over the abbreviations, initials, rubber stamps and graphs belonged to others, those engaged in planning the journey to death with stops along the way. The Jewish room adjoined the offices of less important workers, the coroners and financial experts. For death was connected with complex financial operations, with neat and clean columns of numbers, with adding machines and ledgers. And in the last room on the ground floor sat the executioner's henchman in a uniform of the lowest rank. He held a rubber stamp which he pressed repeatedly on a stamp pad. He stamped list after list, each time mechanically repeating the word 'Done'.

On a closely guarded upper floor sat the true masters over life and death. They wore uniforms with braids and fringes on one shoulder, or two, according to their military rank, while their secretaries were bedecked with French perfumes and stolen jewellery. The Reich resided in these rooms with their flower-filled vases and portraits of the Leader, with their thick Persian carpets and luxurious antique furniture, with paintings and chandeliers made of cut crystal. Here death wore a different face. Though it was surrounded by comfort and luxury, it retained its military character – uniforms, official reports, clicking of heels, crisp commands. For stolen luxury must never soften an official of the Reich. These were the spoils of a victor; yet an official of the Reich knows that he must strike hard to pay for such luxury, he must eradicate, liquidate and root out all enemies, those identified by the signatures, symbols and initials. Once the enemy is turned into numbers, then the numbers must be transformed again into graphs. At first the graphs go up. They keep going up and up, regularly and steadily. And then they go down, also regularly, neatly, until the numbers fade away into nothingness. The officials of the Reich don't need to concern themselves with these graphs or keep track of these numbers. But they must speed up or slow down their movement according to the interests of the Reich.

There is no room for shouting and excitement in the world that prevails in the upstairs rooms. There the work is done by servants whose final goal was assigned them by the Leader himself. The head of this branch, the one in charge of it all, knows the secret of the final solution. He receives briefings from the head office in Berlin. He travels to conferences, he submits quarterly, semi-annual and annual reports; these are neat and clean, with carefully drawn graphs and photographic enclosures. The text is businesslike and gratifying. It shows precisely how the property in the warehouses is increasing, how many new objects have been acquired. It also specifies by how many the numbers have decreased. The pages covered with meticulous writing are contained in hard black covers.

The head of the Central Bureau was a young man; most of his staff were older than he. For when the interest of the Reich and the eradication of its enemies are concerned, regular promotions and years of service don't count. Yet this agency wasn't an ordinary office – it was a military, fighting unit. Of course the enemy had no weapons. They were powerless, weak men, women and children. But the Reich couldn't be hoodwinked in such a manner. The Reich knew well that this enemy was worse, far more dangerous than foreign armies in the field. That was why the Reich considered it more important to exterminate this enemy than to occupy whole countries with subjected populations.

The head of the Central Bureau had recently returned from the East. He had examined the extermination camps, he had carefully studied the technology of murder. They were obliged to show him everything – he was one of the select circle of the enlightened, after all – he would actually provide the numbers. They complained that liquidation was progressing too slowly, that it required too much ammunition which would serve a better purpose at the front. Other means of killing – clubs, axes, hammers – weren't effective enough; they were even more time-consuming. At some camps they were trying benzene injections, at others the exhaust fumes of trucks. But now that the proposal to use gas had been approved, the operation would go full-steam-ahead. Zyklon B was a speedy and safe medium.

The commanders of the camps, of course, had no idea who had conceived of the idea that saved them so much work. The commanders didn't know that it was the man personally entrusted by the Leader with the execution of the whole campaign: Reinhard Heydrich. They assumed that he was simply the Acting Reich Protector, who was keeping order in Bohemia and Moravia. But his mission was greater, encompassing all of Europe. It was he, the enemy of all enemies, who would carry out the final solution.

Only a few people were aware of Heydrich's true mission. Even he, the head of the Central Bureau, learned about it merely by chance from Eichmann. For while Eichmann was ostensibly responsible for all orders and was in charge in the main city of the Reich, the real commander, the source of all orders, was actually here, quite nearby. But needless to say, the head of the Central Bureau never dealt directly with Heydrich. He always went through the agency of his staff in the Reich.

The head of the Central Bureau smiled to himself. One

of the common features of all members of the National Socialist Party was this: they never revealed their goals. Thus they were able to lull and gull and dupe their opponents. Nobody in the Protectorate knew what was going on in the East. Even his own staff did not know, though they could guess certain things because some of the spoils, the stolen goods, came from there. And those who passed through the gates of the Radio Mart with numbers hung around their necks, carrying bundles of their belongings, hurried along by kicks from the SS men, even those did not suspect what was awaiting them at the end of their journey.

Knowing the secret means invisible power. It means standing high above all people and looking down on them in scornful safety, like a statue. It means being made of stone or bronze. Here on the upper floors, everything is clean, no sounds of screaming ever penetrate these walls, no blood has ever flowed here, nobody ever writhes with pain here. Here you can smell the flowers in vases, and sometimes, when they have parties, you can hear music here, classical music, none of your common popular songs or marches. He wouldn't stand for any other music. Heydrich is his model in that. After all the head of the Central Bureau had majored in Oriental Studies at the University of Göttingen. Even then he'd been preparing himself for his future service. Of course, he had prepared himself because he foresaw the Leader's goals – he had diligently read his writings and knew long ago what his task would be. He knows the alphabet and language of those inferior races, that is, the former alphabet and the former language, for the majority of Jews have never learned it. He is even knowledgeable about their literature. He can talk easily with any learned Jew from the Community, with

Dr Rabinovich, for example. Such knowledge makes his work easier.

To expunge, to liquidate, to tear out the weed with all its roots, yes, that was his task. But why shouldn't he leave them a little bit of hope for a while? Why shouldn't he confuse and lull them? The dirty work is done by others, after all – that is not his responsibility. Only he is the master over life and death. Only he knows the secret, and he doesn't need to bring about death by his own hand.

He looked in his daybook. He kept it carefully, model bureaucrat that he was. He fulfilled his daily obligations precisely, and he demanded the same from his staff. They must understand that they weren't in the Protectorate to have an easy time of it, to obtain furniture and rare delicacies. They must understand that their service here was the same as at the front, perhaps even more important.

The first entry in the daybook was about the fortress city and the transports. That was his most important task. The Acting Reich Protector himself kept careful track of it and required regular reports. He took a folder listing the areas designated as 'ghettos' out of the cabinet. His first command from the Acting Reich Protector had been to find all enclosed Jewish settlements. Death was supposed to stop briefly in some ancient Czech town. That was a necessary part of the plot to deceive foreigners. It was also important to give the victims temporary hope, so that they wouldn't be inclined to resist.

Next the command travelled from his office in the form of an order to the Jewish Community. It directed them to find the settlements and prepare them for transports. Among his papers were maps with suggestions of various towns and villages in Bohemia and Moravia. The investigation proceeded swiftly but carefully. It examined the various advantages and disadvantages. And finally Terezin was chosen.

He announced the selection to Frank, who later informed him that the Acting Reich Protector himself was satisfied with the choice. Such a town could be easily guarded. It had walls and gateways. It was not an industrial centre but an old fortress town with little shopkeepers' and tradesmen's houses stuck on. The inhabitants wouldn't put up a fight when they were moved out. The Jews could be stuffed into the barracks as well as the little houses. It didn't matter how many of them there were – it would even be good to have the town overfilled. An excess number was always easy to eliminate. Right next door was the Small Fortress, an annex of the Gestapo prison. That meant more security, even though the Gestapo was a different division.

Other documents gave evidence that the project was in full swing. There were reports of the first transports, made up of workers who had to put the emptied barracks in order and prepare the lodgings. The first family transports gathered at the Radio Mart. The schedule was strictly adhered to. Reception camps were set up in the countryside. Simultaneously, the machinery was set into motion for the confiscation of property. Warehouses began to fill up with carefully sorted objects. Moving vans and handcarts travelled all over the city. Seized apartments were refurnished and scrubbed to provide a clean welcome for their new tenants. Architects provided them with new furniture. Bed linens, paintings, refrigerators, rugs and curtains made their way to them from the warehouses.

Then the graphs began to appear, careful and reliable curves neatly drawn and issued in quarterly reports. The machine gained momentum, reaching ever farther, ever deeper. The first transports were already leaving for the East with a brief stop in the fortress town. The death camps in the East, with their gas chambers and crematoria, were already in full operation. It was a well-run organisation, the very sort of organisation that the Reich could thank for all its triumphs. Nobody could escape it, and everything was planned in advance. The documents and graphs gave a reliable picture, and the head of the Central Bureau could use them to follow everything that was happening. The numbers enter the Radio Mart, the trains leave for the fortress town, and from there still other trains leave for the East. In the camps the crematorium flames blaze from morning to night, and the ashes are carted away in bags to the Reich to serve as fertiliser for future crops. And the gold is caught in collection sieves with jewels and dental fillings among the rest, while other things pile up in warehouses, sorted according to categories. Property is going up and the numbers are going down. The unnecessary is decreasing, and the useful is increasing – the charts show all this to be true. He is satisfied with his work. He will receive the same decoration for it that German men in the field who are conquering the world for the Reich and its Leader receive. And the Acting Reich Protector is satisfied, too, because the task assigned to him by the Leader is being carried out according to plan.

The head of the Central Bureau closed the folder and put it back in the cabinet. He looked at the next entry, yes, an amusing little business. The Elite Guard of the SS seemed to be encroaching on his territory a bit. On his desk lay a telephone message received by an assistant. The message came from the Chief Elder of the community. It seems that a Rottenführer from the Elite Guard had burst into the Jewish Community, beat up the guard and made him lead the way to the Chief Elder's office, where he demanded that they bring him a learned Jew whom some officials at Municipal apparently needed to identify a statue on the German House of Art. The Chief Elder of the Community put Dr Rabinovich at their disposal. The Rottenführer promised that nothing would happen to him. The Chief Elder didn't quite understand what the Rottenführer meant by 'learned Jew'. Apparently that's what he had been told at the command headquarters of the Elite Guard to get. Another message revealed that Dr Rabinovich had, indeed, returned, but in bad physical condition and that he had not been able to identify the statue.

The nerve of the Elite Guard and the Municipal officials! They have no right to encroach on his jurisdiction. The Jews have been specially assigned to him. If he doesn't call the Elite Guard on this little affair, soon they'll be wanting a share of the spoils, or they'll begin to confiscate things on their own authority. But this isn't Poland. Here the Elite Guard doesn't have that sort of power. After all, the Acting Reich Protector himself lives here and he won't stand for any irregularities. He'll give them hell, no matter what their rank.

But wait a minute. The Acting Reich Protector, why that's where the original order comes from. The head of the Central Bureau had also been at the opening of the German House of Art and he had heard Heydrich's speech. Afterwards someone, maybe it was Geschke from the Gestapo, had told him that the Acting Reich Protector had had a fit when he saw a statue of the Jewish composer Mendelssohn on the balustrade. That's it – those imbeciles from Municipal didn't know what to do, so they turned for help to the Elite Guard. And it was easy to understand why they went to the Elite Guard and not to the Gestapo or his own branch. Because they were afraid that Heydrich might hear of it. Therefore this is not an important matter at all, just a stupid little thing. He'll deal directly with the commander about it and won't drag in anybody else. But he mustn't let the Elite Guard get away with anything – he'll rap their knuckles soundly for this. Still, it was gratifying to hear that the 'learned Jew' hadn't managed to identify the statue. How could he identify it, when he was a Talmud scholar and hadn't the foggiest idea about worldly subjects like music. It didn't matter in the least that they beat him up. A few blows wouldn't harm him.

The last entry in his daybook was a private matter: a present for his mother's birthday. The head of the Central Bureau daydreamed for a moment. The image of a white-haired lady, the widow of a university professor, floated before his eyes. She lived in the small family home in a university town and took meticulous care of his father's library, though it never occurred to her to look at a single book herself. Daily she dusted the desk and the armchair as if the old man were to return any moment. She wouldn't allow any of the maids to touch a single object that he had ever laid a hand upon. Several times a day she looked at his portrait in the large gold frame hanging above the mantel. But she also took the same care of her son's old toys and school notebooks. She pulled them out of the cabinet occasionally and leafed through them lovingly. The old lady lived in her memories, and her one and only hope was her son. She was better off than others in the Reich. The criminal pilots hadn't reached her city yet, and she had enough food, because he sent her weekly packages from the Protectorate.

He thought a great deal about what sort of present to send her. Then he remembered that his mother was very fond of old Meissen. All the cupboards and cabinets and shelves in her house were filled with figurines made of Meissen porcelain. He must find the most beautiful piece of all the confiscated Jewish property. Such a piece was surely to be found in the warehouse. The rich Jews had good taste sometimes. He gave the job of finding it to Fiedler, comparatively the most intelligent member of his staff. Once he had been an official in the Prague German Bank, and he came from a fairly wealthy family. He knew porcelain trademarks and was unlikely to bring him an imitation or a tasteless modern piece of junk. Better to wait until after office hours, but the head of the Central Bureau was too impatient. He looked forward to the gift and hoped Fiedler wouldn't fail, hoped he'd bring him something really fine. He rang, and a few moments later Fiedler returned with a carefully wrapped package under his arm. He carried it gingerly, as if it were a holy relic.

'What is it?' the head of the Central Bureau asked eagerly.

'It's guaranteed genuine old Meissen. Very valuable Meissen.'

'What does it represent?'

'I'd rather not tell you. It's a surprise.'

They unwrapped it with excitement, completely disregarding the wood shavings falling on the immaculate rug.

Finally a figurine came into view, actually a group of figures.

'My God, how beautiful!'

'It's one of the most valuable pieces. Please observe that

it's a group representing the Judgement of Paris. Only a very few of these were manufactured. They have one of them in the Meissen museum, but this one is better. The Prague Museum of Industrial Design has a large collection of Meissen china, but they don't have this one. I looked up the literature. This group was commissioned directly by King Augustus, and the models for the three goddesses were Augustus's three mistresses. It appears that there is one other in private ownership in England, but that one is probably a fake. This piece, however, is guaranteed to be genuine. I had it examined by an expert.'

'Thank you. You've done an excellent job. This will be the most beautiful present for my mother's birthday.'

The figures of the goddesses had the delicate beauty of rococo mistresses rather than the austere look of antiquities. The curves of their bodies were rounded, their hips slender, their breasts small. They stood there naked before Paris, first Aphrodite, behind her Pallas Athena, and then, last but not least, the more substantial Hera. And it was clear that Paris could offer the golden apple to one alone – the goddess born from the foam of the sea.

He gazed for a long time at the sculpted group, unable to tear his eyes away from it. Finally he said, 'Have it carefully wrapped. I want you to guarantee that the gift will arrive in good order. You may request a special plane in my name.'

Fiedler placed the porcelain back in the box and walked to the door. The head of the Central Bureau followed him with his eyes, catching the last glints of the goddesses' rosy limbs glistening in the shavings.

SIX

HE HEARD THE VOICES, but he couldn't see their faces. The voices were arguing fiercely about something, but he could catch only a few words: 'I said it was an important scientific case, that the research has meaning for the Reich.' 'An order is an order. They won't rescind it.' 'They turned me down at the German University.'

He knew they were talking about him. The time had come for the move from the hospital. He didn't know where they would take him, but it didn't interest him much. His days were numbered. There was no help for him, and all the experiments they were doing on him were only meant to prolong their research. Of course he couldn't be entirely indifferent. This meant he'd lose touch with the world, even though the world was now limited to Jan alone. He knew he'd never see Adela and Greta again. But if Jan couldn't visit him, he wouldn't have any news of them.

He had met Jan Krulis in a cafe years ago. It was a fashionable cafe divided into three rooms. There was dancing in one, card games in another, while people sat around tables drinking black coffee in the third. Some of them were reading Rimbaud or Lautréamont or Breton. Others were puzzling over Freud, still others were inventing machines for living, as they used to call homes in those days. Different interest groups would always sit together at the same table, although some people circulated from table to table. There were also regulars at the cafe who did nothing and knew nothing. They attached themselves to one group or another, always letting someone else pay for their coffee or borrowing twenty crowns they'd never pay back.

One day somebody introduced him to Jan – he no longer remembered who, but it certainly wasn't an architect, because architects looked down on Jan Krulis. Krulis didn't like their machines for living, those houses that looked like crates. Jan was usually silent during the passionate arguments that sometimes broke out at the cafe, and for that reason he was thought to be backward, a stodgy traditionalist, a man of the last century. Nobody could understand why he even came to the cafe at all. Perhaps he just came to read the foreign newspapers. Maybe he went there to keep warm, as many people did who couldn't afford coal. He might never have become close to Jan, for he himself enjoyed those discussions about new art forms – for him they meant a breath of fresh air after a day at the clinic, where he witnessed so much human suffering, illness and decay. He needed to leave that world for a while and get into the world of colours, words and tones. But one day Jan let slip that he, too, was a canoeist.

Words reached him as if from a great distance. 'They won't give us an ambulance for transferring him.' 'So how can we move him?' 'By handcart.' The voices grew sharp and angry. 'That's outrageous, Doctor. He'll die on the way.' 'But what can we do? We have to follow orders. They won't let us use an ambulance.' 'But he'll catch cold crossing the entire city in a handcart. He'll be dead before he gets there.' 'We don't make the rules. There's nothing we can do, Doctor.' Then the voices grew silent and once again he was alone. Now he knew that they'd carry him by handcart, and that it would be a long journey. But it didn't matter to him. On the contrary, he looked forward to seeing the city again. He'd been lying in the hospital for two years now, and during that time he hadn't been outside once. Now he'd see how the city had changed. He'd see its new subjugated face. He might even meet some of those foreigners now holding sway over the city, the ones who had issued the insane laws that caused him to be thrown out of the hospital and taken away in a handcart.

He loved the river and could listen to tales of it for hours. Perhaps it had something to do with his profession. Sometimes during night service in the emergency room he'd pull out a map of Czech waterways and plan trips along barely navigable rivers. He'd imagine himself paddling from one bank to the other, cautiously avoiding the shallows, keeping the boat from scraping and damaging its canvas bottom on rocks. These were trips he could never manage alone – they called for too much strength and endurance. He thought of buying a kayak. Though it was less comfortable, it would be easier to navigate by himself. But then he arranged to go on the trips together with Jan.

Nobody said goodbye to him when the two men came with stretcher and blankets. Obviously everybody was ashamed to see him thrown out of the hospital. Just as they were carrying him out of the door he caught a glimpse of the nurse taking down the identifying board and wiping off the chalked letters of his name.

It looked like a funeral procession. The men carried him carefully and he didn't feel any jolts, perhaps because his body was immobilised. But when they went out into the courtyard where the cart was waiting for him, the cold, sharp air struck him in the nostrils with such force that his head began to spin. Suddenly everything seemed phantom-like, even the trees in the park, bare on this autumn day. Everything seemed unreal, even the squeaking of the ungreased wheels of the cart, even the houses they passed, even the sky covered with clouds.

Then when they went out into the streets, it seemed to him that the city had become greyer somehow, that it had fallen into decay, that it was disintegrating, that everything was covered with dust and mould. Paper boxes and useless objects were displayed in the shop windows. People walking along the street were joyless and careworn. They seemed to be oppressed by a heavy weight. The city was under a spell, as if it had been enchanted by an evil magician, as if spectres and lifeless shades were moving about it. The children's cries were oddly muffled – even they seemed afraid to disturb the deathly quiet.

The men with the cart avoided the main streets. The cart bounced along the broken cobblestones. At first the streets didn't seem any different. Then he noticed the flags. They were hanging on flagpoles attached to houses with cracking stucco. They fluttered in the breeze, decorated with the enemy's spider, and beside them waved other ones, red and white without the blue triangle. The men with the cart wore stars on their chest. He noticed that only now as they stopped at a crossing. They positioned themselves on either side of the handcart, probably checking to see if he was still alive. Only the yellow of those stars with their black scraggly letters shone brightly in the grey streets.

It wasn't until later, long after he and Jan had paddled down several rivers together, long after they had bounced around numerous freight cars carrying boats and people to faraway stations, long after they had camped on many deserted riverbanks, that he came to understand why Jan was called a traditionalist, and why his ideas were rejected by all the competition juries. Jan loved a city that followed an orderly plan, a city established as a seat of kings, a spreading city that contained palaces and hovels, grand merchants' houses and blocks of tenements with fire escapes, a city surrounded by smoky suburbs filled with shanty-towns, factory buildings and wastelands covered with briars and nettles. He championed this city; he wanted to keep the formless and monotonous machines for living from encroaching on it. Not that he rejected the new glass-and-concrete structures out of hand, but he wanted them to serve the city, not break in like intruders. He didn't want the old palaces in its centre torn down, he didn't want drab apartment houses and office buildings to disturb its rhythm, to dull the musical cries and sighs resounding from the heights of its hills to the depths of its slums.

In the name of the city he guarded every old house and fought against its destruction. He struggled to preserve the old arcaded palaces. Everyone laughed at him, because it was an era that said, 'Tear down those old houses, get rid of all that junk, give people housing modules where they may gaze at painted ceilings rather than at paintings. Let them sit on cushions rather than chairs, let them fold up the couch and push it against the wall.' He had nothing against housing modules measuring a little less than four square metres. But he was concerned with the gradual disfiguring and debasing of the city. Its silhouette, dating from the Middle Ages, was being ravished. Its gardens were being chopped up to make way for prefabricated houses.

Greta and Adela were hiding somewhere in this grey and humiliated city. As long as Jan was in the world they would not be abandoned. Jan would surely manage to find him. At the hospital they'd surely tell Jan where to find him. He must say farewell to him and thank him. But maybe they wouldn't let Jan come to see him. Maybe he'd be shut away somewhere so that no one could get to him. Maybe they'd deny he was there, to avoid any unpleasantness, since he had only a few days left to live. But surely Jan would let nothing scare him off. He'd find his way to the Jewish hospital even if he had to put on a star to get there.

Suddenly the cart began to go faster. Both men quickly pushed it into a little passageway and hid themselves behind it. Something very strange must be happening in the street to frighten them so. Yes, death was parading by in the form of soldiers in foreign uniforms. At the head they carried horsetails. They were accompanied by fife and drum. They seemed to be setting forth on some marauding expedition, one that required an accompaniment of violent and clashing music. They seemed about to serve in some secret bloody rite known only to its participants. He had never seen such a parade. The people on the sidewalk tried to hide in doorways of houses and shops, to avoid saluting the flag with the death's head. Only when the blaring music faded away in the distance did the two men wheel the cart out of the passageway. Only then did the sidewalks come to life again.

They considered Jan Krulis an eccentric, a man fixed in the past, because at architectural meetings he championed the city so fiercely. At first he had thought of Jan the same way, because everyone around was talking about bare walls, white tiles, hygienic fixtures, piped-in music and built-in kitchens. Only after he climbed a hill with Jan one day and looked down at the city through Jan's eyes, only after he saw the city rising and falling away, embracing the river with its quays and bridges, flowing with the current and against it, unshakable and indestructible, only then did he understand why Jan loved it so much.

The cart stopped in the old-city section directly in front of a new building that stood beside a rather old synagogue in the Eastern style. They had reached their destination. This must be the hospital. Some people hurried out of the building and took hold of the stretcher. Just before they carried him inside, he caught sight of people wearing stars who were carrying heavy boxes into the synagogue. One of the boxes fell from a moving wagon and its contents crashed noisily to the ground: toys – teddy bears, dolls in dresses, rocking horses, little rubber animals, little wooden dogs and cats. They scattered on the pavement and the moving men scooped them up. Some of the toys were shabby from years of use by childish hands. That was the last thing he saw in the city: pathetic spoils torn from the hands of children.

They placed him on a clean bed. They put up a chart with his name. Again there was nothing for him to do but look at the ceiling. But this hospital was more pleasant than the other. Everything was glistening and new. They must have fixed it up out of former apartments, and the little room in which he lay quite alone must once have been a bathroom. A doctor with a star on a white coat came up to him and spoke to him in a kindly, warm voice. He was grateful for the friendly words. He realised that in this hospital he was a patient, not a scientific object of study fought over by the authorities. He knew that death would come to him more quietly and inconspicuously here, that it wouldn't be surrounded by consultations and arguments.

No, the trip through the occupied city had not helped his condition, but still he had no regrets. He had seen Prague once again after two years. No matter that the city had been silenced and subjugated. In the end, nobody would ever conquer it. It would awaken one day to rejoicing and flags waving. He wouldn't live to see that day, for the end was approaching. The Jewish hospital couldn't keep him alive – they didn't have the means to do it. But he would certainly die more comfortably among his own people. Breathing was difficult now, and he could barely speak. If only Jan would come before he lost the power of speech entirely. How would he communicate with him if he couldn't speak and his hands were paralysed?

It was quiet there, high above the city. The neighbourhood they were strolling through had lost all signs of life. It should have been noisy, filled with sounds of singing and shouting as in old Parisian streets. People should have been sitting in outdoor cafes, sipping coffee or alcoholic beverages at the bar. But life seemed to have vanished, even though people must still live here, must still sit on balconies that were once arcades of palaces and look down on gardens hidden by house façades. They were under a spell. Life went on only behind thick impenetrable walls. Women did their laundry in metal tubs out in the courtyard, children ran around in the little gardens and picked fruit from the trees, men worked in little workshops. The streets and squares were silent and lifeless, as if plunged into an eternal sleep. Even the dogs that occasionally appeared on the streets walked around gravely and didn't bark. They crept around the cornerstones as if the silence oppressed them.

As they came down again to the city's main streets, the noise overwhelmed them. Trolleys clattered and jangled by them. Car brakes screeched. Heavy lorries rumbled past. A stream of people crowded the pavements, stopped at the crossings and overflowed into the street. Newsboys shouted out the latest news, assailing them with murders, mine disasters and scandalous lawsuits. Their ears were further assaulted by the cries of hawkers selling lottery tickets and noisy flower vendors. Strains of strident music came pouring out of an open shop door. Here the city seemed to be squealing and writhing, as if stabbed by the neon lights and letters that appeared in bright rows announcing the results of a soccer match. The end of the city seemed at hand. Perhaps it wanted to have its last say in the screeching and clattering, the flood of lights and the provocative music.

Overwhelmed by the din, they pulled away from the crowd and escaped to an unfamiliar cafe. As they walked into the large room, they were struck by something decidedly strange about the place, but they didn't know what it was at first. It seemed to be an ordinary cafe with marble tables and mirrors. Only after a few moments did they realise that what struck them was the quiet, the preternatural quiet. Not the usual familiar quiet of regular cafes where people are reading and you can hear the rustling of papers and muffled conversations. Though all the tables were occupied, not a single person uttered a sound.

When they sat down and ordered two cups of coffee, their voices rang out as if they had shouted in an empty room. They didn't dare talk to each other after that and just drank their coffee in silence. Then they looked around the room. People were moving their fingers rapidly, communicating in this way across great distances, from one end of the cafe to the other. The waiter who was serving them also knew sign language and brought them everything they ordered. Suddenly they realised that the cafe was occupied by deaf-mutes and that they were the only people there who could speak, apart from the waiter, and even he didn't speak. They were unable to enjoy themselves. They were afraid of making the smallest movement, afraid that the deaf-mutes might misinterpret it and take it as some sort of insult. They sat there silently, like uninvited guests, and only after they walked out into the street did they find their own voices again.

One day Jan appeared at the hospital and told him that he needn't worry. Adela and Greta were doing well. They were in the hands of reliable people. They didn't have ration cards, but he was managing to get food for them – it wasn't that hard to arrange, because there were always good people to be found. Even in hiding the children found ways to amuse themselves. And they sent him greetings.

He thanked Jan. The disease prevented him from talking much, but there was no need for many words. Jan understood him.

And now the time of peace is beginning. Now all motion is about to end and things will stay fixed in their places. Now everything will turn to stone. The memories and images will fade and the river will cease to flow. Even its waves will turn to stone, even the sky will remain suspended above, its clouds frozen in place.

SEVEN

ROTTENFÜHRER Schulze II hurried Dr Rabinovich along the street. Schulze II was in a rage, and would have preferred to beat the Jew to a pulp and then finish him off with his service revolver as he lay there. That was the way he used to do things in Poland. But he had to bring him back alive, since Wancke had given him an order to do so. Still, all this had caused him considerable unpleasantness. The Chief Elder of the Community hadn't been afraid of him at all and had spoken to him in a way that no other Jew had ever dared before. Yes, that one must have some powerful protection. Still, he should have slapped him in the face at the very least. Somehow he had forgotten to do it while the Jew was in his office, or else he had allowed himself to be muddled by the highest Jew's self-confidence.

'*Los, los, schnell, schnell,*' shrieked Schulze II at Rabinovich hurrying ahead of him. The street emptied out. Everyone disappeared into building doorways. It was a strange spectacle, the uniformed SS man pursuing the cowering man with the red beard. Terrible things were happening everywhere, but everyone was astonished to see this happening to Dr Rabinovich, who had never been harmed before, who always behaved so high-handedly because he was aware of how important and irreplaceable he was. Why, distinguished visitors were sent all the way from Berlin to have him show them his museum and explain Jewish customs. The head of the Central Bureau himself called Rabinovich in to Stresovice for consultations. And now things had taken this turn – an SS man was taking him away, who knows where. Dr Rabinovich would surely come to a bad end, because once you fell into the hands of those people, you never escaped unharmed. You considered yourself lucky to get away with your life.

Dr Rabinovich was hurrying, trying to follow the SS man's command, but he couldn't walk as fast as the well-nourished Schulze II. Rabinovich's body was twisted and misshapen from poring over books endlessly. His head, stuffed with knowledge, overpowered his body, which was just a bothersome appendage. Now he had to make it jump in accordance with the wishes of one of the murderers. There is a time to weep and a time to kill, as it says in the Bible. In the end, even he had become a victim. But more than Schulze II he blamed the Chief Elder: to deliver him defenceless to the mercies of his enemies and to call it an expert opinion! The Chief Elder had claimed that nothing would happen to him, but how can anyone know what those mad murderers might dream up, especially when one doesn't even know what they actually want from one? Maybe they'd drag him off into the barracks and make him entertain the troops during their carousing. Maybe they'd force him to eat forbidden foods so they could laugh at his suffering. There was no suffering on earth they might not think of.

He had come to understand that there was no humiliation on earth that he wouldn't endure. But now he knew that something much worse was awaiting him. He had come to understand that there was no sin on earth that he wouldn't commit if he was forced to do so, even though he hadn't had to eat forbidden foods yet. He knew that if they ordered him to do it he would submit, as he had submitted before when they forced him to perform impure acts and desecrations. Yes, they brought important visitors to see him, and perhaps there were some people who envied him for having patronage in such high places. Those people were probably convinced that performing services for such guests would guarantee his life and protect him from the transports. And he thought so himself, why else would he do it? Of course, he liked life – even his religion commanded him not to give it up. If he had been alone, if he hadn't had a family, he would not have accepted life at such a price. What about all those martyrs who joyously accept a terrible death and allow themselves to be burned alive or pierced by arrows rather than give up the true faith? They could have saved their lives if they had agreed to be christened like many others did. But they wanted to hold on to the faith of their forefathers. Why didn't he do likewise? Perhaps because he lived among people who hadn't preserved any religious laws, who didn't go to synagogue, who ate forbidden foods with great pleasure, and who tried not to differ in any way from the others. No, that was not the real reason. After all, he had lived in this country for a long time without losing his faith, without ever giving in to impure impulses, without ever touching forbidden foods or ever lighting a cigarette on a Saturday even though cigarettes were his only pleasure. No, he had never renounced the faith of his fathers. Even his sons had to follow his example. He made sure that they weren't seduced by the bad example of those wavering members of their religion. Only now, in this time of dying, had he allowed himself to be persuaded to spit on everything he had held sacred all his life.

No it wasn't because his flesh was weak or because he

wanted to avoid suffering, but because he had chosen an earthly mission over a martyr's crown. His mission in the world was his family. As long as he found safety for himself, his family was safe, too. Perhaps the others didn't know what was waiting for them when they were called up for the transports and herded into the Radio Mart. But he suspected and even knew a little something. Because sometimes the head of the Central Bureau would loosen up a bit and he'd drop a hint, especially when he was in a good mood. Then he'd say, 'Be glad I'm protecting you – otherwise you might go up the chimney in smoke.' It sounded like a joke, and it was meant that way. Yet there was some truth behind it, though he didn't want to think about it, though he denied it to himself. But fear forced him to believe it.

Rottenführer Schulze II finally got Dr Rabinovich into the barracks building and shoved him quickly up the steps to the second floor. There Wancke and his visitors were impatiently awaiting him. They were bored and had exhausted the various jokes they'd been whiling away the time telling each other, not political ones, of course, but dirty ones – that was allowed. Because they didn't trust one another, they finally had to parrot news from command headquarters about success on the battlefield, about the perspicacity of the Leader and about the war which would certainly be won, just to keep the conversation going. That kind of conversation, however, only gives rise to a foul mood.

Rottenführer Schulze II clicked his heels and announced: 'I've brought the learned Jew, as requested.'

Wancke exploded at him: 'You certainly took your own good time about it, Schulze. What were you doing there so long with all those Jews?'

'I smacked one of the Jews a few times.'

Wancke frowned. 'That wasn't what you were ordered to do. Just remember that if there are any consequences you'll answer for it yourself. Out!' he ordered. Schulze II clicked his heels and left.

Rabinovich stood in Wancke's office and looked at the three men in uniform. The one who screamed at his subordinate was definitely from the barracks. But those two whose uniforms didn't fit them well were probably from Municipal.

'Come here,' said Wancke. 'So you're the learned Jew. Go with those men and tell them everything they want to know. And remember, you're not to breathe a word about this. You'd better not open your dirty mouth among your disgusting friends. This is a state secret and nobody is to hear about it. Take him away.' He nodded to Krug and Schlesinger.

They were embarrassed to have to take a Jew with them. They didn't know how they were supposed to address him. The Elite Guard was obviously more experienced in these matters. Krug decided to proceed as if he were communicating with a foreigner.

'Go with us to German House of Art. Go up to roof, and find statue of Jew.'

Rabinovich knew that he had to walk in front of the others. They walked along rather slowly and Rabinovich was relieved that they weren't rushing him the way Schulze II had done. These officials from Municipal didn't seem so bad. He was happy that they hadn't left him at the barracks, that the SS man had only threatened him and hadn't forced him to do knee bends, as those killers were wont to do. But the task before him filled him with misgivings. What statue? What did he know about statues? 'Thou shalt make no graven images.' Statues could only bring bad luck. It was one of the worst sins, the sin of false idolatry. Today, he remembered, the shop was supposed to deliver the model of a Passover seder. The human figures gathered around the table were made of papiermâché, to look like real people. The head of the Central Bureau had dreamed up this project himself and insisted on ordering it from the shop personally. And now some other statue was persecuting him. Who was he supposed to identify on the roof of a building about which he knows nothing except it was once the Czech parliament, which the Germans had fixed up as a concert hall?

All three of them mounted the steep steps. As before, Rabinovich had to go first. He was afraid he'd get vertigo, that his head would begin to reel. Never in his life had he done any climbing and he was mindful of the saying: Out of the depths we cry to thee, O Lord. Even tradition forbade high places, though not expressly. But he had to go up, were it the Babylonian tower itself. He had set out on this path and there was nothing he could do but continue on it. A small sin couldn't make things worse.

Schlesinger didn't want to go up on the roof either. But of course with Krug there, and what was worse, the Jew, he couldn't avoid it. All of them stood on the roof. Rabinovich's knees were shaking and he tried not to look into the abyss. He saw the statues. He couldn't help seeing them, for they stood on the balustrade a small distance away. Whose statues they actually were he didn't know. Krug gave him an order: 'Walk around balustrade, look around well, tell us which is Mendelssohn statue. Surely you know which one Mendelssohn.'

They're lunatics, Rabinovich said to himself, they want me to identify a statue. How can they know that Jews never carved any statues, that their religion forbids it. Only in recent times, but by then they had turned into pagans who had come to resemble the others. Of course, he knew the name Mendelssohn. Moses Mendelssohn, the founder of the Reform movement; all bad things began with him. He truly led the Jews astray with his enlightened ways, and it ended with violence, licence, and the slaughter of those whom he had led into a trap. He couldn't understand why they should build him a memorial on a building that was dedicated to the cultivation of the arts. He wasn't an artist, after all, but a religious reformer. He did have descendants, but they weren't Jews. They had themselves christened and married Christians, and so nobody cared about those descendants. One of them was a composer and he had two names. Of course, he must be the one the Municipal officials were looking for. He turned respectfully to Krug, because he recognised that Krug was in charge.

'Please excuse me, I cannot identify the statue because that composer you are looking for wasn't a Jew.'

Krug and Schlesinger looked at him. They were stunned. The nerve! What kind of nonsense was this? Krug couldn't control himself and began to scream: 'How dare you, you filthy Jew! If the Acting Reich Protector says it's a Jew, then it has to be a Jew!'

Rabinovich was sweating with fear. Maybe that other hoodlum would push him off the roof. These people were capable of anything. But he couldn't answer any differently.

He apologised humbly: 'That musician Mendelssohn was christened. In fact, I just remembered he was christened as a tiny baby. And so by our laws he can't be a Jew.'

Rabinovich's humility enraged Krug. He struck him so hard with his fist that Rabinovich reeled.

'Shut up. Those explanations of yours don't interest us. Just tell us: can you identify the statue or not?'

'No,' Rabinovich answered in a quaking voice.

'So get out of here and crawl back to your lousy Jewish rat hole before I change my mind!'

Rabinovich quickly disappeared through the gate, as fast as his collapsing legs would allow him. Krug and Schlesinger remained on the roof alone.

'What now?' said Krug in a cold fury. 'It was your brilliant idea to go to the Elite Guard. Meanwhile, Giesse is about to call. What am I supposed to tell him? That I have an idiot assistant who can't do anything properly, and when he has any ideas at all they turn out to be so colossally stupid that even a Jew can't believe his ears. What you need is a turn of duty at the front. You'll meet real men there and you can prove your loyalty to the Reich and the Leader by dying a hero's death. Nobody will ask for any of your ideas there. And as an SS candidate you'll have to apply to the Elite Guard. They'll certainly be glad to see you there, because the way things have turned out, I'm not going to give Wancke anything. Besides which, they'll be very favourably disposed towards you, since the Central Bureau will surely go after them about the guest appearance of their Rottenführer at the Jewish Community.'

'But Herr Scharführer, I really . . . '

'I don't want to hear another word out of you. Return to Municipal. Get your things together, and hand the whole business over to Dr Buch . . . '

Schlesinger ran quickly, as if afraid that Krug would dream up something even worse for him. He wasn't even thinking about the front. Bad enough to think about the hell facing him at the Elite Guard – they certainly knew how to make life miserable if they put their minds to it. And they'd put their minds to it, never fear, because Wancke would get nothing from Krug, and the Chief Elder of the Community had surely sent a report to Stresovice. He should have volunteered for the army long ago and then he wouldn't have committed that mortal sin. Now he'd never get to Rome and the Pope would never give him absolution. All his hopes were dashed. He'd die a sinner and his body would rot somewhere on Russian soil.

Krug remained on the roof alone. Only after a few moments did he descend the stairs and return the keys to the guard. He was thinking furiously about what he should say to Giesse when he asked about the statue. There was nothing left but to ask his wife for help. Official regulations forbade him to confide official secrets even to his nearest and dearest, but not fulfilling an order was an even worse offence and he'd end up in Schlesinger's boat. Meanwhile, his wife was a college graduate and knew a lot of people. Surely she'd come up with someone who could identify the statue. He'd go right home.

Dr Rabinovich returned slowly to his office. It was actually a museum created at the request of the Central Bureau and also, perhaps, through efforts of certain shrewd people in the Jewish Community. The museum collected confiscated objects from the defunct synagogues, everything to do with religious ceremonies. It was to be a storehouse of trophies commemorating the Reich's victory over its enemy. Thousands and thousands of ark curtains, prayer robes, Torah crowns and pointers had been sent from rural communities to Prague, where they were marked, catalogued, priced, dusted, repaired, restored; the most valuable were selected to be displayed in exhibits. From seven in the morning to seven in the evening, office workers, movers and hired hands worked at the museum. It was a very complicated job, and Dr Rabinovich was in charge.

Sometimes distinguished visitors arrived from Berlin and asked for a guided tour. The museum was supposed to be a victory memorial, for the objects displayed here belonged to a race scheduled for annihilation. Nothing would remain of that race but these dead things. The visitors were fascinated: they had already read so many mysterious hints about the power of this deadly enemy that they expected to see charms, magic and mysteries of some sort. The exhibited antiquities, however, were made of perfectly ordinary fabrics, silver and wood, though in rather uncommon forms. It was therefore necessary to help things along with darkness and special lighting effects to give the exhibit a feeling of mystery. All the objects that had formerly been used for worship – the scrolls, ark curtains, mantles, crowns and pointers – lost their original purpose and now became merchandise, exhibition pieces that would never come to life again in a living faith. Rabinovich helped the desecration along. Under his supervision everything was received, uncrated, sorted and catalogued.

The head of the Central Bureau was as proud of his museum as if it were his own creation. He even showed off his learned Jew with pride and forced him to read from the scrolls, to sing like a cantor, and to wave the palm sprig in the air before visitors. Dr Rabinovich lent himself to all this. He had to, because he wanted to save his wife and his sons. He had to endure everything because he knew. He recited a verse from the Psalms to give him strength when he was afraid: 'Like sheep they are laid in the grave; Death shall feed on them.'

A high minister of the Reich arrived, one of the Leader's favourites, and the Acting Reich Protector himself took him around Prague. Behold, this golden city of a hundred towers now belongs to the Reich, these proud and ancient buildings will stay in German hands for ever, that river mirroring the royal castle and dividing the city into two parts is now a German river. Unlike the usual thugs, this one was an educated man, an architect by profession whose head swarmed with fantastic projects. The Leader had picked him to be in charge of industry and to extract the maximum work from foreign labourers and prisoners in concentration camps. He conscientiously fulfilled his duties, but his dream was beauty – new cities, magnificent buildings, squares, parks. When the war was over he would carry out his plans. Now he was glad to be able to admire the beauties of a city he didn't know, glad he could look at its monuments in peace and quiet because no bombs had fallen on this city yet and its architecture was intact. Like Mozart's music, its palaces were in perfect harmony, unchanged from the day they had emerged from the workshops and foundries of the German masters. Yes, Germans had built this city and filled it with beauty. Who else could have done such a job? The Czechs had merely taken over for a time. Now their reign was finished.

The former architect and the present Acting Reich Protector made a long tour of the city. The minister was heartened to find so knowledgeable a person in such a position – he had expected someone resembling other favourites of the Leader, narrow people who knew only about military or slave-driving trades. But Heydrich understood music. It was his strong point.

Heydrich showed him buildings where the German composers Mozart and Beethoven had stayed when they visited Prague. He introduced him to the perfect acoustics of the Rudolfinum, a concert hall now returned to German art. He took a great deal of his own valuable time in order to personally show off the beauties of Prague. He was sorry that he couldn't also take him for a tour of the Jewish quarter with its curious sights – the Old-New Synagogue, the old Jewish cemetery, the Jewish Town Hall and the museum the Reich was setting up, but the head of the Central Bureau was better suited for that.

The head of the Central Bureau was deliriously happy to have so distinguished a visitor. The head was the son of a university professor and had been in Oriental studies before receiving this assignment. Now he was the absolute lord and master of all Jews in the Protectorate. His power was unlimited and no one could encroach on his territory. The minister was glad to meet so well-informed a person, an expert on Jewish monuments who knew the exact dates they were constructed. Once, the head of the Central Bureau explained, Prague had been a virtual bastion of Judaism, where Jews had lived uninterruptedly for at least a thousand years. This was because the Czechs lacked the racial sensitivities of the Germans, who had been trying to get rid of the Jews from at least the beginning of the Middle Ages; often, when the king's power was weakened, they actually succeeded. But soon not a single Jew would remain in this golden city. Of course, the monuments would remain. The head of the Central Bureau wouldn't allow them to be razed or burned down, as had happened in the Reich through human anger and bitterness. They were too valuable; they must be preserved. The minister was surprised to find a person engaged in such crude work who understood so well the need for preservation. He decided to mention him in Berlin.

In the Jewish quarter, the head of the Central Bureau sent for Dr Rabinovich, his servant and slave. The contrast was striking: behind the slender, tall man with muscles hardened by sport and games, whose uniform and coat looked as if he had been poured into them, stood a twisted shadow, hunched over, looking down at the ground. In a briskly military and rather patronising fashion, the head of the Central Bureau ordered Dr Rabinovich to describe the ceremonies for the guest. The servant and slave spoke softly in good German with only a slight accent. The minister was interested in everything, even the embroidery on the ark curtains, even the variously shaped spice boxes – the little towers, fish and the locomotive. And then he saw the ram's horn, a real ram's horn.

'What's this?' he asked with amazement. He was surprised that such a primitive object still served a religious function. But how else to explain its presence among the exhibits here?

'Explain it to the minister,' ordered the head of the Central Bureau.

Dr Rabinovich spoke the words he had often been obliged to repeat to various visitors: the ram's horn was called the *shofar*. Formerly it had served as a military bugle, but now it was used to announce the beginning of the Day of Judgement; the Day of Atonement, the highest and most terrible of the Jewish holidays, the day when one thinks about one's sins, repents of them, and begs for forgiveness.

'I see,' said the minister. 'It's a sort of musical instrument. I'd like to hear what it sounds like.'

'Blow it,' commanded the head of the Central Bureau.

'But I . . . ' stuttered Dr Rabinovich. He was being forced into a further sin. He mustn't commit such a blasphemous act. He'd be lost for ever and the vengeance of the Lord would afflict his issue for four generations. For these accounts are settled on earth!

'Blow!' bellowed the head of the Central Bureau in a threatening voice.

And so he blew. His flesh was weak, he was not of the martyr's breed, he had a wife and sons who wanted to live.

It wasn't a pleasant sound, not at all, rather a prolonged croak. He wasn't a trumpeter, after all! He had never held this instrument in his hands before. Other people were meant to blow the *shofar*, people who knew how to produce sounds with it.

'Well, it's certainly not pleasant,' announced the minister. 'Nevertheless, it's interesting.'

'Next time blow it better,' the head of the Central Office reproached him sharply. 'You need practice.'

And he left with his grand visitor.

Rabinovich remained alone in the exhibition room. He looked around at the cases and the hanging ark curtains, feeling pangs of remorse.

This had been a terrible day, a day of sorrow not unlike the day commemorating the destruction of the temple in Jerusalem. First he'd been sent up on the roof of an unclean building to identify some statue, then he was beaten on the head. But none of that was as bad as the blowing of the *shofar*. He believed that blowing the *shofar* on a day that was not a Holy Day would provoke the Lord's anger, which would then fall upon the innocent. Because of him people would be tortured, tormented and sent to a terrible death. For by blowing the *shofar*, he had allied himself with the murderers. He had become their helper. Indeed, he was even guiltier than they, because they believed they were annihilating an enemy, while he had betrayed his own people. He had desecrated his own religion and allowed himself to perform a shameful deed. For such a sin everyone must be punished.

And still the miserable day was not over. A parade of movers marched into the exhibition hall. Strapped to their backs were heavy packages shaped like human figures, which the movers carried carefully as if they were made of valuable and fragile porcelain. They were followed by the young and cheerful designer of the exhibition. He was full of smiles, as if this had to do with some light entertainment.

Rabinovich gave him a furious look. Yes, it's easy for him to laugh, the faithless little wretch. He doesn't even know what these things mean, nor has he ever set foot in a synagogue. Before this he was making scenery for a famous left-wing theatre and now they've made him designer of the exhibit rooms. But even Rabinovich had approved the appointment, because who else could have done the job but someone who wouldn't really care about objects that generations of believers had worshipped with the deepest respect. Dr Rabinovich felt like cursing him under his breath, but then he realised that he was accursed himself, that he was a greater sinner than this little prig who had done nothing in the past but think up costumes for loose women and paint backdrops for lustful entertainments.

The designer, Frantisek Schönbaum, greeted Rabinovich with a nod of his head – they did not shake hands. They disliked each other and had nothing in common apart from the fact that they were compelled to work together. Schönbaum knew he was better off here than working in a quarry or digging trenches. He knew that Rabinovich, though the director of the museum, still couldn't throw him out. Rabinovich couldn't manage without him.

'Now, fellows, unwrap them carefully and let's see where they go,' said Schönbaum gleefully. 'This is going to be quite a show, at least as good as the Grevin Museum, maybe better.'

The movers unwrapped the packages and brought out figures made of papiermâché all in sitting positions. They were dressed in the fashions of the 1840s, and one of them – an older man – wore a white vestment.

'Now let's arrange it and see how it's going to look.'

The movers dragged in an ancient table and chairs and positioned the various figures according to the directions of the designer. The whole scene created the impression of a feast.

'Now put a book in that old one's hand and set the table nicely. Then throw in these props.' The movers set various papiermâché objects representing holiday food on the table.

'Well, that should be it. Let's just have a look and see whether the figures are arranged correctly. They must be in chronological order, from the oldest to the youngest. The youngest one must look foolish. Does it look all right, Dr Rabinovich?' he asked.

'I gave you instructions, but I won't give you any more advice. That's not my job,' snapped Rabinovich.

'Well, don't take offence,' said Schönbaum calmly. 'I'll work it out. But it turned out well, didn't it? The figures look almost alive. And when I put it all in a darkened room and throw a little light on it from the side, people will really think there's a feast going on here. Nobody will know that these are just dummies. The visitors will be startled, won't they, fellows?'

The movers agreed enthusiastically. They were strong, healthy young men who were referred to as 'gladiators'. They were just as indifferent to religious objects as Schönbaum was.

'Let's leave it in this room for the time being. Then I'll test it out after I find an electrician. Maybe I'll need you again then for moving it around.'

The movers and the designer left, and Rabinovich was alone again. Suddenly he felt the presence of the figures. They were seated at a round table, a family engaged in pious devotion, celebrating the Passover feast of the Seder. During the meal the grandfather tells how the Jews were delivered from their Egyptian bondage, their slavery to the Pharaoh. The grandfather was the figure in the white vestment holding the book.

The head of the Central Bureau had ordered this exhibit and demanded that the figures be life-size and realistic to the smallest detail. Rabinovich gave Schönbaum the order along with careful instructions about what such a Seder should look like. And Schönbaum followed the instructions well, it couldn't be denied. He was an able craftsman with a good sense of theatrical effect.

Yet it was another sin, another desecration. 'Thou shalt not make graven images.' And a mockery of religion besides, a mockery of the ancient holiday.

The cup of his sins runneth over. He'd never find grace in the eyes of God after this. What good would following all the commandments and observing the Sabbath and praying and chanting do him when he had committed so many sins in a single day!

The faces of the figures were cheerful, for the holiday they were celebrating was a joyful one in which everyone, even the youngest and humblest, was allowed to participate. But he sensed that even they, with their calm good humour, were reproaching him for his sins.

He left the exhibition room quickly and returned to his office, which was on a different street.

EIGHT

TO BE MASTER of a conquered land on its way to becoming a German land is tiring and enervating work. Life was better in those long-ago days before they seized power, when he could fight the enemies of the Reich directly, when he could chase them around the room at meetings and then connect with a fist to the jaw. Life was better when he could see the enemy standing before him, visible, blood trickling down his face, and he could stamp on him with his high boots, polished until they veritably glistened. Life was better at Columbia-haus, where he could interrogate conspirators of the Night of the Long Knives, watching the blood soak through the plaster walls of his office. Life was better in the Polish campaign, dropping bombs on villages from his own plane and then, because the Poles had no anti-aircraft guns, flying low, barely above the ground, in order to see the cottages burning, the confused human vermin racing back and forth, the dead bodies lying on the ground, frying in the flames.

He had fought the enemy face to face in those days. Now he only gives orders to bring about its destruction. He is the master of hundreds and thousands of subjects, setting a complex machinery into action, making sure it operates well, checking its various parts, improving them, perfecting them, introducing technological innovations, all the while remaining invisible himself, receiving figures, reports and graphs, signing death sentences without ever seeing the condemned, going in to check the results only on occasion.

But to be master of the land is the task assigned him by the Leader. It means that he must renounce everything personal, that he must be alone, that he must have no friends, that he must be inscrutable and inaccessible even at home among his family, even at parties and dinners. All that remains for him is music; it always helps when he feels tired; it offers peace and contentment; the tensions of the day melt away in it. He remembers listening to Beethoven's Fourth after the Night of the Long Knives, remembers how it gave him renewed strength to carry on, to continue interrogating enemies and beating confessions out of them. The music cleansed everything that time, even the blood.

But now he can no longer listen as he pleases. Though he has an excellent gramophone in Panenske Brezany, one that is not for sale anywhere, but was a personal gift from the director of Siemens, and though he has records of virtually the entire classical repertory, still he rarely plays them, because he doesn't like canned music, however well produced. He no longer plays in an amateur quartet – his playing has got too rusty and his hand can no longer hold a bow, because he has used it too often on police duty.

What about concerts and opera performances? Nowadays these bring him little pleasure. They're official occasions organised to honour some important event or visitor; mainly they serve as background for official gatherings. Even the house concerts of chamber music at the Waldstein Palace aren't actually 'house' concerts but social evenings to which he is obliged to invite all sorts of people – generals, big shots of the SS Elite Guard, the highest officers of the Gestapo, chance visitors. These people have no interest in classical music – they would much prefer operettas or films with Marika Rokk. They attend these concerts because they don't know how to get out of it tactfully, while he, on the other hand, has to invite them to discharge social obligations.

Small wonder, then, that they're bored, that they yawn, inspect their fingernails, cough and clear their throats, clean their monocles, and even doze off. How can he possibly enjoy music under such circumstances? What good is it to invite the finest musicians and conductors of the Reich to Prague, when they must perform for such uneducated audiences, who applaud only dutifully and never with enthusiasm. And, of course, the artists sense this immediately; they have a well-developed instinct about their audiences. Therefore, they play and sing any old way, without distinction, and instead of demonstrating the strength of their artistry, they spend their entire day running around the city shopping for goods and foodstuffs. They demand special rations allowing them to bring home bacon, poultry and woollens.

Even tonight he is expected to attend an opera performance, Mozart again, *Don Giovanni*, at the Stavovsky Theatre. The opera had its first performance there and it would be performed there again today, the day the stolen theatre is to be restored to German hands. What better opera to invite the minister of the Reich, the Leader's favourite, to attend? He had escorted the distinguished guest around for the whole day before entrusting him to the head of the Central Bureau who was to show him the Jewish memorials. The Acting Reich Protector's kindness did not go so far as actually showing him Jews. Besides, the head of the Central Bureau was better suited to it – he himself knows nothing and wants to know nothing about the Jews besides the Leader's command – that they be annihilated. This command would be carried out, but it was easier to do so if one saw the Jews only as numbers instead of having to actually meet them in real life.

They rode along the quay together. He had the roof of the car down so they could better inspect the city. They looked at the river and at the royal castle. The view was most beautiful from there. The quay had been completed a hundred years earlier, when Prague was a German city. He sat beside the minister and spoke to him about the monuments, about musicians and composers who had visited Prague. The minister knew a great deal about the city – he had undoubtedly studied a number of illustrated books back in Berlin. It was strange to discover that this former architect, well known for his grandiose plans for the reconstruction of Berlin and for the construction of an art centre in Linz, took such pleasure in this city. Surely it must seem small and provincial to him compared to Berlin or Vienna. The minister said, 'Music in stone,' and truly this phrase, bandied about by authors of art books, described Prague well. The city was, indeed, steeped in music and brought into harmony by it. The guest wanted to see the German House of Art and expressed a desire to visit the opera. Fortunately, they were playing *Don Giovanni* at the Stavovsky Theatre. It would be a good performance and something to boast about.

They continued across the Charles Bridge to the castle. He particularly singled out the statue of Roland as incontrovertible evidence that Prague had always been German. The guest admired the statue on artistic grounds but didn't seem to get the symbolic significance, nor did he take any notice of the sword the statue was clutching in its hand. He was more interested in the statue's face. But of course the former architect was one of the few intellectuals in the

Leader's inner circle. He had never been a soldier, he didn't wear a uniform, and he had come to Prague in a civilian coat and hat.

Slowly they drove uphill towards the castle through the old neighbourhood called the Small Side – and the minister asked to have the car stopped every so often in order to admire the palaces' façades.

'It most certainly is a German city,' the minister thought out loud, 'erected by German builders, but . . . '

'There are no buts,' his host interrupted him sharply. 'The Czechs always lived here as temporary guests. It's German, to the core.'

'Yes, you're right, you're certainly right. The Leader, after all, said the same thing when he returned from Prague. Its architecture seemed more German to him than the architecture of Vienna. But . . . the German builders hired Czech artisans. We architects have a trained eye, we can see that they brought a foreign element into their work. They worked in their own fashion. When you picture Nürnberg . . . '

'But Prague is Baroque,' his host interrupted him a bit peevishly.

'Of course, but after all, the Prague Baroque is different from the Baroque in other cities – Munich, for instance, or Dresden.'

They drove up to the castle and walked about the courtyards.

'What sort of army is this?' asked the minister when he saw the castle guard. 'I've never seen uniforms like these with canary-yellow lapels.'

'That's the Czech national guard – a real joke. The state President lives in one wing here.'

'I hope we don't have to visit him.'

'No, he comes to visit me. Or rather, he doesn't come, but Frank brings him. That flag of theirs is also just for show. We had to leave them something.'

They stopped by the Cathedral of St Vitus.

'The Czechs have always had a megalomaniac streak. Wouldn't you like to go inside? They have the vaults of Czech kings there, and the crown jewels as well. I have the keys to the crown jewels, but of course I don't carry them with me.' He smiled. 'Shall we go in?'

'I'm afraid we have little time,' said the minister 'and I've kept you from your official duties long enough.'

'Not at all,' he protested. 'I'm very honoured to be able to acquaint you with the beauties of Prague.' In fact, he was glad he didn't have to enter the cathedral.

He had unpleasant memories of the cathedral. The state President, though he barely reached Heydrich's shoulder, had hunched even lower as he handed him the keys to the crown jewels and humbly thanked him for returning three of them. He was repulsed to see the old man kiss the death's-head of St Vaclav, as if hoping St Vaclav would have mercy on his land.

On the other hand, he was happy to point out the statue of St George to the minister. The Leader had admired it enormously after arriving at the head of his armies to take possession of the conquered land for Germany. It seemed to symbolise the Reich itself. Snakes and lizards slither at its base and a ferocious dragon rears its head out of the mud, dirt and mire. The hero in armour stabs the dragon with his pennanted lance. That's how the Reich triumphs over its enemies! The Leader had first thought of moving the statue to the Reich Chancellery, but after looking it over again carefully he changed his mind. His unfailing artistic and political instinct warned him of something. He called in a professor of Art History from the German University, an expert on Prague, and confirmed that his instinct had been right. The statue had originally been German; indeed, commissioned by Charles, Emperor of the Holy Roman Empire. It was a Gothic statue. But then in the sixteenth century it had been recast by some Czech bungler. That's why it didn't have the proper German proportions. The hero was smaller than the horse and his face didn't have the properly severe, constricted, emaciated look of a German hero. He looked like a regular Czech pancake of a fellow. Thus the corrupted statue could not be an embellishment of the German Chancellery but remained in the castle courtyard.

'I'll show you the spot where the Leader looked out over Prague. It was actually from a second-floor window, but the view is the same.'

They were silent for a few moments as they looked at the view.

'The German students rightly named Prague the "Golden City". Fortunately, Göring didn't have it bombed. Otherwise we'd see only ruins today.'

'I've seen enough of them in Berlin,' complained the minister bitterly.

Heydrich frowned. He disliked hearing about the bombing of German cities.

The minister continued: 'We'll build a new Berlin after the war, a Berlin with broad, airy streets and parks, with grand squares and modern buildings. The conquered nations will pay for it, so we won't have to count pennies. But this city will probably remain a museum.'

'Yes, a museum.' Heydrich suddenly remembered. 'The head of the Central Bureau is waiting for you in the Cerninsky Palace. My chauffeur will take you there. I must leave you now, but I'll see you tonight at the opera.'

The minister sat back again in the car. He was annoyed with himself for getting into a dangerous conversation with Heydrich. One had to be very careful with these military types. He had noticed Heydrich's reaction when he had mentioned the bombing of Berlin.

The head of the Central Bureau courteously opened the door of his car for the minister. They drove back down to the city.

'You're about to see an entirely different neighbourhood, the former Jewish ghetto. Unfortunately, it's no longer a ghetto. Otherwise, we'd keep the Jews there temporarily as they do in Warsaw. But there are interesting historical sights: the old Jewish cemetery, the Jewish Town Hall with the clock that runs backwards, and then our great secret, a Jewish museum.'

The head of the Central Bureau was certainly better company than Heydrich. He obviously didn't stand on military ceremony, nor was he a stone-face like Heydrich, before whom one had to watch one's every word. And the tour of the exhibits really intrigued him. Even the blowing of that curious horn in the gloomy half-light of the museum amused him. They said their goodbyes at the hotel near the main railway station. He needed to rest a bit, take a bath, and change clothing before going to the theatre . . .

'I'll be at the theatre, too,' said the head of the Central Bureau. 'May I have the honour of visiting you during the interval?'

The Stavovsky Theatre was especially illuminated in honour of the Reich minister's visit. In the presidential box he was greeted by Heydrich, who presented his wife to him, and then the wife of the Secretary of State, Frank, and finally the Secretary of State himself. Heydrich offered the minister a seat next to his wife. Standing behind them, at respectful attention, were his adjutants. The minister stood out in his evening clothes: looking out over the audience, he saw only men in uniforms and women in formal attire. This preponderance of tassels, cuffs and epaulettes seemed inappropriate for such a lovely and delicate theatre, with its gilded rococo ornamentation in which angels were the predominant motif. Chubby angels and bemedalled military types in high boots that squeaked at the smallest movement of the feet – these did not go together. Actually Mozart himself was not suited to people in uniform. But the audience listened quietly and attentively once the music began. Perhaps the music was so strong that it penetrated even brains dulled by murder and alcohol. Perhaps they forgot about their bloody trade – at least for a while. It was also pleasant not to have this outstanding performance disturbed by the screaming of sirens.

During the interval Heydrich's wife started a conversation with him. She questioned him about Berlin as if she were longing to return to the main city of the Reich. She tried to give the impression of being in exile among barbarians here, but her rounded, well-nourished figure suggested that life in the Protectorate suited her well. This time he was careful not to say a word about bombing. He talked about the inner workings of the Reich Chancellery, about the Leader's cabinet, about receptions organised by Göring in the Karinhalle . . . And of course also about

Prague. He had come to appreciate its beauties, thanks to his most-competent guide. Even Frank joined the discussion about Prague, describing what the city had looked like during the Republic, when he'd fought against the thieving Czech parliament.

'They stole this theatre from us. They took a theatre dedicated to German art and they degraded it with perverse French drawing-room comedies and yokelish hodgepodges by Czech authors.'

It was clear that hatred and spite were pouring out of Frank, that his words did not reflect the feelings of a ruler and master of the land such as Heydrich but rather those of a person who had finally quenched his desire for revenge.

The adjutants brought refreshments – French wine for the gentlemen and real orangeade for the ladies. They chatted easily in the comfortable box, everyone smiling. Only Heydrich stood to the side, his face expressionless.

When the head of the Central Bureau suddenly appeared, young and full of good spirits, as if exhilarated by the music, Heydrich interrupted the conversation in a commanding voice, without any regard for his guest: 'I haven't had a chance to read your report. Is Terezin in full swing? Have all the Czech inhabitants been moved out?'

'Yes,' announced the head of the Central Bureau. 'The order has been carried out, the Czech inhabitants moved, and transports dispatched regularly. Some of them stop just briefly and then continue immediately to the East. The construction of a special Terezin-Bohusovice line is being considered, to facilitate the operation. But the Jews would have to put it up themselves!'

'Good,' said Heydrich, and then he thought of another thing. 'Giesse' – he turned around – 'has the statue of that

Jew on the balustrade been torn down? You seem to have forgotten to inform me about it.'

'I haven't had a chance to do so, sir, but everything is in order. The statue was torn down this afternoon.'

Heydrich fell silent again. But the mood was spoiled.

Heydrich's wife complained to the minister: 'You men can't stay away from business even in the theatre! And the Jews, on top of everything! Really, people shouldn't speak of them in polite society.' The rebuke was aimed at the head of the Central Bureau.

'You can be sure, madam, that in the nearest future there will be absolutely no need to talk about Jews in any sort of society.' The head of the Central Bureau smiled and stepped away so that the minister could resume his interrupted conversation.

The head of the Central Bureau looked around the hall which was beginning to fill up again. The gold of uniform and women's precious jewels glistened everywhere. Some faces were joyfully agitated by the music, others were calm and cheerful. As if there weren't a war going on at all, as if they had all met here to celebrate a victory, as if they had put on their dress uniforms and ordered their wives to wear their most expensive jewellery. How strange it all was . . . and at that moment he thought of his most recent trip to the East. He had just returned from there two days ago and now, as he stood in the box decorated with the sovereign emblem of the Reich, it seemed a different world.

A desolate countryside in the rain, a black, barren plain shrouded with smoke and fog, the loading platform of the railway station, the cattle cars out of which staggered the half-suffocated people with stars – men, women and children with bundles and suitcases. And the SS policemen beating them with clubs, hurrying them along, pushing them into the thick mud and then stamping on them with their heavy studded boots. Cries and blood, screaming children, blows and pistols, the long road to the camp and the dead bodies lying along the roadside. And the smoke from the chimneys pouring out day and night, fog and mud, barbed wire and high towers with machine guns. Dirt and blood, the hiss of gas in tiled chambers that resembled bathrooms, ashes covering the earth, fields of the thousands cremated.

He smiled contentedly. They all pretend they know nothing. They don't want to know anything. They can't even bear to hear a word about the Jews. He is happy that he knows what is going on in the East. Heydrich, of course, knows, too, but he never lets on that he is pleased with the good work of his subordinates.

The orchestra was beginning to tune up. It was time to say their goodbyes, above all to the distinguished guest who was returning to Berlin that very night. A little later the sweet music of Mozart rang out through the theatre once again.

NINE

KRUG KNEW THAT the statue must be torn down today. Heydrich forgot nothing. He was not the sort of person to wait for a report from a subordinate. Schlesinger had failed abysmally – now Krug had to take matters into his own hands. He ordered the workmen to stay at Municipal even if they had to wait all night, and he went home to get his wife's advice. He couldn't borrow an official car and there was little time left. Fortunately, he didn't live far away.

His wife was frightened when he burst into the apartment so unexpectedly. She thought they must be sending him to the front. How terrible it would be for her and the children to be alone in this hostile city! Everyone had envied her when her husband got the job in the Protectorate. People said that this country was a paradise on earth, that there was plenty of everything: food, clothes; that German children received fruit, even oranges and lemons! They gave them a nicely furnished apartment with central heating where there truly was everything you could possibly want – modern furniture, nice linens, books in gilded bindings, rugs, paintings, dishes, a refrigerator and kitchen equipment. Everything became their property and it cost them almost nothing. They even received toys for Horst and Hildemarie. At first all those beautiful things hadn't made her happy, because she hadn't chosen them herself; somehow, they seemed to resist the hands of a new owner. Then she grew accustomed to them and felt as if she had owned them for ever.

They told her it was a German city, but it wasn't German. They lived here as if in a besieged fortress. Everywhere, whether in the lift or at the local shops, she was met with looks full of hate. She saw that everyone detested her, even inanimate objects, stone houses, bridges and parks. As long as her husband was with her he could defend her. But what if he had to leave?

The morning paper which Krug had left as he hurried to his office was lying on the table, waiting for him to finish reading it in the evening. It was folded to the last page, which was covered with military crosses. The death notices. Lately the number had been mounting. If her husband was to fall on the field of honour and glory too, what would become of her then?

But it wasn't a transfer to the front. Something else was bothering Krug. His wife sighed with relief.

'A composer, a composer,' she repeated. 'That's very easy. I'm surprised it didn't occur to you. Don't you remember the Ohnesorgs – they had dinner at our house a while ago. He's an official with the same rank as you and comes from a Prague musical family. His brother is a famous pianist and his wife studied at the Prague conservatory – she plays the harpsichord.'

'But I can't go to see him at the Protectorate office. That would be very dangerous. I'd have to explain to him what this is about. Who's to guarantee that it wouldn't get back to Giesse or Heydrich?'

'Don't worry,' said his wife. 'I'll take care of it. Wait right here for me. I'll run over to see his wife – it's just around the corner. She knows all the composers and musicians as well as her husband does, and she's also from Prague. She'll tell me where that statue is. I'll make you some real coffee –

that'll calm you down.' Coffee was a great rarity and they drank it only on special occasions.

His wife came home before long and immediately spilled out her news. It would be easy to identify the statue; she had written down its description and location. Krug ran to Municipal.

Antonin Becvar and Josef Stankovsky had been sitting in the guardhouse for over two hours, holding the noose. That's what they'd been told to do. They were waiting for Krug and for further orders. They were rolling cigarettes out of local tobacco.

'Yeah, sure,' said Becvar. 'This statue business is endless. Maybe they'll send us out on the roof again to look for that statue and it'll be the wrong one again.'

'Those Krauts are all crazy,' Stankovsky reflected aloud. 'Like that Schlesinger. Now, if he was some kind of official, that would make sense, but he was a working man before, a locksmith. He went crazy, too. I'm telling you, it's just something inside them, and nothing you can do about it.'

'Yeah, sure.' Becvar exhaled smoke. 'They're a real pain. I'll tell you something – that Krug is even worse. He's from the Reich – those are the worst bastards, because if he was a decent person he wouldn't come crawling here. A decent person always stays in his own home.'

'Do you know what happened?' The guard spoke to them through the little window. 'They fired Schlesinger and he's going to the front.'

'You think we don't know that?' Stankovsky frowned. 'We've got Krug leading our Wild West round-up. Don't you see our lasso?'

'You know, that Schlesinger wasn't necessarily bad, he

was just totally stupid – ' Becvar chimed in. 'You didn't know him the way I did. He kept going to those courses on World View and they went to his head. And then he decided he'd conduct a course for us in Czech so we'd understand the Reich way of thinking. You were lucky you were in Vrsovice that time, but I had to sign up. I'm not going to tell you all the stupid things he lectured about there; I hardly remember a single thing, because I slept through most of it. But once I did have a run-in with him about Gypsies.'

'What do Gypsies have to do with the Reich World View?'

'You're really out of it – Gypsies are very important. So he was telling us about race and Aryans and all, and he said that Jews and Gypsies are a hostile element because they're not Aryans and that the Leader had expelled them from public life, so nobody is supposed to have anything to do with them. Well, I knew all about the Jews. Don't we see new announcements about them all the time here at Municipal? But that stuff about Gypsies – that was news to me. See, I once read some kind of book, or maybe it was in a news magazine, I can't even remember, saying that the Gypsies come from India and that in India they're Aryans. Somehow the whole thing didn't make sense to me. So I went and said to Schlesinger: "Those Gypsies come from India, right? So I read somewhere that Indians are Aryans." Well, you should have seen him begin to yell and scream: "That's treason! You can be punished severely for that. If the Leader says Gypsies aren't Aryans, then that's the way it is and no dimwit is allowed to open his trap about it around here." After that I never asked him about anything. I preferred to sleep.'

'Well, since Schlesinger is so well educated, now he'll

have a chance to pass this information along to his army buddies,' added Stankovsky. 'Except I don't know how much good it will do him when he gets knocked off.'

They chatted a while longer, then they fell silent and dozed a while.

Suddenly Krug burst into the guardhouse and immediately began to yell: '*Marsch! Auf!*'

Krug spoke only German. Becvar and Stankovsky knew hardly any German, but they were used to orders like that.

He hurried them along. They knew where they were going, and they knew what they were supposed to do. On the roof he showed them which statue they were supposed to knock down.

They threw the noose around Mendelssohn's neck. Then Becvar had an idea.

'Look, pal, the Kraut's gone back to the guardhouse, so he can't see what we do. I'll tell you what. That statue must be important since they're making such a fuss about it. We've got to knock it down, obviously, but let's do it really carefully. We can just, like, roll it over, so we don't break it. And then, when this is all over, our fellows can put it back up again. Okay?'

'You bet,' Stankovsky agreed. 'Let's go.'

They tugged at the statue carefully. It came down so slowly that only a hand broke off.

'Who cares about a hand. That doesn't matter. That can be glued back on.'

Then he called out one of the German words he knew in the direction of the gate: '*Fertig!*'

Krug looked out. The statue was lying on the floor of the roof. It would not be visible from the street. The order was carried out.

'*Marsch! Auf!*' Krug yelled. He hurried to Municipal to make a telephone call.

Becvar and Stankovsky raced out so that Krug couldn't change his mind and return to inspect the statue. But dusk had fallen by now, and it was hard to see its features. They hurried home. Stankovsky had the rope under his arm.

'What are you going to do with it?' asked Becvar.

'Nothing, but it's a good pre-war rope, it's not made of paper. Maybe my old lady will hang clothes from it.'

'It's no good for clothes, it's too thick, she'd never get the clothes-pegs on it. And besides, it belongs to the Reich.'

'Well, if not for clothes, then it'll be good for something else. And as for it being the property of the Reich, don't worry. In all that rush I never gave them a receipt for it. So they'll never find out I kept it.'

'See you later,' said Becvar in parting. They lived in different sections of town.

Krug rushed into the office all in a sweat and grabbed a telephone. It was already late, extremely late. What if Giesse wasn't in his office? Luckily he remembered that an important visitor was scheduled for today – the Reich minister had arrived. One of the officials must still be on duty. If Giesse wasn't there, someone else would be who could take messages for Giesse.

He couldn't get through for a long time. Finally one of Giesse's assistants answered. Krug told him emphatically that the order given by the Acting Reich Protector had been carried out and that he must get this information to Giesse immediately. The assistant promised that he'd call Giesse at home. He'd surely be home because he was getting ready for a gala performance at the Stavovsky Theatre.

Krug sighed with relief. The statue was down and there'd be no more unpleasantness. Or would there? That imbecile Schlesinger had got him involved with Wancke, and in addition Wancke's little flunkey had kicked up hell at the Jewish Community. The head of the Central Office would surely have something to say about that. What would it take to get the Elite Guard off his neck? The garrison was here on leave, in any case, and would soon be leaving for the front. Of course he might end up the same way Schlesinger did. Good thing he'd got rid of him – now he could blame everything on him. Though it was actually he himself who had dealt with Wancke, acting as Schlesinger's superior. No, the whole business with the statue was dangerous and would lead to no good for anyone.

Dr Rabinovich went home at the end of his working hours. Like everyone else, he worked until seven in the evening – no exception was made for him. Indeed, he had very few extra privileges, though he had quite a high position in the Community. He was able to take advantage of a little fresh air at the cemetery during the workday to study the Hebrew inscriptions on the gravestones – that was a part of his scholarly work and nobody could hold it against him. Nonetheless, there were those who were jealous, people confined to their desks in offices who worked uninterruptedly from seven in the morning to seven in the evening, and had to be home by eight because there was a curfew. The curfew applied to Dr Rabinovich also. But every so often, when he had extra work to do at night, he'd receive permission to exceed the curfew. He had the same food allotments as the others and bought nothing on the black market, but it wasn't hard for him to live on a vegetarian diet – at least he could observe the dietary laws that way. It was worse for his sons. There was nothing else for them to do but get used to slim pickings.

But now he knew there was no escape. He was mixed up with murderers, he served them, and yet he'd always thought he'd get the better of them. Though he had set up this museum according to their wishes, as a memorial to an extinct race, in reality he had hoped to save the sacred articles which would otherwise be destroyed as they had been in the other conquered countries. Now he knew that the articles would remain but not the people. Whoever gets mixed up with evil types commits evil deeds and becomes their accessory whether he likes it or not, no matter what excuses he might make to himself, even if his intention had always been to deceive them. For evil is their dominion and Death is their companion. They assign Death to guard each person: guard and bark, they command. And Death guards his victims and his barking increases their fear. Fear makes his victims sink deeper and deeper into the mud from which they can no longer fight back, from which they can no longer even deceive themselves into thinking that they are doing it for a good cause. He said to himself: 'My heart is sore pained within me and the terrors of death are fallen upon me.' But repeating the words of the Bible was useless – the words brought no comfort. For if he was cast out, what help could the Bible bring? Just one more day of life, a bad, bitter day. Just one more day of life for his wife and sons, a hard day in a time of shame.

Following orders, Julius Schlesinger handed over his schedule of affairs to Dr Buch. Dr Buch was a runty fellow, always complaining of stomach troubles. He wore glasses and false teeth. Nobody'd ever get him to the front, you could be sure of that. He was evil and mean-spirited, clearly pleased that things had turned out so badly for Schlesinger. Let him wallow in mud at the front, let him freeze to the bone – all those things Buch wished him, and more – let him hang as a deserter. He didn't even wish him a hero's death.

Schlesinger saw how happy Dr Buch was and it filled him with fury. They're all evil, especially that bastard Krug, who had promised him the Iron Cross and then sent him to the front, in spite of the fact that the whole business had turned out all right, as he later discovered. Somehow Krug had managed to identify the statue. And the statue wreaked its revenge on Schlesinger, a heavy revenge. The end of the good life at Municipal. But if everyone is evil, if everyone is out to harm him, why shouldn't he be evil, too, why shouldn't he let out his anger on someone else, someone lower? Becvar and Stankovsky, those Czech dimwits who ran to Municipal right behind him to see him taken away in the black car. He must have his revenge on them somehow while he still had the chance. He just needed to say a word to Dr Buch and he'd take care of it – to do a bad deed was a pleasure for him. But he couldn't turn him loose on both of them – that would be too obvious. He had to pick one of them. Becvar had ridiculed him about those Gypsies. Yes, Becvar was the right one. If the statue had its revenge on him, then let it hound someone else as well.

He said, 'I want to inform you about one more thing, Dr Buch. It's that workman, Becvar; you know, the one I took with me to tear down the statue. He's a dangerous person, a secret enemy of the Reich. I saw his true nature at once when I was teaching the course.'

'So. Becvar,' mused Dr Buch with a smile. 'I know something about him.' Dr Buch was a confidant of the Gestapo and knew quite a lot about everybody. 'I've had my eye on him for a long time. So he showed his true colours after all. Don't you think this might be a case for the Gestapo?'

'No, he's too sly. He puts on a good act. They'd never pin any treasonous act on him.'

'That's not a problem. The Gestapo would beat the slyness out of him. They have their methods over there.'

Schlesinger resisted. He didn't want to go that far in his revenge. 'No. It will be enough if you kick him out and send him to the Employment Bureau with a bad recommendation.'

'Of course. Whatever you say. I'm delighted to be able to help you out in this little thing, especially' – he grinned – 'especially since you're going off to fight against the savage barbarians.'

Then he bade him farewell with great sincerity and wished him a lot of luck, and may he achieve heroic acts on the field of honour and glory.

Out in the hall Schlesinger exploded: 'That little rat, that cockroach. How it pleased him to talk about those heroic acts at the front. I'm surprised he didn't wish me a heroic death.'

Maybe he shouldn't have denounced Becvar to that little rat. But why shouldn't Becvar get it, too? Why should he be the only one to suffer?

Richard Reisinger returned to the guardhouse. He was still bleeding at the mouth, and asked the person who had stood in for him to stay a little longer while he went to wash and stop the bleeding. When he returned, his temporary replacement told him not to resume his watch, that they had just called to say that Reisinger was fired and that he was to go to ask for a new job at the Work Force Division.

'So it goes,' sighed Reisinger.

He hadn't liked being a guard anyhow. Sitting closed up in an airless little room behind a little window all day long – that was no work for him. He was used to working in the quarry and doing heavy hauling with a cart out in the fresh air. And then that constant weeping and moaning and complaining, and also the physical abuse.

At the Work Force Division of the Jewish Community an official pulled out his card: 'You're in category A, Roman numeral I. That means perfectly healthy, capable of the hardest physical labour. So office work is out.'

'Sure, I'm not afraid of hard work – the harder the better. I'd be happy to go back to the quarry or to do heavy moving.' He preferred not to mention digging trenches. The SS were overseers on those jobs and they were merciless.

'The quarry is out of the question,' announced the Community official, formerly a travelling dry-goods salesman. 'Ever since the transports began they've stopped all outdoor work. Moving and hauling is all booked up. We can't send a single person there. The only thing left is trench digging, but I really wouldn't recommend that – you should see them carting off seriously injured people from there all the time. How they got injured and by whom I hardly have to tell you. But I do have some work for you. Actually, it's a position I have to fill at any cost. And here you are at just the right moment. Forgive me, but I can't send you anywhere else. It won't be so bad, I assure you.'

Reisinger was alarmed. What sort of job was it that made

the official talk about it so vaguely, so cautiously? If it turned out to be carrying dead bodies to the morgue, that wouldn't be so bad.

'You know' – the official seemed to be weighing his words – 'it's a warehouse job, moving and the like.'

'But not at the Collection Agency?' Reisinger spoke a little impatiently. 'Why, you just said a few minutes ago that all the jobs there are taken.'

'No, it's not at the Collection Agency,' the official continued quietly. 'It's not an office connected with us at all. We received this order from higher up. You know, we have to accommodate them at any cost.'

'So tell me, for goodness' sake, what kind of job is it?'

'Well, since you're so eager to know' – the official shrugged his shoulders – 'it's the Gestapo warehouse. They've got a lot of work there now because they're confiscating the property of executed people and they need a moving man, one who wouldn't breathe a word. A Jew is suitable for that sort of thing. So. Now you know what kind of job it is.'

Reisinger's knees began to shake. He had got used to all sorts of things, and he had lived through all sorts of things. But this? They were handing him over directly to the worst beasts of prey. What might they do to him there? As soon as they stopped needing his services, they'd find a way to make sure he'd never tell, the only way they knew how.

'No, not that . . . not the Gestapo . . . '

'I can't help you,' said the official. 'I don't know any other job for you. And it won't be so bad. Fischman was there just before you. He left on his own because he got a hernia. And he said that the Gestapo were fairly decent to him; that is, as decent as they are capable of being. They certainly didn't beat him, and they didn't scream at him either. They're mainly interested in making off with as much as possible there, so they don't have time for anything else. The manager there is a woman. Of course, she's one of their women. You'd be worse off digging trenches.'

He gave Reisinger a paper with an address and told him to show up the next day.

TEN

ADELA AND GRETA sat in Mrs Javurek's little cubbyhole. The house was old; many people lived there. From morning to night feet trudged up the steps – there was no lift. An overcrowded apartment house where things are in an uproar from morning to night and nobody pays attention to a stranger is the safest hiding place. Adela and Greta had to sit quietly. If anyone rang the doorbell they knew they mustn't open the door, for nobody should find out there were strangers in the house. Mrs Javurek spent almost the entire day tracking down food and standing in queues. Mr Javurek was a tram driver and came home at different times, depending on his shift.

The day dragged along slowly. The children looked at books their Uncle Jan had brought them. But it's not possible to read books all day long. They drew pictures with coloured pencils and paints, and they played the sort of games that don't require much noise. They also cleaned the apartment and carefully washed the dishes. When the neighbours were home they would have noticed any unusual sound coming from the apartment, because they knew that Mrs Javurek had gone shopping.

Now they'd never get outside! Maybe when the war ended, but nobody knew when that would be. Their names were already on a list of the disappeared. All policemen had these lists and it would be very dangerous to go out on the street, since nobody in the building knew they were there. There was not much air in their little cubbyhole. They weren't allowed to go into the living room or kitchen when they were home alone, nor were they allowed to go near the windows. The best idea would have been to board up the wall. But in a house like this, where the arrival of a bricklayer or a roofer is a big event, boarding up was impossible. When word got around that they were doing spot inspections, the Javureks hid the door of the cubbyhole by putting a large wardrobe in front of it. Nobody unfamiliar with the apartment would ever dream that there was a little room behind the big piece of furniture.

But sometimes Adela and Greta simply couldn't overcome their curiosity and they peeked out from behind the curtains into the street. It was a suburban street, not at all a lively one, only paving stones, apartment houses with cracked paint, and a few little houses without gardens dating back to the days before the village had turned into a suburb. There were many children who played on the street when school was out; they jumped and ran around everywhere, because no trams ran on the street and cars rarely drove by that way – only the dustbin men and an occasional coal delivery. Adela and Greta liked to watch the dustbin men. And-a-one, and-a-two, up and over, and the dustbin was empty – they wished they could learn to do it, too. The coal wagons were pulled by horses, gigantic animals, but the children preferred a little horse who delivered packages. He'd show up on the street on occasion and paw at the ground with his right foot as if he were begging for something, maybe sugar. But nobody gave him sugar these days. Sugar was rare. Sometimes he'd get a crust of bread. He said thank you for everything, even if it wasn't sugar, by nodding his head up and down. As soon as the weather grew warmer and the sun came out, the children were happier; they heard voices because the windows were open.

There was a tomcat who used to show up regularly on the street. They even knew his name – a funny one – Bretislav. They had learned about a historical Bretislav when they were still going to school and they remembered something about him – that he had abducted somebody called Jitka from Germany. The tomcat didn't look like the abducting type. He sauntered along in a dignified way, a nice fat cat, which made him stand out somewhat in wartime, when people and animals were all losing weight. He must have been catching lots of mice – they weren't rationed. The whole street hated this cat. He belonged to the janitor of the house across the street, who watched over him carefully and obviously cared about him a lot. Such a fat cat was a highly unusual sight nowadays. The janitor was a card-carrying Fascist; he was always threatening people in the neighbourhood and he had already denounced quite a few. That's why many people disliked the cat and would have preferred to see him in their frying pans.

As soon as they could, Adela and Greta got into position to peek out of the window. The cat took a long time to show up. Not until the sun was broiling did he deign to stroll out of his house and on to the street. By then it was almost noon. The girls ran the danger of being caught by Mrs Javurek when she came home to make lunch. They'd really get it if she caught them, and they didn't want to make Mrs Javurek angry. They loved her. They knew she was risking her life for them, that the Germans would kill Mr and Mrs Javurek both if they found out they were hiding someone. The punishment for that was death. The children knew something about death – they were with their mother as she was dying. Their father had disappeared even before that. The Germans had probably killed him.

The cat was a great temptation, and especially a famous cat about whom they had heard so much. No, they couldn't resist watching him. Why did he jump out of his window only at noon? Someone should persuade him to come out at other times.

Adela spotted him first. Quietly she let Greta know. 'Look. Here comes Bretislav.'

The cat walked along slowly, not at all furtively. He walked along self-confidently. He probably knew that his master was watching him out of his window. He paid no attention to the people around; he had a definite destination. The street ended in a small square, with a little prayer stool in front of a statue of the Crucifixion. Women coming home from shopping often stopped at the statue, put down their bags, knelt and prayed. That was the cat's place in the noonday sun. Right on the prayer stool. The clasped hands of the woman praying there on the bench didn't bother him at all. But who wants to pray with a cat? The woman always got up and left indignantly. But nobody dared kick the cat or chase him away with the janitor keeping a close eye on him.

One evening the Javureks had a talk about the cat.

Mrs Javurek said, 'Somebody ought to put a stop to this. You know I'm not a religious type and I don't go to church. But when that cat is sprawled out there and women want to pray, it seems like a sort of desecration. Besides which, the cat belongs to that Fascist who's always looking to catch somebody and get them sent to prison.'

Mr Javurek argued with her: 'It's not the cat's fault that his master works for the Germans. And if a person is religious and wants to pray, then they don't have to pay any attention to their surroundings.'

Adela and Greta observed Bretislav. He was lying all stretched out and he didn't seem to mind that the prayer stool was on a slant.

Greta whispered: 'Cats are really clever, aren't they? I'm sure I'd fall off if it were me.'

'You ninny,' her older sister, Adela, answered condescendingly, 'you're bigger than that cat.'

'I don't care,' Greta insisted. 'If we were cats we'd have a better time. We'd walk around the rooftops and places like that. We wouldn't get caught by the Germans. We wouldn't have to sit here in this hole.'

'You ninny, you'd be so small that anybody could do whatever they wanted with you, like pull your tail. And all you'd be able to do is meow.'

'Oh no,' argued Greta, 'I'd hiss and scratch and bite. Cats are brave.'

Suddenly the doorbell rang. They jumped away from the window and quietly crept towards their cubbyhole.

The doorbell gave a second ring and then a third. It was the prearranged signal.

'We must open the door,' said Adela. 'It's Uncle Jan.'

'I'm scared,' Greta said, trembling. 'He never comes at this time. Maybe it's you-know-who behind the door, and they've got guns.'

'Don't be scared,' Adela reassured her. 'If it was you-know-who they'd be stamping and screaming.'

It was quiet outside.

They tiptoed up to the door. Adela looked through the peephole.

'It's Uncle Jan,' she said, and opened the door.

Jan Krulis closed the door behind him carefully. Adela and Greta clung to him, one on each side. They loved him, and besides, he always brought them something. He also told them about what was happening in the world. His visit always meant a few happy days for them. But Jan didn't joke around with them today; he didn't seem at all jolly.

'What happened, Uncle?' asked Adela. 'Do we have to move again?' They had moved three times already and it took them a long time to get used to strange people. They liked it at the Javureks'. The Javureks were kind to them.

'No, it's not that,' said Jan. 'It's your Uncle Rudolf . . . you know . . . '

Yes, they knew, they were able to figure it out. When they visited him once, long ago, Uncle Rudolf's face was different from other people's, so thin, as if the skin just covered the bones. It was waxy pale, a face full of pain. He looked like that statue that stood behind the prayer stool.

They wept. Uncle Rudolf was the last remaining member of their family. Now they had nobody. Death had come for everyone, for their mama and for their papa. Now it was their uncle's turn.

Jan Krulis was silent. He waited for them to cry their fill. They would forget. Life would bring them many other things to worry about. Yet what sort of life was it to sit all day in a little hole, to be afraid every time the doorbell rang, never to go out into the fresh air, to the river, to the park. People used to say that the sun and the air were free. But they weren't free. These children might pay a heavy price for them: their lives. Life had become the common price for everything. And keeping them in hiding was very difficult. They mustn't stay anywhere too long, that was the most important rule. Even when everyone was very careful, disaster might strike. The neighbours might notice a tiny movement of a curtain in the apartment at a time when they knew nobody was at home. On streets like this, women look out of their windows for hours at a time – that's their major entertainment, even though nothing ever happens outside. They notice every little thing and then people begin to talk, to speculate. One fine day you-know-who might break into the house – they have their spies. Hiding too long in one apartment was dangerous.

But it was difficult to find new hiding places. People were afraid, and it was hard to blame them. The penalty for hiding someone was death. It didn't matter whether you hid children or adults. Some people did it for the money, but you couldn't trust people like that. They were capable of betraying for money, too. The only people you could depend on for such a task were high-minded, honourable, good people. There had to be plenty of them, but try to find them in a big city.

Also, people were used to living according to certain rules. They had their favourite chairs, places at the table, stools by the kitchen stove. They held their knives and forks in their own way, they drank their water or their beer either during the meal or after. Everything strange, everything unusual bothered them, prevented them from enjoying their normal lives. And if you added fear to that, fear of death, fear residing somewhere deep inside, then that fear could explode at any time in the form of a sharp word, a reproach or an insult – people couldn't always control themselves. Adela and Greta were familiar with this. They realised that they were always at people's mercies, that they were the cause of fear and sorrow and despair. They felt they were in disgrace here. They were afraid of making the tiniest move. They were afraid of uttering the slightest sound. Anything they did might make someone angry or irritated. It was a bad situation for everyone.

He was taking care of Greta and Adela as he had promised, though actually, as a member of an illegal organisation, he wasn't supposed to do that sort of thing. He sought out hiding places for them among acquaintances or at addresses he received with the help of his organisation. He had to find food for them because they didn't receive any food rations and they couldn't deprive their hosts of food. That meant having enough money to buy provisions and rations on the black market. Still, money could always be found. There were always people who would give money without asking what it was for. And food could always be bought on the black market. The hardest thing was to ask people to place their own lives in danger. Drummers and pipers walked up and down the streets, waving horsetails; red decrees with long lists of names hung on every street corner: Condemned and executed for unfriendly acts towards the Reich. Everybody could read the red decrees. They never said what it was that people had done, nor was it necessary, for the punishment for everything was death. But the signature was there: Reinhard Heydrich.

Adela and Greta stopped crying.

'Look what I've brought you,' he said. He unwrapped a little package. There on top lay a bar of real, true, pre-war chocolate. Chocolate was an absolute miracle that year.

Greta reached out for it and wanted to take a bite.

'No, no.' Adela stopped her. 'Here's how we'll do it. Mrs Javurek will get a half, because she is so nice. We'll divide the other half into four pieces. Each of us will get one piece now. That way it will last us a long time. You can't wolf down the whole thing all at once like that.'

Greta was regretful, but she agreed to the plan.

Only then did they look at the other things in the package. They weren't so interested in them: soap, margarine, two cans of something or other, sugar, pasta.

They would forget, of course. They had practically forgotten their parents. That was good, that's the way it should be. They'd forget their uncle Rudolf Vorlitzer, too.

Death is all around. It is waiting for him, it is waiting for the two little girls. Death is always lurking. It is motionless, petrified. But there's no point in thinking about it. The point is to take care of ordinary things – where to place Adela and Greta at the end of the three months, how to get money and food.

'Uncle Jan' – Greta pulled him by the sleeve after she had eaten the chocolate – 'would you like to see Bretislav? There he is. Look behind the curtain. He's the cat sunning himself in front of the statue.'

Obediently he looked out at the cat. Yes, everything was all right.

'Goodbye, Adela and Greta,' he said to them. 'Give my regards to Mrs Javurek.'

He looked through the peephole to see if anyone was out in the hall. Then he quietly opened the door and tiptoed out of the apartment.

ELEVEN

HE SHOULD HAVE LEFT at nine that morning, but he was delayed because the children kept begging him to tell about his trip: What does Paris look like, what city did his plane fly from yesterday?

They hadn't seen him in the evening because they were already asleep when he arrived. For Lina to let them stay up late – that would have gone against her principles: discipline must be maintained from early childhood. He brought home many presents – the Paris Gestapo took care of everything – even in 1942, Paris was a wealthy city. Silks for his wife, fine underwear, perfumes, toys for the children, French wines, cognac, olives, shrimps.

He shouldn't have allowed himself to be delayed by the children when so much work was waiting for him in Prague, and when he was obliged to fly again the next day to Berlin, and from there to Holland. The great plan of the final solution was in full swing. Of course, he'd have to keep everybody on their toes. Things were going well in Prague; the head of the Central Bureau was a capable fellow, and besides, he could supervise him personally. But nothing was working in France – not surprising, in view of French sloppiness and self-indulgence. Instead of chasing the Jews into detention camps, the Office for the Solution of the Jewish Question kept publishing its stupid pamphlets, translated from the German; nobody read them, even though they were distributed free. The French police were unreliable. The Jews escaped across the border into the 'free' zone, often with the help of the French authorities.

The most vulnerable ones hid away in Nice, where the Italian authorities gave them a hand, probably for money – why else would the Italians do it? Eichmann's commissioner was haggling with the locals; here and there they handed over a few foreign-resident Jews. They made excuses, saying that they were unable to recognise who the Jews were unless they had a list of them. One of their stupidest ideas was to hire physiognomists who claimed they could reliably pick out Jews on the street simply by their appearance. He paid those good-for-nothings real money, though they recently picked out the ambassador's secretary.

All of France was a mess. He had a folder in his briefcase containing all the plans, the figures and quotas. The final solution depended on reliable fulfilment of plans. How was Auschwitz to work properly, how could it use the crematoria and gas chambers at full capacity if the quotas didn't arrive regularly, if everything was done in a makeshift way, if instead of the required number of Jews from France the Reich's functionaries had to fish for Jews all the way to the Peloponnese? He'd send Eichmann to make order there, to show those Frenchmen that the Reich wouldn't stand for such sloppiness. They knew how to steal property, but to send the quotas with regularity, that didn't interest them.

And in Holland, where he was to go tomorrow, the situation was even worse. There the inhabitants were rebelling against the Jewish laws, and everyone in Amsterdam was deliberately pinning on the Jewish star. He'd show those fat Dutchmen that the Reich could treat them the same way it treated the Jews. The task would be accomplished, no matter what.

Today he had a meeting scheduled with those clowns that called themselves the government of the Protectorate.

First he had scared them to death with the red decrees. Now he'd encourage them a little with some promises.

The children had asked what the Eiffel Tower looked like and whether the Reich flag flew from it. Yes, he'd seen the Eiffel Tower – if you're in Paris you can't help seeing the Eiffel Tower. But he hadn't gone up. What would he have done there? He had other things to do. In fact, apart from the streets he drove through in a closed limousine, he saw nothing of Paris. His wife was curious about French food. He couldn't tell her about it. He'd eaten whatever they set before him at the German officers' mess – he couldn't even remember what it was – he simply gulped down the food and hurried to his next meeting. He had nothing good to say about Paris, a spoiled, good-for-nothing city where nobody wanted to work, where people sat around in pavement cafes as if there weren't a war going on, as if there weren't air raids and bombings. Except that nobody was bombing them. Paris was undamaged, while Berlin was covered with rubble. But the French would pay heavily for it after the war.

He was impatient. The day had started somewhat inauspiciously because of the delay; Frank was surely waiting for him in his office by now. Everyone had grown accustomed to discipline and punctuality – he set them a good example. This was the first day he hadn't left at the exact time he was supposed to. And Paris? He had only taken a quick look at the Madeleine, because the Leader had stopped there on his way into the subjugated capital city.

A driver wearing an Oberscharführer's uniform brought Heydrich's open car to the back wing. The clock read ten past ten. Heydrich sat next to the driver in order to hurry him. Two flags bearing the sovereign insignia of his rank flew from the front bumper. The driver could ignore the local highway rules. They flew through villages where nobody at all appeared on the road; the poultry and geese were shut up in their sheds, according to his orders, and the people didn't come out of their homes. Good, a dead village, while the lord and master rides by. He only wished it really were dead. They hurtled through Zdiby and Chabry towards Kobylisy, the driver paying no attention to the speed limit. The troopers and police had already sent out word that the Reich Protector was on his way. The road was empty, not a soul in sight, not a single person standing in front of a house or a shop, even though it was a weekday, a beautiful day in May.

He filled his lungs with the sharp fresh air. He loved to drive fast, to have everything rush by. He loved the illusion of flying through a dead countryside accompanied only by wind, sun and clouds. Slowly his mood improved, his bad humour lifted. Now he didn't care whether he came late or not. So what, they'd wait. Why shouldn't the various officials and Frank and the government clowns wait for the ruler of the land? He was tempted to tell the driver to slow down, but that would have deprived him of the joys of speeding. Then he thought of something else. He'd allow himself one more pleasure. He screamed into the driver's ear: Let's go in by Hradcany Square.

The driver nodded. He'd drive through the majestic wrought-iron portal. On each side of the portal were statues standing on pedestals; the Acting Reich Protector had taken a particular liking to them the first time he'd marched through this portal on the way to the castle courtyard and been welcomed by a guard of honour as the future ruler of the subjugated land. The statues had impressed him even then. Even then they symbolised his power. Above the mighty backs of the vanquished enemy stand two giants. One of them holds a club, the other a dagger. In a moment the club will crush the spine, in a moment the dagger will plunge into the soft back. No mercy will be shown the adversary – that is clear from the faces of the victors. The blows will fall, blood will flow from the crushed body, from the pierced heart. These figures stand on their pedestals at the entryway of his seat of power, to remind him of his mission – when the fight begins he must show no mercy or pity. And his flag, the sovereign flag of the ruler of the land, waves in the breeze, that all may know he is here to rule this land in the name of the Leader and to transform it, with the help of club and dagger, into a part of the Reich. Today he'll be in residence in his office and the whole city will know, thanks to the flag, that he has returned. His signature will once again appear on the red decrees.

They drove at full speed along the main highway without stopping at the tram stop. People ran like rabbits, out of the car's way.

'Drive more slowly,' he ordered the driver, 'that curve is dangerous.'

The driver nodded. They drove the same route every day, didn't they? He didn't need driving lessons.

He looked at his wristwatch: 10:31. Good work. If they drive through town at the same speed, they'll be at the castle by a quarter to eleven. But you really can't drive as fast in town and besides one has to take into account the sharp climb to the castle. Let's say eleven. They'll have been waiting for him an hour and a half. Good work, a good German machine, the Mercedes-Benz.

They took the curve slowly. A tram was coming towards them and it halted at the stop. The driver turned on the high-pitched siren of the car of the highest lord of the land. Then a man ran into the road directly in front of the car. Idiot – he was running around like a lunatic. If he didn't jump to the side the driver would run him down without a thought. But then he saw that the man was holding an automatic pistol in his hand. Mechanically he reached in the glove compartment and took out a revolver. Mechanically he drew the briefcase closer.

Two members of the London parachute team known as Anthropoid had been waiting there since nine o'clock. They had figured everything out long before. They knew what time he left Brezany. They could calculate what time he would arrive at the curve. They picked that spot after studying the whole route long and hard. They were experienced. They'd been sent from England to get rid of Heydrich. Arriving by parachute, they wandered through the countryside, running, hiding. They were turned away from many a door; they saw the red decrees and understood that people were afraid. Finally they found a hiding place. They obtained false papers, food, cigarettes, money. They walked around the city and hardly recognised it, having been away for many years. The city was different, changed, beaten down. But there were still people who were unafraid, who were willing to help. They had to fulfil their mission: to kill.

They jumped off their bikes and leaned them against the fence of a vegetable garden. Then, calmly, they took their places at the tram platform. Under his raincoat one of them had an automatic pistol. The other had a hand grenade in his briefcase. Above the curve two other men were keeping watch, to give them a signal with a hand mirror when the car was approaching. Only the two at the tram stop were supposed to strike, one with the automatic, the other with the grenade. No mercy would be shown the adversary, the blows would fall, blood would flow from the bullet-torn heart, from the shattered body. They stood and waited nonchalantly at the tram stop.

The sun was extremely bright. It was a beautiful May day. They waited and waited endlessly, and yet no signal came from their associates. Something must have happened, how strange. They knew that Heydrich had returned – someone at the airport had informed them. They knew he must go to the castle, because he had a meeting scheduled there with Frank and the Protectorate government. They had received reliable reports from the castle. Why, in that case, wasn't he here yet? He always left Brezany at nine o'clock – they had confirmed that themselves. They kept waiting and waiting, never giving up hope. Maybe something had gone wrong with his car, a breakdown. But he had to go this way, there was no other way, and he had to get to the castle if there was an important conference scheduled, one he had instructions from Berlin to hold. That meant to keep on waiting. According to the wristwatch bought in England, it was ten past ten. They'd been hanging around the station here for over an hour, letting tram after tram go by. People might begin to notice them. But people at tram stops obviously have other things on their minds. Also, there were no windows nearby for anybody to look out of. It was an ordinary weekday, everybody was working.

At last the light signal flashed. One of the Anthropoids automatically looked at his watch: 10:31. He's coming. At that moment a tram arrived at the station heading for Kobylisy. Bad luck. Maybe it would leave quickly – nobody was getting on. One of the Anthropoids, the one with the automatic pistol, jumped on to the tram tracks. The other was only a stand-by, in case something unexpected happened.

Holding his automatic, the Anthropoid marksman stood in front of the car. He was calm, he aimed carefully. He pressed the trigger, but there was no report; the gun had failed to fire. The car was beginning to move slowly along the edge of the pavement, continuing on its way.

Suddenly the second assailant moved away from the lamp-post at the edge of the curve, took two or three steps towards the car and threw something.

A loud noise was heard, as if a tyre had blown out. The windows of the tram shattered, the doors of the car crumpled and tore out of the frame, a coat flew into the air and caught on the electric tram wire. Then slowly it fell to the ground. The assailants fled. One of them, the one who had vainly tried to fire, threw the useless gun away. The other, as if slowly waking up after tossing the grenade, only began to run after a few seconds.

The driver was unharmed. He jumped out of the car with his revolver and began to shoot.

A dull, unbearable pain in the back. As if someone had broken his spine with a club. He must control himself. He must force himself to get out of the car, to stand next to the driver and shoot. The assailants pull out revolvers and shoot back. They stop running for an instant and the driver takes off after them. Heydrich wants to run with him, but the pain, the dull and unbearable pain, holds him back. Though the pain makes him stagger, he must stand up straight. Only subhumans hang back and throw away their weapons, subhumans like the ones who finally got him.

Confused people are running around like insects, like ants after someone has poked their anthill. They run away from the shots, and then they run back out of curiosity. They jump in and out of the tram. They'd like him to be lying on the ground, face downward, back uncovered. No, he must remain upright, even if the pain tears him to pieces. He must show these subhumans how the highest lord of the land behaves.

He wants to stand with revolver in hand, shooting, even though the pain is paralysing his hand. He leans his other hand against the metal fence. He cannot pursue the assailants, who flee. He feels that he will collapse, after all, that he will reveal his back with its gaping wound. This is the end. They got him. He drops the revolver.

Suddenly he is alone. The driver has vanished long ago, chasing the second assailant. People nearby are running around, coming closer, then receding. Curiosity brings them nearer to him, fear makes them retreat. Now they must know who he is.

That's good. He doesn't need help from this scum. He doesn't need help from slaves for whom a worse fate than his own lies ahead . . . Again he hauls himself up. A German hero dies upright. He must show them his superiority. He forces himself to pick up the assailant's automatic, though it causes him incredible pain. But he manages it. He tosses it aside scornfully. Then he walks slowly towards the car, and leans against the broken door.

His thoughts are confused. He knows he has forgotten something. Just as he almost remembers, a new wave of pain overcomes him. Yes. The club and the dagger in the back. Sharp and dull pain. But he is not lying in the dust, head downward.

At last he remembers. The briefcase with the folder, with the graphs and quotas, with all the plans worked out to the last detail. The deadlines and figures. The task assigned to him by the Leader. He must find the briefcase. It was right beside him. He bends down and has to grab on to something again. Again the pain overpowers him, the sharp and dull pain.

The people nearby are watching his every move. They've recognised him. His name is on the red decrees. His flag flies above the castle. His photograph is published in every newspaper. The Acting Reich Protector.

Then the silence is broken. An overdressed blonde is coming towards him. Obviously she is not one of the crowd watching his every move but probably got here by chance. She is prattling in German.

'Herr Protektor.' She is handing him her coat.

He grimaces and waves his hand contemptuously. He doesn't want any help from these subhumans. Why are they staring at him like that? They probably don't want to miss seeing him die. But he won't give in. He'll show them how a German soldier in a subjugated land behaves. He'll deprive them of the pleasure they are expecting. He won't lie on the ground, his face in the dust, writhing with pain.

'The hospital,' the woman is saying in broken German, 'nearby . . . by foot.'

He looks at her with fury. How dare she tell him what to do, the nerve of such a whore to even speak to him, the lord of the land. He does not answer, and merely gives her a malevolent look. The prisoners in Columbia-haus and in the Prince Albert barracks knew that look well. It always meant death. Now death is waiting for him. He must wrestle with it in front of all this scum. If only there were a single fellow-countryman nearby. He has to endure the sympathy and help of some floozy.

He touches his back. Blood is dripping from his torn military shirt. His German blood is falling on the filthy pavement. Then the pain again, dull and sharp. The dagger and the club. And the confused thoughts keep running through his mind. He must find it, the briefcase. It mustn't fall into anyone else's hands, not even a near and dear one's. It contains the secret task assigned to him by the Leader.

He finds it and firmly presses it to his side. Nobody will wrench it away from him. Now he can give in to the pain, let it overpower him. Now he can show weakness.

He is fainting, he is unconscious as they place him on boxes in the van. He is awakened by the shaking of the van and by pain. He is lying with one foot hanging out over the edge. He clenches his teeth. He tries to straighten up and pull the leg in. But he can't move. He holds on to the briefcase with the folder and the secret plans. He holds on to it, holds on tightly.

The van arrives at the hospital entrance. They transfer him to a hospital trolley.

His flag is still fluttering over the castle, the flag with the sovereign symbol and the swastika. This means that he still reigns over the subjugated land. The day he first stepped into the courtyard accompanied by music of fife and drum, the flag was unfurled for the first time. That time he greeted it with outstretched arm and the entire guard of honour greeted it with him. The statues look out at him from their pedestals at the portal. The flag is still flying, it will keep flying, he will not surrender.

He continues to clutch the briefcase as they wheel him into the operating room. He will not release it to anyone. Only to the authorised person, and that is the head of the SS.

Now a crowd rushes to the deserted car. There is a lot of debris and broken glass all around. People bend down and eagerly gather the bits.

'Why are you taking it?' someone asks.

And one of them answers, 'For good luck.'

TWELVE

THE LARGE ROOM looked like a junk shop. It was full of every possible kind of thing – furniture, chandeliers, refrigerators, radios, gramophones, clothing, vacuum cleaners, paintings, framed photographs, pots and pans, serving dishes, toys, binoculars, typewriters, irons, tennis rackets, oars, kayaks, footballs, a garden ornament in the shape of a dwarf. There was none of the orderliness here he had grown used to at the Collection Agency, where everything was sorted according to type and every type of object had its own special stockroom: an eiderdown stockroom and a refrigerator stockroom. There, every object had a tag with a number. Here, everything was just thrown together. Of course, there was a simple explanation for the sloppy state of affairs in this warehouse.

The theft of Jewish property was a part of the larger mission aimed at the extermination of all Jews. The Reich declared this property to be its own, and organisers from the Jewish Community had created a safe and reliable net to catch such property in the warehouses of the Collection Agency.

This warehouse also depended on theft. But the objects came by a different route – they came as a result of the red decrees. It was not possible to predict the number of those who would be executed and to plan for the disposal of their property. There were periods when the number of red decrees went down, others when it rose. Right now, in the wake of the assassination of the Acting Reich Protector, the number of names on the red decrees was rising so precipitously that everybody in the warehouse was going crazy with the flood of things. The small objects – gold, jewellery, fountain pens, watches – went their own way and never reached the warehouse. But the room was constantly filling up with heavy objects – furniture, chandeliers, kitchen sinks.

Now the dealers were coming virtually every day. These were the vultures who used to buy goods from pawnshops. The lady manager of the warehouse sold them everything for a song, just to get rid of them. Requests for clothes and furniture for bombed-out families kept arriving at the warehouse from various Reich relief societies. The lady manager threw these into the wastebasket, saying, 'The Gestapo gives nothing for free. The Gestapo only sells.'

The lady manager, a Baltic German, spoke German with a Russian accent. She called herself a baroness, though people said she once ran a brothel in Riga. Gestapo members used her office as if it were their bar, but they brought their own drink. They also brought along various provisions from the confiscated goods – rare delicacies, Hungarian salami and real coffee. They'd arrive there half-drunk, stamping around as if they were trying to shake off something. Sometimes, when they were very tight, they'd try to shoot off their guns and break dishes. But the baroness knew how to keep things in hand.

'You're not going to make a pigsty here. Go somewhere else for that. I've seen plenty of your type in my life, and I've always known how to handle them.'

'Madam,' Erich teased her, 'a whorehouse madam.'

'Shut up, you idiot,' the baroness said sharply. 'Where did you put that gold cigarette case? Don't think I didn't notice it. The one with the initials J. P.'

'They're gone, old girl,' Erich squealed, 'rubbed away.'

'You imbeciles, why don't you at least learn to keep your mouths shut,' the baroness said heatedly. 'Richard is right behind that door. He can hear every word.'

'Come on.' Karel grinned. 'What's all this Richard business? He's just a Jew. Who's he to blab? He's going up the chimney.'

'As long as he's here, he's Richard, as far as I'm concerned,' snapped the baroness. 'Whatever you do with him later, that's not my business. All I know is, he's a good worker, he doesn't drink, he doesn't use bad language, and he doesn't throw up in my flowerpots.'

'He can't,' said Erich. 'He'd like to, but he can't. He's a subhuman, see. But otherwise he's a good-looking guy.'

'Call him in,' bellowed Karel. 'Let's have him drink to the Reich with us. Oh damn, not to the Reich. That's forbidden. So let him have a drink just for nothing.'

'Behave yourselves,' said the baroness menacingly. 'You're not at headquarters here and I won't let you hurt Richard. If you try to pull something I'll get you for it, even if I have to go to Geschke himself.'

'We don't want to hurt him,' Erich reassured her. 'We're off duty here. We'll just give him a swig.'

The lady manager called in Richard Reisinger.

'Here, bottoms up.' Erich offered him a glass. 'It's real French stuff with three stars. It used to belong to some banker. Well, we just did him in – maybe that bothers you.'

'Oh no,' said Reisinger. He knew he mustn't provoke the Gestapo. 'I'm still on duty here.'

'The hell with your duty.' Karel waved his hand. 'The baroness here says it's okay.'

'But I'm a Jew,' Reisinger tried to argue. 'There're rules against it.'

'Those rules don't count for us. They only count for ordinary people. We're the Gestapo,' bawled Erich.

Reisinger took a drink. The cognac was really good, pre-war French Courvoisier.

'Here's some salami – you don't want to drink on an empty stomach.' Karel handed him a plate. 'Go ahead, eat and drink, you're a dead duck anyhow.'

'You know too much and you've seen too much. Types like you are usually dead ducks.' Erich lit a cigarette.

'We know too much and we've seen too much and we're not dead ducks,' said Karel.

'Maybe we are,' answered Erich.

'Cut it out with talk like that. It's treason, and I'll knock you off with my own hands. Even in front of the Jew. I don't care.'

'Stop yelling. Couldn't you be quiet once in a while and drink like decent people do? A treat like this, real Courvoisier, and they swill it down like pigs,' said the baroness.

'Shut your trap, madam,' shouted Karel. 'I can knock you off, too. We're allowed to do anything.'

'You better keep your grubby hands off me, or I'll turn you in for stealing,' the baroness threatened.

'And you? I suppose you don't steal? What about those bangles? I suppose they're from Riga, too?'

'Maybe they are from Riga. It's none of your business where they're from. But I can deal with you, if it comes to that. I know exactly who to speak to . . . '

Karel was drunk, but he had just enough sense left to recognise the baroness's threatening tone and know that she really meant it. God knows how that woman does it!

She's got contacts with the biggest bosses, she even drops in on Geschke without an appointment. She probably does various transactions for them on the black market, things they wouldn't dare do themselves. Naturally she divides everything up with them, and also gives them presents. Moreover, she knows a lot about them.

He gave her a foolish, drunken smile. 'Don't get mad, Baroness. We were just joking around. After our kind of work a fellow's got to have a little fun. Right, Erich?'

'Of course,' babbled Erich. 'You're our little darling, our honey, our little mama.'

'Keep your sweet talk to yourself, and get going. I'm expecting a visitor. Our colleagues from Kladno are coming to look at the stock.'

'We don't give a damn about them. They can kiss our . . . They're this small,' Karel sneered.

'But you're in the way now. Get out of here. *Marsch*!'

Erich and Karel obeyed. They belted up their trench coats as if they were uniforms and said their goodbyes.

'*Grüss Gott*, Baroness.'

And they made an exit, still walking straight.

The baroness spoke to Richard, who was sitting in the office with his half-filled glass. 'Clean this place up after those pigs so it looks decent. And hide the bottle somewhere. They're sure to forget there was anything left over.'

The day they sent Richard Reisinger to this warehouse from the Work Force Division he had imagined it would all be different. He assumed he'd be working under conditions similar to the trench diggers – under the command of the SS, with beatings, kicks and curses. The best he could hope for in such a case would be for the SS to abuse him to the degree that he'd have to be carried off in a handcart to the

Jewish Hospital, no longer eligible for heavy physical labour and unable to return to the warehouse. That was the only way to get out of the Gestapo's clutches. He didn't know any other.

But what he saw in the warehouse was something entirely different. It was more terrifying, even though nobody actually beat him and nobody was patrolling in uniform. Everything he heard and saw there seemed incredible to him, a crazy dream or something he had read about somewhere in an adventure book. It was as if he had fallen into a den of thieves, though the house was near the centre of town, a relatively new house with a gate wide enough for a removal van to go directly into the courtyard. You could enter a room on the ground floor from the courtyard, a room that was lit up day and night. That was the stockroom, from which a little door led to a small office. The baroness, who managed the warehouse, sat in the office. She was a fat, old, heavily made-up woman who wore many necklaces and bracelets that jingled with every step she took.

She took his paper from him and welcomed him in quite a friendly way. She used the polite form of address with him and behaved decently to him, much to his surprise. She described his various duties: mainly he'd be in charge of ordering the removal vans, supervising the movers, overseeing the storage of things in the warehouse. She showed him the handcart he'd use to take various things to various apartments whose addresses he'd be given. If a piece of furniture was too heavy, he could hire a helper. Then there'd be various side trips, perhaps even to the country, to pick up pieces of furniture, but of course he could go there only with an escort.

He had plenty of work to do. At the Collection Agency he

had been obliged to move and carry heavy furniture himself. Here he'd only be supervising. The lady manager was probably a beast, but she didn't speak to him unpleasantly, nor did she threaten him in any way. She warned him that he must hold his tongue, that a careless word meant death, but he knew that already from the official at the Community. The warehouse was a mess, but that wasn't part of his job; he wasn't responsible for the warehouse.

Then he met the Gestapo. Quite a few of them came there, most often Erich and Karel – they had no other names. They were responsible for the confiscation of furniture from apartments, and of course they did other work as well. But he preferred not to think about that. They didn't wear uniforms but, rather, street clothing. Still, they did wear something that reminded him of a uniform: leather coats in the winter, trench coats in the summer, and always green hats with tufts.

They didn't scream at him the way the SS man had done, that one who made him run to the Jewish Town Hall, bleeding from the mouth. These men called him Richard, quite affably, and didn't lay a hand on him. Nevertheless they inspired fear, greater fear than the uniformed ones did. Their eyes seemed to be mad, and they always kept one hand in their bulging pockets. That's where they had their revolvers, undoubtedly cocked and ready to fire.

When they were drunk they were terrifying: they raved, they waved their revolvers and seemed ready to fall on him at any minute. They resembled bloodthirsty animals. But the lady manager knew how to handle them, and nothing bad ever happened while they were in the warehouse. Once they were outside, once they were on duty, they knew how to control themselves. But because they were so high-strung and because their bloody work made them so nervous, he could never be sure they wouldn't kill him. He knew that this kind of person would never be satisfied with merely knocking out a few teeth or cracking a few ribs. For such a person only death would do.

Thus it was that he found himself in the midst of robbers, thieves and murderers, joining them on their various expeditions, though only to pick up their booty. They weren't careful in the least about what they said in front of him. They calmly chatted about whom they had 'knocked off' or 'done in', and how. They used certain technical terms during these discussions that they must have learned at some courses in murder. That they spoke so casually in front of him was the most terrifying thing of all. It meant that he was doomed from the start, that he had only as much time left to live as they might assign him. That was why they didn't have to hold back in any way before him. He was a living dead man.

He had to be incredibly careful when they asked him about anything. The fact that they didn't curse him or beat him, that they spoke quite pleasantly to him sometimes, meant that such behaviour didn't cost them anything. It was clear to him that they could shoot him any time they wanted, either because they had an order to do it or without any order. Murder was a small detail to them. They didn't have to work themselves up to a fury or a fit.

'Come and have a beer with us,' Erich once invited him when they finished emptying an apartment and the movers were already carrying out the furniture. 'There's a tavern right near here.'

'But there's a sign there: NO JEWS ALLOWED.'

'You can sit there with us even with a star on. We'd take

care of it if anybody objected.' And he motioned to his right pocket.

They sat at a table near the window.

'To your health,' Erich toasted. 'Go ahead, clink glasses with us. Let everybody see this farce.'

It was evening, after work. There were quite a few people in the tavern, but as soon as they saw the queer little group they began to leave quickly. Soon nobody was left in the room besides Richard and the Gestapo.

'See what big shots we are,' Karel boasted. 'You're completely safe with us, even if we don't pay the bartender, even if we slap him in the face instead of paying. He'd still bow to us. Isn't that true, Erich?'

'Too bad you're a Jew, Richard.' Erich clinked his glass against Richard's. 'We'd take you with us. You'd have a great time. Money, women, we've got everything.'

'Too bad. You're such a good-looking guy. What did you do before the war?'

'I had a small hardware store. Nothing special. But I made a living from it.'

'I was a plasterer and Karel here was a shop assistant. See how we've come up in the world,' Erich boasted.

Richard had read about things like this in books. Things like this didn't happen in real life. In books he had read about gangsters or gunmen from the Wild West. They also got drunk and shot at people. Of course, in those books a sheriff always showed up who got rid of them somehow.

'I'll tell you a story,' said Erich, in a talkative mood, 'it's sort of a story with a moral about five old-fashioned overcoats. Some guy named Fischman was still working at the warehouse the time this happened – a good-for-nothing fellow, scared shitless. In any case, there was a certain farmer, a rich bastard who lived out in a village somewhere – what was it called? – well, I've forgotten, I can't remember all those Czech names. Anyhow, he found an apartment in Prague and was moving there with his whole family. He had a son and daughter over fifteen years old – that's important. And then there was the grandfather. He was supposed to wait in the village for the family to move to Prague and fix up the new apartment. So they took all his things away in the moving van and told him they'd let him know when to come and join them. Then somebody denounced that farmer, one of his enemies, and reported that he had provisions hidden in the moving van. So we went to check it out.

'Well, he did have some provisions there – that wasn't so bad. But we also found some hunting guns. And of course you know the penalty for that today. So we had to sort of liquidate that family. The only one of them left, finally, was that grandfather out in the village. Naturally we confiscated their things, so grandfather in the village didn't even have an extra shirt to change into. Then some smart aleck advised him to write to us saying that he hadn't done anything wrong and therefore his things had been wrongfully confiscated, and to request that his things be returned. But you know the way we operate. Nothing hangs around very long around here. Those things were gone ages ago. Only the five old-fashioned overcoats of Grandpa's were left – nobody had wanted them. So we sent them to him. We really made Grandpa happy, don't you think?' Erich cackled as he finished his story.

All the Gestapo's stories were terrible, but the way they told them was even more terrible. Even gangsters in books didn't talk like that.

Every two weeks Mr Smutny came to the warehouse. He was a bit different from the other second-hand dealers: round, pink-cheeked, well-dressed and courteous. He addressed the manager as dear lady and kissed her hand. He leaned confidentially towards Richard when they were alone and spoke in a pained voice: 'You know, my heart bleeds when I look at these things: Imagine my coming across Mr Netousek's portrait here, and he was one of my best customers. What can I tell you, we became friendly over all those years we did business together. Well, I didn't buy the portrait. Just between us, Mr Netousek didn't take my advice that time and ordered the portrait from a second-rate painter – Mr Netousek didn't know much about art. I bought back the things I sold him, for the right price, needless to say. Mr Netousek was just too trusting and he paid through the teeth. Well, my heart was bleeding, but I bought them. I said to myself, Smutny, you have a duty to buy these things. If you don't buy them, someone else will. At least they'll be in friendly hands.'

Richard didn't really like to get in a conversation with him. It was like talking to a hyena.

'Mr Smutny, you're an Aryan and a member of the National Confederation, so you're not allowed to talk to a Jew.'

'But I don't have anything against Jews,' objected Mr Smutny. 'I used to do business with them in the old days, though they were certainly sly. Still, I don't hold it against them, you've got to be clever to do well in business.'

Mr Smutny dealt only with artistic objects; he didn't buy junk. He had a shop on the main street with many select customers. The lady manager was gracious and polite to him. She offered him liqueurs.

Mr Smutny looked over the antiques carefully. He didn't buy any old thing. He was on the lookout for rare pieces, examining everything for a long time, picking up objects in his hand, studying the signatures on paintings. He never chose many things. Reisinger delivered them to his store personally, perfectly wrapped. He always received a box of good cigarettes as a tip.

First, of course, Mr Smutny haggled for a long time with the lady manager over their glass of liqueur. Mr Smutny knew that the baroness knew nothing about art. The baroness, on the other hand, knew that Mr Smutny offered a third of the actual value at most. They always came to a friendly agreement in the end.

One day, during Mr Smutny's usual visit, after he had picked out several antiques and was getting ready for his usual negotiations with the manager, the baroness stopped him.

'I want you to buy this statue also. Otherwise I won't sell you anything. It's in my way here, and I don't like to look at it.'

The statue was half a metre tall, a bronzed plaster casting. Of course the baroness didn't understand all that.

Mr Smutny looked at the statue. 'My dear lady, what would I do with this? Who's going to buy it? A modern sculptor made it, this is no antique. It's a copy of the statue of Justice that's standing or used to stand in the main courtroom at Pankrac. You tell me, dear lady, who cares about justice these days?'

Justice held a sharp sword in her hand. Her eyes were blindfolded.

The baroness insisted. 'Take it away. I don't want to look at it. Justice or injustice, I don't like it either way. Why should I ruin my nerves here on top of everything else? I'll give it to you cheap. Maybe for only fifty crowns. That's only five marks, after all. The main thing is, I'll get rid of it.'

'Dear lady,' Mr Smutny replied, 'I can't give you more than twenty crowns for it, and that's only to do you a favour, because it'll just sit in my shop.'

'Good,' agreed the lady manager, 'take it for twenty crowns, then, and I'll be rid of it.' She turned to Reisinger. 'Richard, wrap this statue up right away and put it on the handcart, before Mr Smutny changes his mind.'

'I'm going to lose out on this, you can take my word for it, dear lady,' complained Mr Smutny, 'I'm only doing this as a favour . . . '

'So much talk for twenty crowns,' the lady manager said scornfully. 'Don't worry, you'll foist it off on someone. Hurry up, Richard.'

The copy of the statue of Justice was soon packed in sawdust and put in a box on the handcart together with the small objects Mr Smutny had picked out. Reisinger waited by the handcart while the dealer and the lady manager settled on a price for the other things.

After a while Mr Smutny came out. He was grumbling to himself: 'Justice, what a stupid idea in this day and age!' He turned to Reisinger. 'You've wrapped it up too well, my friend. It'll never break this way. Well, it's only twenty crowns, so the hell with it.'

It wasn't far to Mr Smutny's shop. Reisinger carefully unloaded the crate and received the usual box of cigarettes.

When he returned the lady manager greeted him: 'Thank God it's gone.' She was drunk. She must have been tossing them down the whole time he was away.

She poured some liqueur into a glass.

'Have a drink, Richard.' She began to complain. 'What a life, surrounded by skunks here! I've seen a lot in my day, but never anything like what goes on here. When I see these things I feel like crying.' The drink was making her sentimental.

'Don't believe what they tell you, Richard. They're playing cat and mouse with you. They don't care about anything. They'd do me in, too, if they could. But they can't get me. Do you like it here, Richard?'

What was he to say to a direct question? How to answer a drunken floozy who is bad-mouthing the Gestapo while she's in with them up to her neck?

'Well, you're very kind to me, Baroness, but otherwise . . . '

'I know,' wept the lady manager. 'I'm a real softy. But you know, life is hard and a person has to be tough to survive. I used to live differently, once upon a time. I'm sorry for you, Richard. I used to know somebody who looked like you. And when I think that . . . '

Suddenly she caught herself. It was as if the drunkenness had suddenly lifted. She began to speak in a different tone of voice. 'Oh, I almost forgot. I have another errand for you. Look over there in the corner – you'll find some framed photographs. Here's a package with some other photographs a certain gentleman sent me from Bredovska. Go to the framer's, tell him to take the old photos out of the frames and put in the new ones from the package. Tell him I need them in a hurry.'

Reisinger was glad to get out in the fresh air. He remembered seeing a shop with the inscription PICTURE FRAMING AND GILDING somewhere quite nearby on a parallel side street. He was wearing his workday smock without the star, which he wore in the warehouse. He didn't want to embarrass the framer.

The owner of the shop, an older man with a grey moustache, stood alone behind the counter. Reisinger unwrapped the framed photographs and said to him, just as the lady manager had instructed him, 'Throw away these photographs and replace them with the ones in the package. And hurry, we need them soon.'

Hardly had the framer taken the framed photograph in his hand than tears began to flow from his eyes. 'Good Lord! It's Frantisek! Jesus Christ, here's Ruzena and Jaroslav! That's my cousin. Why, they . . . '

He began to sob. 'This can't be true,' he gasped. 'My God, where did you get these?'

Reisinger made a great effort to answer calmly. 'Please. It's better not to ask. And please do the job quickly. I have nothing to do with this. I'm just the servant.'

'But whose servant are you? Who sent you?'

Reisinger realised that he must tell the truth. 'If you must know, then, the Gestapo.'

The framer stood stock-still, like a pillar of salt. Reisinger left the shop quickly.

'What a job,' he said to himself. 'What a job. It would be better to be kicked to death by the SS than this.'

Three weeks later, as he was unpacking objects from another confiscated apartment, he had a sudden shock.

'Baroness, Baroness, please come here,' he called to the office. He could tell by a scratch mark on the left side that this was a statue that had been here before.

The lady manager waddled into the warehouse. She almost fainted when she saw the unwrapped object.

'I can't believe it.' Her eyes were popping. 'Why, it's that statue, that Justice! Call Smutny immediately,' she screamed, 'tell him to come here at once, to drop everything and come.'

She ran back to her office and locked the door behind her.

Mr Smutny came very soon. He obviously thought this was going to be some exceptionally good business deal.

'Well, how d'ye do,' he said, all smiles. 'Here I am again. What little gem do you have for me today?'

'This.' Reisinger pointed to the statue.

'Ah so.' Mr Smutny didn't allow his feathers to be ruffled. 'Well, well, there're a lot of strange things in the world.'

As soon as the lady manager heard Mr Smutny's voice, she ran into the warehouse and began to scream hysterically: 'You must take this statue away immediately. Richard, wrap it up!'

'Dear lady,' said Mr Smutny apologetically, 'I'm sorry you're taking it so hard. Please don't get so excited. You know, I did sell that statue, after all, although to tell the truth I didn't make anything on it. It was bought by, let me see, yes, a certain Mr Krajicek, yes, that's who it was; he'd been a major in the Czech Army and now he's a bank official . . . I mean, actually, what am I saying, well, so it's come back again . . . '

'Take the statue away. I'm superstitious. It'll drive me crazy.'

'My dear Baroness,' Mr Smutny said slowly, 'please forgive me, but I won't take that statue. I'm also superstitious and I don't want it in my shop.'

'What am I supposed to do with it, then?'

'That's easy, dear lady. Tell Richard here to go out to

the courtyard and break it. That's all. And then throw the pieces in the dustbin.'

'Richard,' the lady manager commanded, 'take it out to the courtyard and smash it.'

Richard put a hammer in the pocket of his smock and carried the statue out to the courtyard. The lady manager and Mr Smutny watched him go.

'Let's have a drink, Mr Smutny,' said the baroness invitingly. She was calm now.

Reisinger began to destroy the statue with the hammer. First he knocked off Justice's head, with her blindfolded eyes. Then he knocked the sword out of her hand. Then he struck the head again to smash it completely. Then he attacked the body. Finally all that remained were some dirty white bronzed pieces lying on the courtyard floor. He swept them up and threw them in the dustbin.

Justice would no longer stand in anyone's way.

THIRTEEN

THE TRANSPORTS CONTINUED to leave from the Radio Mart. The Hangman's death changed nothing in the carrying out of his task. The dead lines and quotas for each individual country were set in the plan, the plan was hidden in the folder, and the folder was in the briefcase. The briefcase ended up in the hands of the highest Reich police officer, who came to town in a Panzer tank. He came at the request of the dying man, who wouldn't relinquish the folder to anyone else. The two from the Anthropoids had got him, after all. His coffin lying on the gun carriage passed through the castle courtyard and the portal for the last time. The statues with dagger and club stood there, silent, motionless. He'd never see them again, he'd never return to this city again. The flag with his sovereign symbol flew at half-mast. Death, once his constant companion, went on a rampage at his extinction. The red decrees appeared daily and the list of names grew longer. Death stalked the city. It even found the two from the Anthropoids.

The body on the gun carriage passed through the city accompanied by fife and drum and left the subjugated land. It passed the statues on the bridge, it passed the statue of Roland. It passed along the river, it wound through the main streets, and the tramp of heavy military boots accompanied it all the way to the railway station. The strangled city fell silent. The flags at half-mast were harbingers of death. People sat behind darkened windows. As death marched by, they turned on their lamps and read the words of poets.

The body on the gun carriage, followed by a parade of dignitaries, left by special train for the capital city of the Reich. There, too, it passed through the streets accompanied by an honour guard, but these were different streets, with broken buildings, crumbled walls and shattered windows. Death already held sway there as a trusted friend. The city belonged to it entirely. The broken city greeted the dead body with a twenty-one-gun salute by the light of blazing torches. Thunder and lightning from a storm of nature joined the thunder of the cannons.

The city in the subjugated country was plastered with notices. Loudspeakers attached to street lights rattled off the names of the executed. But because it was warm and the sun was shining, people lay on the banks of the city's river, swimming, jumping into the water and laughing. Because life is stronger than death. Because people have to sleep, eat and love.

Death walked all around the town. It even paid a brief visit to Mrs Javurek's house. The city was under martial law then and the tramp of metal-studded boots and the blows of gun butts on doors were heard at every house. They searched the apartment, but they didn't find anything, for they never dreamed there was a little room behind the cupboard. Besides, they were in a hurry. The old house was overflowing with people, children suddenly awakened from their sleep were yelling in every apartment. The stifling smell of poverty was everywhere, for it was forbidden to open a window.

Adela and Greta barely peeped. They knew that every little sound could mean death. They only heard the voices, sharp, blustering. They gave a start and almost cried out when they heard a crash. It was a rifle smashing to the floor, either by accident or deliberately, to scare the Javureks. Then suddenly everything was quiet. The night callers were gone, but nothing moved in the kitchen. The Javureks didn't speak to each other, as if afraid that the night's guests were still listening outside the door. Adela and Greta were just falling asleep when the Javureks moved aside the cupboard and opened the cubbyhole door. Drowsily they let themselves be carried into the kitchen and seated at the table. They had been locked up all day and had eaten nothing.

Now the Javureks began to talk loudly, almost too loudly. That's how people behave when some danger has passed and they feel elated. All at once they felt like talking long and loud. They wanted to go over everything bit by bit, how those two had rushed into the apartment, how the smaller one had a gun and used it to poke around under the bed, how the bigger one searched the parlour and kitchen, pulling out dishes from shelves, searching the cupboards and rummaging through the linens, even messing up everything in the kitchen cupboard that stood in front of the cubbyhole.

The Javureks described it all to Adela and Greta and praised them for being so quiet. The danger had passed. But fear stayed on in a place deep inside.

The very next day Jan came to visit.

'How are you doing, little submarines,' he said, seemingly jolly and carefree. But everything was very bad now – house searches, arrests, ID checks. Food had vanished – the black marketeers were scared. They were hanged and shot, too, as it was expedient to mix them in with the other names on the red decrees. But he had to find food, he couldn't ask the Javureks to share their meagre rations with the children.

They spent only a short time together. Jan was in a hurry. He had a date with a man who was perhaps the only person who could get him food now that the city was in a state of siege.

The person Jan was going to visit was a Jew. He was in hiding, even though he didn't actually need to be. He was not persecuted, because his name was not listed at the Jewish Community or at the Central Bureau. He had Aryan papers – genuine ones, moreover, and so nobody was after him yet. Still, he preferred to remain at home. There were quite a few people who lived in the city that way. They were registered properly, they picked up their ration cards regularly at the janitor's, but they didn't show up in public very often.

He had been a photographer for a picture magazine before the war, and he accepted every assignment he could get: important visitors, sports events, exhibitions, new acquisitions at the zoo. He took very different photographs for his own purposes: the temporary shacks of the unemployed, queues at the employment agency, people on breadlines and in shelters, mothers and children begging for food and money, demonstrations, shantytowns being knocked down. Nobody paid him for these pictures; they served a different purpose: to show how the unemployed live in a country that boasted of its democratic ways. Communist delegates submitted the photos to parliament: they travelled around the Republic in small travelling exhibitions to gain support. Nobody knew who organised these exhibitions. Nobody knew that these shots of policemen beating people at demonstrations and shooting into crowds of children were taken by a photographer with an official licence.

The photographer had a common name – Otto Pokorny. Some of the many people with the name Pokorny were Jews. He had a studio in a large modern apartment house with a steady turnover because the rent was high. Even the janitors kept changing, because the landlord didn't want to pay them for operating the central heating. The house actually belonged to a bank that was represented by an accountant. Nobody pays much attention to anybody else in a house like that.

After March 15, several German tenants moved into the house. They were quiet and inconspicuous, not wanting to attract attention. They went off to murder at regular working hours, while pretending to be ordinary office workers at home, carefully wiping their shoes on the doormat and politely stepping out of the lift to make room for ladies.

Pokorny signed the 'Aryan declaration' for the new editor-in-chief of the magazine he worked for. But nobody there knew him very well – the magazine employed several free-lance photographers. There was little work to do, since most of the magazine's pictures were provided by the German news agency – pictures from the front, sessions of the Reichstag and military parades. The only local pictures were sentimental ones, used for diversionary purposes: springtime on the river, lovers in the park, a country market. But even such pictures could be dangerous. For instance, a view of a city square might include a monument that had not yet been removed.

Pokorny worked with a heavy heart. He was sick of grinding out the same old sentimental pictures. His passion was to uncover old and unusual things. And so it happened that he almost got his editor sent to a concentration camp.

He took a photograph of a trained dog, a mongrel named as an outstanding circus artist by the German Commission. This remarkable dog received special allotments of meat and rice which supported his whole performing family. The editor printed the picture with the caption *A Deserving Dog* in the same issue that carried a portrait of the Acting Reich Protector. At the very last minute someone noticed it and the whole issue was pulped.

From that time on, Pokorny was not trusted at the magazine. Even his shots of animals didn't seem safe. Slowly but surely Pokorny withdrew, into semi-illegality. Occasionally he'd send a girl he knew to the office and identify her as his secretary. He took fewer photographs, only enough to stay inconspicuous and to keep from being conscripted to the Reich, for he had other, more important work to do. He had become an expert at making false documents. At first glance, the system of control over the inhabitants of the land devised by its present masters seemed ingenious and truly foolproof. Every person was required to have an ID card – the *Kennkarte*, as it was called. You also needed a Residence Card, as well as working papers. If you moved, you had to get a cancellation certificate for your former residence. Without this cancellation you couldn't move to a new place.

But you had only to break one link of this chain and everything fell apart. You could buy the Residence Card blank at any news-stand, fill it out, and then have it stamped with a false stamp. Once you had this false Residence Card you could, with a little nerve, obtain a real cancellation certificate and then, through perfectly normal channels, get a real Residence Card for a new place of residence. You could get *Kennkartes* in various ways – for instance, by saying that you had lost yours and applying for a new one or by not turning in a *Kennkarte* of someone who had died. Blank *Kennkartes* were the most valuable of all. It was relatively easy to get working papers from Czech officials at the Employment Bureau. Consequently, what was usually falsified was the stamp.

Jan Krulis knew nothing about Pokorny's various activities. He knew him only as a photographer, having bought pictures of various preserved landmarks from him. Once Pokorny had procured some coffee for him; he probably had contacts with black marketeers. It was difficult to ask a person he knew only superficially to help him get food, but Jan had exhausted all other possibilities. Under martial law the German and Protectorate bureaus had sealed off the silenced city from all sides and strengthened their checkpoints at the railway stations. Troopers with automatics guarded the exits from the city. And nobody wanted to sell their ration cards.

He rang the doorbell for a long time before Pokorny answered. Perhaps he was waiting for a different visitor. At first they just made small talk and Krulis couldn't find a way to get to his subject. Pokorny seemed to be trying to get rid of him. The studio smelled of chemicals. It was actually used as a darkroom, with an enlarger and trays with developing fluids. They chatted for a while, then there was silence. The pauses grew longer.

Finally Pokorny eased the awkwardness by bringing out a metal box and carefully counting out coffee beans. He took down a coffee mill from a shelf and concentrated on grinding.

Coffee, real coffee at a time like this – it was almost too much hospitality. Pokorny turned the handle of the mill energetically but without a word, as if he were performing a ceremony. There was nothing for Jan to do but look around the room. Suddenly his gaze fell on the corner of something poking out from under a pile of papers. Surely that could be nothing but a *Kennkarte*. But why was it lying there, as if someone had quickly covered it up with papers but hadn't had time to hide it completely? Ordinarily, people kept their *Kennkarte* in their pocket, for ready access. Or else they'd leave it out on a table to have at hand in case of an unexpected inspection. But to throw papers over it as if to hide it – that was strange. Perhaps it didn't mean anything, perhaps it was a complete coincidence. But he kept having an odd feeling about Pokorny, partly because of his awkward embarrassment, his long silences, and also his strange behaviour when he opened the door. A name kept running through Jan's head, and suddenly it came to the surface: 'the Comet'! When people in his organisation needed false papers, they always said, 'You have to wait for the Comet to arrange it.' It could have been a person or a group. In an organisation with many branches, everybody knew only a few other people, and nobody asked questions about anyone else. But now it appeared that he had unexpectedly come upon a member. He glanced over at Pokorny, who was still concentrating on grinding the coffee, and their eyes met. Pokorny seemed to sense something, because he looked at him uncertainly. He stopped grinding and the atmosphere grew unbearably tense. And that caused Jan almost unconsciously to say out loud the name that was running through his head: 'The Comet.' Quietly, as if to himself.

Pokorny started, and for a moment seemed filled with doubt and indecision. And then suddenly, as if at a given signal, they both began to laugh. The laughter broke the tension and cleared the air. Now Krulis spoke freely. The coffee smelled delicious. Its aroma overpowered the chemical smells. Everything was all right; now he could tell why he had come. He needed food, at least a little food, or a few food coupons.

He apologised for having come with such a trivial request. He would now look for other sources. He didn't have to explain why he was apologising.

'Don't worry about it. And if by chance anybody stops you and asks what you were doing here, show him these photographs of the Hrzansky Palace. I'll give you a bill, and keep a copy. But I don't think it will be necessary. And I can get you some food, too, but nothing much – just sardines, Dutch cheese in a tin, Hungarian salami. I don't have anything else.'

That's some 'nothing much', thought Jan, such rare things as sardines, Dutch cheese and Hungarian salami, at a time like this.

'I'd rather give you some lard or meat, but those are hard to find these days.'

They drank the coffee and smoked the cigarettes which Pokorny offered Krulis. They were American cigarettes, Chesterfields.

'Thank you for everything,' said Jan Krulis as he was leaving. 'It will get to the right place.'

The story behind these delicacies was a strange, even unbelievable one. In a street that ran down a steep incline from the castle, the street named after a poet, there was a single modern house. It blended in somewhat with its surroundings; nevertheless, it contrasted sharply because of its new red paint and the doorbells without names at the wooden entrance. People with secret telephone numbers lived there, members of one of the Reich intelligence services, but only part of the time. The rest of the time they travelled to other countries with false papers. They travelled under various disguises – even as Dominican monks or Orthodox priests.

One of them, who bore the noble prefix 'von', had already earned a bad reputation during the First Republic. While serving as a temporary attaché at the German embassy then, he had organised meetings with some dishonest Agrarian Party politicians. Forced to leave when his activities were discovered, he didn't return until after March 15. He voluntarily chose Prague as his main base. Now, under the Protectorate, he worked in the Balkans. He could have settled in Vienna, but he chose the city he had been kicked out of – perhaps to even the score somehow. Or perhaps he had come to love the city; this sometimes happens to adventurers who have no home of their own.

He avoided all public places. He had a feeling that he was surrounded by spies, not only from other countries, but even from other Reich services, who worked for the Reich Ministry or favourites of the Leader. They all fought and set traps for one another.

He needed a housekeeper who would clean his house and cook for him, not full time, but at irregular intervals and odd hours, because he never knew when he'd return from his travels and how long he would be in town. The housekeeper should not be too clever, so that she wouldn't understand anything and wouldn't meddle in anything. She mustn't be a German – a German might be a plant from one of the other Reich services. He searched for such a housekeeper for a long time, and finally found one quite by chance. Back when he was still working as an attaché he had met a career diplomat, an Austrian baron who had enlisted as an officer of the Reich when Austria was occupied and had himself transferred to the German embassy. After March 15, the German embassy was abolished, but the baron stayed in town for several months longer. He had some business to complete. And also, one could eat and drink well in the Protectorate if one had enough money and the right connections.

The former attaché ran into the baron in front of the German House. The baron was just coming out from dinner and couldn't pretend he didn't know him. They talked about various unimportant things, not a word about the front – it paid to watch one's tongue. Officials wearing dress uniforms and monocles were everywhere to be seen, and the baron gave a little sneer. He didn't like Prussians and their uniforms. Nor did he like the former attaché, who he knew was an agent and involved in various dark affairs, including murder. But he acted perfectly politely. When you live with wolves you have to behave nicely towards them. He talked only about special rations and parties at the Press Club, as if those were matters of the utmost importance.

The baron remembered that he knew of a housekeeper. She had cooked for him back in the days he had worked for the Austrian embassy. He recommended her highly. She was old and ugly. She was unlikely to attract a lover. She didn't know how to read or write and spoke Czech badly because she came from the easternmost part of Slovakia. Some Czech state trooper had brought her to Prague a long time ago and then abandoned her there. But she was a great cook.

And so the agent found a new housekeeper at last. She didn't have much work to do, since her master was constantly on the road, but whenever he returned she created veritable feasts for him. And she kept the apartment meticulously clean. When she emptied the wastepaper basket she had instructions to throw the various torn-up scraps of paper directly into the furnace. But she only threw the newspapers there. She removed the scraps of paper and took them elsewhere. Where she took them was her affair. She couldn't read them herself, but she took them to someone who was able to decipher them.

The housekeeper lived well – there were plenty of provisions in the pantry. The agent with the prefix 'von' received special ration cards. But that wasn't his main source. He brought salamis from Hungary, canned vegetables from Bulgaria, coffee from Turkey. The sardines were Portuguese. His servant stole them from Red Cross parcels for English prisoners of war, as she did cigarettes and chocolate. Because he was on the road all the time, the easily transportable small delicacies went on the road in other directions. That's how it happened that Jan got two cans of sardines, a Dutch cheese in a tin and a piece of Hungarian salami for the Javureks, Adela and Greta.

FOURTEEN

WHEN RICHARD REISINGER left the warehouse in the centre of town to go home in the evening, he had to ride the tram a long way through the darkened streets. The faces of people coming home after a long and exhausting day's work seemed green and corpselike. He had a haunted feeling as the tram crawled slowly ahead, clacking along and stopping at the stations.

The star sewn on his left breast, just above the heart, should have forced him to follow the regulations and stand on the outside platform, but he usually covered it with his briefcase, sat in the corner and dozed off. Indeed, half the car was sleeping. It was as if they were all riding through a lifeless city, disintegrating and silenced, where the only sound to be heard was the screeching and rattling of a tram going off to an unknown destination.

Still, he was glad he could sit in the corner and doze until the tram-car clambered up the hill to the stop near his house.

He had grown up in this neighbourhood. He owned a little house with a little hardware store, now closed and cleared out. The house was so small that it didn't even have a yard. The wooden steps creaked as he went up to his apartment – a single room with a kitchen. He turned on the light – a bare light bulb – and then turned it off again immediately in order to open the window and air the room out. Then he drew the blackout shades again, put a pot on a small electric hotplate and waited for the water to boil. In the winter he had to use a small heating stove, but sometimes he was too tired even to make a fire. Then he'd eat a little, get in bed and read. He read a lot lately. Before the war he had hardly touched a book, buying only an occasional sports magazine and listening to the radio.

Books helped him slough off the ugliness and horror of his work. In the old days he used to like going to dances, hanging about with his friends and boxing. There was never much business in his shop. Customers went there mainly to pass the time of day; at the most they'd buy a few nails or a hook. Generally the neighbourhood was concerned with local problems: someone was born, someone died, someone else was taken to the hospital, a girl took poison because of an unhappy love affair. When one is young everything seems simpler. No need for soul-searching about what to do, no need to make plans, so long as a living could be eked out from the shop. Some day he might get married, but God knew when that might be. The store would hardly support two people. If they had children he'd take a job as a shop assistant in a larger store. But if his future wife had money, they could open a shop in another neighbourhood. Of course, he'd never marry a girl just for money. Then the Depression came, and the new chain stores took away a lot of customers. But if a person has only himself to support, if he lives modestly, if his only amusements are boxing, hanging round with his friends, playing soccer and going dancing occasionally at Deutsch's, he can always scrape by.

The mobilisation came, in 1938, and like everyone else he was happy to go. Then came Munich. The Vlajka Fascists cropped up everywhere and wrote all sorts of abusive signs on his shopfront. The writing could be washed off, and the neighbours didn't pay much attention to such foolishness, but in the end he lost his shop anyhow in accordance with the law regarding the confiscation of Jewish property. At first he wasn't too upset by this either. He was strong and healthy. He'd always find work of some sort.

But after the occupation on March 15 the merry-go-round began. As it turned faster and faster, he found himself alone on it. No more friends, no more dances; the Boxing Club had been dissolved even earlier. And the rest of it was like a terrible dream, except that he was forced to live it. All that remained was the apartment he came home to every evening. But that wasn't enough. The old way didn't work any more – to take life as it comes and not worry too much about anything.

His group of friends broke up. Some of them were conscripted to the Reich, some of them were arrested, new friends were hard to come by. Things were better when he was working on the highways and in the quarries – there was a spirit of camaraderie among the labourers. Even at the Collection Agency everybody stuck together – there was no other way, though people with different occupations were thrown together there, each with problems of his own. The main problem was to avoid being called for the transports as long as possible.

He'd talk with the neighbours about the war and they'd tell anecdotes about the Führer, his marshals, ministers and Czech collaborators, about news from the General Headquarters claiming that the Reich armed forces in the East had succeeded in breaking away from the enemy and reducing the front. These conversations about good and bad news had two beliefs in common: that justice would prevail in the end and that the Fascist murderers would eventually be destroyed.

Reisinger had hardly any time for himself on weekdays. But Sunday belonged entirely to him. He had a day off on Sunday – the warehouse was closed.

When the weather was nice he'd stretch out on a hillside overlooking the city. He could see only factories and tall chimneys. Smoke poured out of them even on Sundays.

He knew that the transport lay ahead for him. He did not comfort himself, as many others did, with thoughts that the war would end in two months, that freedom would come, and that there was plenty of time for the people in the Central Bureau to accomplish their task. He did believe, however, as most people did, that the war would end, that the Russians would win and bring justice and peace. Sometimes he felt a wave of anger, and he had to control himself to keep from smashing Erich or Karel when they boasted about their devilish work. The trouble was that he'd enjoy only one satisfying moment. Then they would kill him.

One afternoon he decided to go for a walk. He was tired of the bare rubbish-strewn hillside, scorched by the sun and over-grazed by goats. He walked down the road that followed the river. Above it the hill was blooming with acacias. He felt as if he were out in the country, because there were trees here and the river was quiet on this Sunday afternoon. He didn't feel like thinking about anything. He just wanted to look at the river, at the trees, at the garden of an isolated little house. He felt as if he were saying goodbye to something he might never see again.

His head was full of confused thoughts that kept cropping up as he kept trying to push them away.

Suddenly he bumped into someone. That could have meant real trouble if it was one of them. But they never came this way. He mumbled a few words of apology. Then the person caught him by the sleeve.

'Are you so blinded by that sheriff's star of yours that you don't even recognise me?'

It was Franta, his friend from the Boxing Club. He used to work in the Rustonec factory.

'So what are you doing now?'

'I'm with the Gestapo.'

'Come on, Richard, stop pulling my leg.'

Reisinger told him about his adventures. He was glad to have someone to confide in.

They talked for a few more minutes. Franta looked around.

'There's nobody here, but still, it's better not to have long chats out in the open. I'll tell you what. Next Sunday take off that star and come to the Sestak pub. We could go a few rounds. Everything's the same as it used to be there.'

They went off in opposite directions.

The next Sunday Reisinger went to Sestak's. It was an ordinary corner pub with a bar and a small side room. Before the war the owner used to lend the room to the Boxing Club at no charge. It brought in hardly any business, because the boxers drank very little or nothing at all. But the owner was a boxing fan. He even turned on the heat for them in the winter.

The pub was unchanged. People were sitting around the bar, playing cards. The owner stood behind the counter, pouring beer. He recognised Reisinger, but he gave no sign of it. He just muttered a greeting and indicated the door of the side room with his eyes. There were sounds coming from that room, dull thuds. When he entered, Reisinger saw Franta and two young men he didn't know. They were hitting a punchbag – those were the dull, inexpert thuds he had heard in the bar-room. Franta was apparently giving them lessons.

The little room looked the same as in the old days. Pictures of famous boxers hung on the walls. In a glass case were polished trophies won at various matches; the boxing gloves must have been in the cupboard. Either the owner had declared the things in the room as his own private property when the inventories of the various workers' sporting clubs were confiscated or perhaps the officials didn't want to bother carting away that small amount of junk.

'This is Louis and this is Tonda,' said Franta, introducing the two young men. They shook Reisinger's hand. Their hands were strong, work-hardened.

'Not to keep you in suspense too long,' continued Franta calmly, 'I didn't really invite you here for boxing. We have to keep punching this bag so that people in the bar-room think we're practising. One has to be careful. But first tell me, do you still live in that little house up on the hill? I haven't been in that part of town for a long time.'

Reisinger answered that he still lived there. They'd probably let him keep his apartment until he was called for the transport, because nobody really wanted it.

Then Franta continued to ask a lot of questions. What time did he come home? Did anybody come for visits? What were the neighbours like?

Reisinger found the interrogation strange, and finally he asked, 'Why do you want to know all this?'

'I'll tell you. These two young fellows are from Suchdol. Do you know it?'

Reisinger was familiar with Suchdol. When he was still working for the Collection Agency they used to pick up furniture there. A former village located just outside Prague in the woods above the river, Suchdol was a neat and clean suburb with little gardens and odd street names. No factories or industry, only market gardening. Once when he was moving furniture out of a Suchdol villa and the sun was shining and the sky was clear and blue, he felt as if he were on an outing to the country. They took it easy that day, smoking a pack of cigarettes the former owner had left in a drawer. They felt as if there were peace, as if this neighbourhood were in a world of its own because everything was so calm there. They ate sandwiches and drank water from their thermoses and watched the river flow away from the city.

'I know it a little. What about Suchdol?'

'The town was always left-wing and always somewhat red before the war. The authorities were after a doctor from Suchdol for unfair competition, because he took patients who were unemployed during the Depression without charge. The mayor of the town was a Communist and so were the majority of people there. Something was always going on in Suchdol. Then, after March 15, the Gestapo began to kick up hell. They wanted to arrest the mayor and the local authorities. Except they didn't pull it off and they haven't caught them to this very day. They tried to find out where they were hiding from their wives, so they arrested them, but they never got anything out of them – good women in Suchdol. Then nothing happened for a long time. But now they're having trouble again. These fellows come from there and they need to disappear. As soon as they get new papers they'll go somewhere else.

So they need to hide out somewhere for a week or two. I thought maybe the way things look today the safest place might be at your house. They'd never search for them there.'

At first Reisinger was a little surprised. But he made a quick decision. Those fellows were obviously not hiding out for no good reason. He was glad to help them. At least he'd be a bit useful.

He told Franta that he didn't mind at all if they stayed with him, but there was a problem about getting enough food.

'Don't worry about that. We'll take care of it.'

The young men didn't take part in these arrangements. They kept punching the bag.

'Well, what do you think? How about going a few rounds, since we're here. Are you still a welterweight?'

Richard and Franta stripped to their undershirts and put on boxing gloves. Louis and Tonda were referees, except it was obvious they didn't know anything about boxing.

'Let's call it a day,' said Franta. 'There's not much time. You go home now, Richard. I'll bring them to your house in the evening, after dark. I won't ring the doorbell and I won't knock. I'll just whistle that signal of ours we used to use when we went to steal pears in the Grabas's garden.'

Later that evening Franta whistled and Reisinger opened the door immediately. It was raining outside and nobody was hanging about on the street. They didn't turn on the lights in the hallway but followed Reisinger, groping in the dark.

'We didn't manage to find any food,' Franta apologised. 'But I'll send something tomorrow. Until then they'll simply have to go hungry. They've been through many worse things. Once, during the rampage after the Heydrich assassination, they had to stand all night in a pond without moving.'

'What about sleeping arrangements?' asked Reisinger. 'There's an old couch in the kitchen and a bed in the living room, but two won't fit on it, so somebody will have to sleep on the floor. How about let's toss a coin.'

But Franta wouldn't hear of it. The guests would sleep in the kitchen and take turns on the couch.

And so Reisinger became one of a threesome. In the evening the young men wanted to talk a lot, mainly about soccer, since they didn't talk during the day. That was partly because they had to be quiet and partly because they had exhausted all subjects of conversation between them. Franta sent food through various contacts.

It was a new world for Reisinger. Until then he had come to believe that one has to give up fighting when the opponent is stronger. It sometimes seemed to him that he had been written off already.

Louis and Tonda persuaded him that it was possible to fight, that it was only necessary to know what one is fighting for. This small country had been sold down the river, then it had been overrun by bandits and murderers; they chained it and beat it down, but they couldn't break it, not as long as there were people to defend it. The people he had been meeting until now didn't know how to defend themselves. Living life just to survive – that would never end well. One had to make up one's mind firmly and resolutely, to be willing to give up comfort, submission and fear; one had to be willing to sacrifice one's own life, if need be, for a cause that would ultimately prevail and bring peace and freedom to other people.

The young men often told stories about Suchdol, their pride and joy, where nobody ever gave in to fear tactics, where the mayor, for instance, distributed the entire town treasury to the unemployed during the Depression and then was arrested for embezzlement. After Munich he had been forced to give up his office, and a Nazi warrant was put out for his arrest immediately after March 15. But they hadn't managed to catch him, and they probably never would.

After quite a long while Franta reappeared one day and Reisinger knew he had come for his guests. As they were leaving Franta said casually, 'Thanks a lot, friend. We won't forget what you've done for us.'

When they were gone the house felt empty and deserted to Reisinger.

FIFTEEN

ANTONIN BECVAR LIVED in Prosek. It was a long walk from the last stop of the tram at the end of the day, and he had to get up early in the morning. But Prosek had its advantages in wartime. People were able to keep rabbits and chickens in the backyards of their little houses. People also kept goats.

He came home from Municipal earlier than usual. His wife was out in the yard doing laundry in a washtub.

'Marena, come in the house,' whispered Becvar, 'everybody can hear us out here. I have some news for you.'

'I know,' Marena scolded as they sat down in the kitchen. 'That Paroubek bilked you out of the wood slats you gave him a down payment for. I always told you he was cheating you. And Santroch is coming for the rabbit hutch the day after tomorrow.'

'It's not Paroubek, not at all.' Becvar waved his hand. 'If he doesn't bring the wood slats I'll find them elsewhere. For your information, I was kicked out at Municipal today.'

'What did you do wrong? You were blabbing somewhere, right?'

'Not at all. It's all on account of that statue I was telling you about. They canned Schlesinger, and so he took it out on me. I was about to go in for lunch, I was hardly out of the door when the guard yells at me that I should go to Personnel. So I went there and they told me I was dismissed as of today and that I was to register at the Employment Bureau. So I said I wanted to know the reason I was dismissed, but they said they didn't know themselves, that the notice was signed by Dr Buch. Imagine that, after so many years of service they give me an hour's notice like you give a maid. All that talk about a job with a pension! I should have stuck to cabinet making.'

'Of course you should have,' said Marena. 'Everything's different now.'

Three days later Becvar received a summons to come to the Employment Bureau. It stated a time and a room number.

He knocked and entered. An official sat behind a desk.

'Morning,' said Becvar. 'I'm here with the summons.'

'Hail to the Homeland,' answered the official, according to regulations. 'Now, let's see what you have here. I see. Becvar Antonin, formerly employed as a worker at Municipal, married, no children. Sit down, Mr Becvar.'

Becvar sat down.

'So what will it be,' Becvar asked, 'CKD or Letov? I'd rather go to Letov, it would be closer to home.'

'Neither CKD nor Letov,' said the official, almost apologetically. 'You are definitely conscripted to the Reich.'

'But that can't be possible.' Becvar jumped up from the seat. 'I'm over fifty. What would they do with me there?'

'The order came from higher up. The file from Municipal states that you are an asocial element and a malingerer.'

'That's baloney,' said Becvar angrily. 'I've been working since I was fourteen, and I've been at Municipal for ten years.'

'I know, Mr Becvar,' said the official, trying to calm him down, 'I believe you. But what can I do?'

Becvar grew even more excited. 'What's going to happen to me now? I'm supposed to leave everything here at my ripe old age and go off to work in the Reich somewhere?'

Suddenly he had a better idea: 'Look, couldn't we make a deal somehow, like that I wouldn't go to the Reich, like that I was sick or something. I'd make it worth your while, you know . . . '

The official shrugged his shoulders. 'It's a direct order from a Reich official. His stamp is on the paper and the Employment Bureau is required to inform him as soon as the order is fulfilled. You must have done something wrong to make them go gunning for you.'

'Yeah, sure, it's a long story,' said Becvar. 'It's on account of a statue. Then I was denounced by a certain Schlesinger because he had to go to the front. I didn't do anything bad at all.'

'You'll have to go to the Reich one way or another. It'll be better if you stay out of their sight.'

'Yeah, sure, but why all the way to the Reich?'

'Look, I like going to the theatre. I saw a play recently called *Harlequin the Comedian*. It's a completely different world there, with real honest-to-goodness people living in it who love, who hate, who are jealous of each other, who kill for love. Meanwhile, these four walls covered with dirty whitewash, and this work of mine – sending people to the Reich – that's all just a dream, it's not reality.'

'Yeah, sure, except I'm a part of that dream, and you're obviously sending me to the Reich no matter what.'

'I can't help you. Here are your papers. Day after tomorrow you're leaving from the main station.'

Becvar left without a word, slamming the door behind him. Out in the hallway he spat disgustedly.

'That one's crazier than the Krauts with that play of his.' And suddenly he felt homesick for everything, even the lifeless streets of his native city, even the rabbit hutches and the little yard in Prosek. They were sending him off to a foreign land he didn't know or care about; they'd give him all sorts of awful stuff to eat, because Germans don't know how to cook and they ruin even the best food. He'd have to sleep on a bunk in some dump there. And in the end he'd certainly be killed by a bomb, because bombs were dropping day and night there.

And then there was Marena. They'd been together twenty-five years and they'd never been separated once, if you didn't count the time Marena was lying-in in a hospital. What would she do without him? Of course, he'd send her money from there, but what good did money do these days? Why, they'd be dead of hunger by now if they had to live off the pay he got at Municipal. It was just barely enough for their rent and coupons. The main thing was those rabbit hutches; they brought in extra provisions. Well, nothing could be done about it, Marena would have to manage on her own. She'd pull it off somehow because she was a tough woman. Boy, would she carry on when he told her the news. 'I always told you to keep your mouth shut, Tony, but not you, His Highness always thinks he knows better, and look at him now – off to the Reich.'

But it didn't happen that way. When he came home to the little yard Marena said to him, 'You don't have to tell me, I can see it written all over you that things turned out badly. Where did they send you? Somewhere out in the country?'

'If only it was the country. The rats are sending me to the Reich.'

'But you're over fifty. How can they do that?'

'They can do anything they want.'

'The dirty bastards!' Marena said angrily. 'Well, they'll get theirs one of these days!'

And that was it. No reproaches, no crying or carrying on. Just anger and hatred. Marena was a fine woman, Becvar thought to himself. Then they began to figure out how to manage things once he left. Marena could trade off some things for food. Today everything had a price. Then there were the rabbits. She couldn't eat them all, so she ought to sell a couple here and there. Marena seemed calm. But she was on the verge of tears.

The neighbours came over. They had obviously heard everything, since Becvar was talking out in the yard. Some offered help, others had malice peeping out of their eyes: Becvar is going to the Reich and we're staying here. Meanwhile, Becvar acted as if he were getting ready for a holiday. He was leaving the day after tomorrow. Marena had her hands full of work and Becvar had a lot of running around to do. He also stopped off at Municipal to sign some papers and say goodbye to Stankovsky.

'This was all that idiot Schlesinger's doing, the lousy Kraut,' said Stankovsky. 'Just be careful you're not clobbered by a bomb like Sehnoutek. All that was left of him was his coat. Actually it was just rags and they sent them to his wife. But they refused to bury just the coat at the cemetery, so she's got it at home now.'

'Don't worry, I'm not croaking. I've got years for that.'

They shook hands.

'So look, come home soon. That statue is still lying on the roof there, you know. Nobody's minding it, and it's only missing a hand.'

'That damned statue.' Becvar sighed. 'It really played a dirty trick on me.'

The next day Becvar said goodbye to his wife at the main station and departed for the Reich. This time Marena cried.

Bad luck had been dogging Becvar from the moment they sent him to the roof of the Rudolfinum. Now he was working in a munitions factory, though doing the bare minimum – what did they expect from an older person, and a politically re-educated one at that. Becvar actually knew various trades, but why should he say anything about it here? In any case, everything was mixed up in the Reich. A barber worked on a milling machine and a worker from Ringhoffer's tapped beer. There were air raids all the time, day and night. At those times they all ran to a shelter and work stopped. In fact, everything turned out just as he had imagined it in Prague: he slept in a bunk and the food was awful. It was only bearable because everybody received packages from home and Marena sent him some, too.

And then disaster struck. They used to sit around in the dark telling stories during the blackout hour organised in the buildings every night. When his turn came around, all he could think of was the time he was a volunteer fireman back in the days when Prosek was still a village and not part of Prague. The building must have had a spy, because he was called in the next day and informed that he was being transferred to the fire brigade. And that was the beginning of a hellish life for Becvar. Not only did the job involve putting out fires – which was futile in any case – but they had to drag dead bodies out of basements and carry off the wounded. All the while bombs were whistling and any one of them could knock him off in a second like a nine-pin.

The fire brigade was made up entirely of foreigners, but the commander was a German and he had a revolver. There were also fifty-five men all over the place, so sneaking off was out of the question. Becvar found a countryman in the brigade, a certain Ruda Vyskocil from Prostejov. He used to work in a clothing store there before being sent to the Reich. Ruda taught him not to get involved in anything unnecessarily – he was a crafty Moravian. It was a miserable job and many of their number were carried away on stretchers when walls collapsed on them or they were struck by shrapnel. Becvar and Vyskocil were lucky; nothing had happened to them yet. But how long could such a streak of good luck last?

'Do you call this living?' Becvar once said to Vyskocil. 'Pulling dead bodies out of cellars and waiting for a bomb to drop on your head. I'm a pretty easy-going chap, but I've had enough of this. I mean it, I'll just crack up and do something crazy. One time they sent us up on the roof to pull down a statue, and later that friend of mine Stankovsky took home the rope and said it was good for hanging, and I couldn't figure it out because the rope was much too thick for hanging clothes. Now I know what he meant.'

'There's time enough for that, Tony. Meanwhile, you better just try to stay alive and out of a concentration camp. They're beginning to lose the war, and if you don't do anything stupid you might live to see the end of it. Then you can settle accounts with them.'

'Yeah, sure, except I'm not the type for that sort of thing.'

And then came the great air raid. Half the city was on fire and the bombs kept coming down. They were crouched near the entrance of a shelter, waiting for the bombing to end. But this time it seemed it would never stop. And they were scared, scared to death, even though sitting in a shelter during an air raid like that wasn't much better than being out on the street. Still, a shelter provided a certain security, however dubious. A person imagined that the danger wasn't so great there. But everybody knew perfectly well that they were kidding themselves, because they often dragged dead bodies out of the shelters.

Becvar stayed close to Vyskocil. If a person had to die, it might as well be near a friend. But they couldn't even talk to one another, the bombs were whistling and exploding all around.

The bombs came nearer and nearer to their shelter. It was a terrible spectacle to see a house collapse before their very eyes or catch fire from the roof down. They were used to this, except the fear was worse as the bombs came closer and closer to their shelter. They couldn't tell what the people in the shelter were doing because the terrible thundering, whistling and crashing kept them from hearing any sounds from below. But people there were surely groaning, trembling and throwing up. They had seen that many times also.

Just then they heard the sound of a bomb falling so near to them that, by reflex, they tried to dive into the shelter. However, the commander with the revolver stood on the steps and wouldn't let them down with the Germans. They had to stay out on the street.

All that was left of the house across the street was a single wall. And on the top of the wall they saw the figure of a woman holding a small suitcase. Her mouth was wide open; she appeared to be shouting with all her might, but in all that noise you couldn't make out a single word. How she got on top of that wall and how she stayed there was a complete miracle. There was no guessing how long she could hold on. The wall was bound to collapse any minute.

Another strange sight was a completely undamaged statue in a niche of that very wall, looking out with a dull, complaisant gaze at the battered street. There had probably been a pharmacy in the building, because the statue was of a woman in a flowing robe with a snake twined around her. The screaming woman stood directly above the serene trademark of the pharmacist.

Antonin Becvar was terrified. His nerves were giving out and the worst thing was that he couldn't confide in Vyskocil; he wouldn't have heard him even if he had screamed right into his ear. Becvar didn't want to look at the woman, who kept opening her mouth wide. But somehow he had to keep looking at her, because if he let his eyes drop lower he would have to look at the ridiculous statue in the middle of the ruins. Her smile annoyed him. It reminded him of his unlucky adventure on the roof of the Rudolfinum. But the woman on the wall with her mouth that opened and closed yet uttered not a sound irritated him even more.

Suddenly Becvar grabbed a folding fireman's ladder that was standing in front of the shelter and rushed out into the street. Ruda Vyskocil screamed something that he couldn't make out, but nobody dared go after him. Becvar found himself alone in the midst of the thundering, whistling, crashing and flames, alone with his anger. Now he had really had enough. After being forced to pull dead bodies out of bombed buildings every day, he could no longer stand living in this roaring hell and being afraid of dying. He was overcome with a senseless fury at his own powerlessness, and that forced him to do something.

He grabbed the ladder, stood it against the wall and climbed up to the screaming woman. The people in front of the shelter watched his race against death with excitement.

Either the wall would collapse before Becvar got to the woman or he'd be struck by a bomb or hit by anti-aircraft fire. Even the commander, who was standing downstairs at the entrance to the shelter, neglected his duties and went up the stairs to watch what Becvar was doing. Becvar climbed the ladder as if he didn't see what was going on around him, as if he didn't care about the bombs, anti-aircraft fire and flames. Now he reached the woman and he could really look at her. She was an old lady completely covered with plaster dust, all dolled up in old-fashioned clothing. She had the kind of bonnet on her head that they wore in the last century. And in her hand she clutched a suitcase, even though she could fall off any minute.

Only now could Becvar make out what she was screaming. It was a single word repeated over and over again: '*Hilfe*! *Hilfe*!' Becvar knew what it meant. The old woman didn't weigh much. He picked her up off the wall quite easily and made his way down the ladder again. She had finally stopped screaming; only her eyes emanated terror. But she didn't let go of the suitcase, even when Becvar tried to carry it for her. She would rather have fallen off the ladder. Becvar himself didn't know what had got into him to undertake such a dangerous rescue. Everything was going around in his head, the stupid statue that survived the bombing all by itself and the statue at the Rudolfinum, the one that got him sent to the Reich, and that old woman opening and closing her mouth like a mechanical doll wound up with a key.

As he descended, he slowly came to his senses. Now fear began to return and he couldn't even get it straight in his head where he was. Yet fear impelled him to hurry, and that's why he quickly dragged the old woman all the way to the shelter. Then he fainted. Suddenly life returned to the old woman. She didn't even cry, but just sat there smiling placidly. They carried Becvar into the shelter and poured water on him. He regained consciousness but continued to shake all over.

The sirens announced the end of the air raid. It grew quiet. And then the quiet was broken by a sudden rumbling, as if an earthquake were occurring and the earth were opening up. It was the wall on which the old woman had been standing a little while ago finally collapsing. The battered bricks and mortar fell right up to the entrance of the shelter.

'Jesus Mary,' Becvar began screaming. Only then did he understand what a crazy thing he had got himself into. He had to struggle to keep from throwing up.

Suddenly the old woman appeared at his side. She was still clutching the suitcase in her hand and talking rapidly about something. Luckily Ruda Vyskocil was standing right there. He knew German, because there were a lot of Germans in Prostejov, especially in the clothing business.

'What's the old bag blabbing about?' asked Becvar.

'That's not an old bag. She says she's a countess, von Sarnow or Tarnow, or something of the sort, who the hell knows.'

'Ask her what's so special about that case that she wouldn't let me hold it for her.'

'She says it's the family jewels.'

'Yeah, sure,' said Becvar.

The Countess von Tarnow or Sarnow was going on and on about something else.

'What does she want now?' Becvar asked Vyskocil.

'I don't understand her too well. She talks all that Prussian double-talk. But I think she's saying something about your being a hero and deserving a reward.'

The commander came up to them and the countess introduced herself to him. When he heard her name, he clicked his heels with respect. Then he addressed Becvar and informed him that he would receive a decoration.

Becvar flew into a rage. 'To hell with his medals.'

The countess paid no attention to the commander and turned to Becvar. Vyskocil translated: 'She's asking what you want for a reward. She says she has a lot of pull in the various bureaus here. Her son is some kind of general or marshal or something. So quick, think of something you want.'

Becvar jumped up and shouted: 'Home! *Nach Hause! Böhmen! Prag!*'

He grabbed at all the German words he knew. Vyskocil didn't even need to translate. The commander looked disgruntled and said something excitedly to the countess. Vyskocil was afraid to translate, net wanting to make Becvar mad again. But he translated the countess's reply.

'I give you my noble word of honour that I will see to it that you return home. Even if I have to go to the Führer personally. Your heroic deed deserves it.'

'We'll see about that,' said Vyskocil dubiously. 'Don't believe that old bag one hundred per cent. But you might thank her anyhow.'

Becvar said, '*Danke*.'

That was also one of the German words he knew.

Becvar arrived in Prague late at night. He guarded the document stating in black and white that he was leaving at his own request with the approval of the Office of Volunteer

Work for the Reich; he guarded it like a holy relic. In addition, the document announced that he had distinguished himself during the bombardment. Becvar knew what the document said – Ruda Vyskocil had translated it for him. They parted as old friends. Becvar promised Vyskocil he'd write to him.

A guard stopped Becvar at the station, but the document had magical powers – it bore the stamp with the sovereign seal and the signature of some big shot. He took the tram to the terminus and then trudged with his suitcase to Prosek. The road seemed endless and the suitcase grew heavier and heavier. It was three o'clock in the morning when he finally arrived at their little house. It had no doorbell, only a dummy push-button, because neither the landlord nor the tenants wanted to pay for the installation of a bell and they had to get around the regulations somehow. But even if there had been a working bell Becvar wouldn't have used it – it would have woken up the whole house. He jumped over the gate and tapped at the window of his apartment. It took a while before Marena woke up. She looked out of the window, sleepy and alarmed. She almost cried out when she saw him standing in the courtyard, but she restrained herself. She indicated that she would come and open the door – all this quietly, without a word.

Only when Becvar was in the kitchen did she whisper: 'You ran away, didn't you? But you can't stay here – somebody would turn you in. We'll have to figure something out. Maybe you could hide out somewhere in the country.'

Becvar said, 'Well, Marena, you could at least give me a kiss.'

Marena realised that she hadn't even greeted him in all the confusion.

Becvar sat down on a chair. He was tired to death.

'For your information I didn't run away. Not at all. They let me go.'

'Because of illness? But you don't look bad.'

'Not at all. It was because of the statue.'

'Have you gone crazy? What statue?'

'It's like this: I got to the Reich because of a statue, and I got out of the Reich because of a statue. The second one, that was an idiotic statue; you know, one of those women with big curls and a snake crawling around her. I couldn't stand looking at her. And because I couldn't stand looking at her I had to look at the old bag who was screeching on the wall, except that I couldn't hear her screeching in all that noise. So it drove me crazy and I saved the old bag. And the old bag fixed things up for me so I could go home. I've got a document, so they can all drop dead.'

Marena was confused. 'I don't understand at all. What does some old bag have to do with a statue or anything?'

'I'll explain it all one of these days. But I can barely talk now, I have to lie down and go to sleep, and I'll sleep at least all day and night, so don't wake me up. The main thing is that I have the document, so you don't have to worry about me.'

Only then did Marena stop controlling herself. Tears began to fall to the ground.

'When you wake up I'll make you a roast rabbit with bacon.'

SIXTEEN

FRANTISEK SCHÖNBAUM SAT in his office in the fortress town. It wasn't really an office, more like a cupboard formed by partitioning off a room. It was not much bigger than a dog-kennel. But Frantisek Schönbaum rejoiced in that cupboard because it belonged to him alone and it was warm. Outside, it was bitterly cold, colder than any of the new residents had ever experienced. He looked at the thermometer hanging behind the window – nine degrees below zero. He was drawing a blueprint. The work helped him avoid thinking, tormenting himself.

Before the war he used to decorate the homes of rich people and design special furniture for them. The only work he had enjoyed, however, was his job at a well-known left-wing theatre. He hadn't even minded designing exhibits at the Jewish Museum not long ago; it still gave him a feeling of doing something useful. Then he was sent by transport to the fortress town. Here, with difficulty, he just managed to keep going.

He designed things here, too, but not furniture, of course. A practical cart to be attached to a human carthorse. A simple coffin that could be produced without much work. Work-benches that could be used for various purposes and other articles that were required in the running of a ghetto.

He threw himself feverishly into his work. Coming to work early that morning he'd had to pass a transport of people getting ready to leave for the East. He arrived at six o'clock, but the people assigned for transport had been gathering in the courtyard of the barracks where he had his office since three o'clock or earlier. They stood there in the cruel cold; men, women and children. They wore their transport numbers around their necks. They stood in assigned groups of fifty people. They were shivering with cold and huddling together. It was still dark on that gloomy, freezing morning when an outcry was heard from the barracks courtyard. It was the troopers and ghetto guards calling together their groups in order to herd them to the railway station. Weighed down with baggage, the procession went out through the gate and began its journey. The ghetto guards and troopers darted about Schönbaum like hunting dogs. He quickly slipped into his office and threw himself into his work. At first he had to force himself to concentrate, but finally he became absorbed in it, and even began to whistle to himself.

And so the morning proceeded. Along with everyone else he joined the queue in the barracks courtyard at noon. Holding a stub with the date in one hand, he waited for the main meal. In his other hand he held a mess tin. The queue moved slowly. As people reached the little window they argued; they whined and begged for more. It did them no good. People were distributing soup and, as the next course, three potatoes in their skins. An old man who had just received his meal slipped on the ice and his soup spilled. The potatoes scattered at the feet of the others waiting in the queue. Someone must have quickly grabbed them, because they never appeared again. The old man lay on the ground, tears falling on the freezing puddle that had been his soup just a moment before. He knew he would have to go hungry the whole day. The people in the queue after him begged the woman doling out the meals to give him another portion. But she was implacable.

Frantisek Schönbaum was lucky to be able to take the food away with him to his office. The others had to eat in overcrowded dormitories where everyone was on top of one another. He ate slowly, having read in a book somewhere that the longer one chewed the more nutritious the meal. He ate the potatoes with their skins, having read in yet another book that there were vitamins in the skin. When he finished eating, he felt like having a brief nap, but suddenly he was stricken with fear. The transports left for the East in the dark, in the fog and frost. When would his turn come? He knew it was foolish to think that he was indispensable, that they needed him to design useful articles. That was nonsense; such people were a penny a dozen. If he went, another person would take his place. That one would sit in his office and delight in the quiet and warmth before they chased him out into the cold to the transport, too. He forced himself to think about the East. Nobody knew what went on there. Postcards arrived from there with the words I'M FINE in block letters, and nothing else. But those words meant nothing. They were the same on every postcard. There was just one thing that everyone knew: things were bad there, worse than in the fortress town.

He tried to talk himself into believing that even though his turn would come, it would not happen for a long time, and by then the war might be over and those who remained in the fortress town would be freed. How else could he manage to go back to work if he had no hope at all?

At three in the afternoon an errand boy with a message burst into his office. The errand boys were always fearless youngsters who were rude to everyone. The errand boy shoved the message into Schönbaum's hand. The boy didn't care that the hand was holding a compass and that the motion caused one end of it to scratch the blueprint.

Schönbaum leaped up. 'How dare you, you little brat! You've ruined my drawing!'

But the errand boy only grinned and handed him a notebook. 'Just sign so I won't have to waste any more time here.' And he slammed the door behind him.

The message was from his boss. It ordered him to come to the technical division immediately. Schönbaum tried in vain to figure out what such an urgent summons might mean. Could the boss be dissatisfied with him? No, impossible, Schönbaum sat in his office from morning until night and did the work of three. More likely the boss wanted to give his job to some other person he cared about in order to save that person from the transport. The boss could always find a fault of some sort in his work. And if he couldn't find any, he could always pass it off as a reassignment.

And now fear struck Schönbaum once again. In his mind's eye he recaptured the people in the barracks courtyard, their bruised cheeks, their eyes wide with terror. Their fear was far greater than his, because they were being sent into the unknown, perhaps to their deaths. The darkness enveloped them, illuminated only by an occasional torch. They had been condemned, expelled from the town; they had become mere numbers. Such a fate awaited him, too, if the director kicked him out, because then he'd be assigned a less important job, perhaps as a sweeper. After that nothing would protect him and they could send him to the East with the next transport.

The office of the director of the technical division was in the Magdeburg barracks, where all the ghetto functionaries were based. It wasn't far, but to Schönbaum it seemed miles away. Finally he arrived at the barracks entrance, showed his summons, and was allowed in to find the office. Even as he stood before the door he thought about whether he should go in or not. But if he ignored the summons he'd be in worse trouble.

The director of the technical division greeted him with unaccustomed kindness, but of course kindness can be contrived, kindness can be a mask covering a harsh decision. A moment later his face took on a more severe and serious look. Here it comes, thought Schönbaum, and wondered whether he ought to beg and plead for mercy, or whether he ought to hold his head up and be proud before the fateful blow.

All at once he heard an agitated whisper just at his ear: 'Swear that you will preserve secrecy; otherwise you face the penalty of death.'

It sounded like a phrase out of one of those cheap novels you buy at the news-stand and Schönbaum was even more confused. But he was obviously not being kicked out. So he answered: 'I swear.'

'Tomorrow there will be an execution in the moat of the Ustecky barracks. Your job is to design a double gallows for the technical division. I hope you realise what a great responsibility this is. The gallows must be strong and simple, so that our carpenters can make it easily, because everything must be ready by nine o'clock tomorrow morning. Now run back to your office. I'll be sending for your design in an hour.'

A gallows – he had never designed such a thing. He didn't even know what one looked like. But in the ghetto library they had many books. Perhaps he'd find a picture of a gallows. He stopped there on his way and borrowed a volume of a technical encyclopedia.

Among the ghetto guards patrolling the transport that had gathered in the barracks courtyard that morning was Richard Reisinger. He had been assigned to the ghetto guards against his will and he hated the job. But the only way to get out of it was to volunteer for the transport himself. The baroness had been right – he hadn't lasted long in the warehouse. They sent him to the fortress town anyhow. In Terezin he was assigned to the ghetto guards because he had worked at the Gestapo warehouse and was used to dealing with SS men, and also because he had served in the army

It was a brutal job. With his fellow ghetto guards he had to get rid of people coming to the Magdeburg barracks with various requests. He checked passes, he quarrelled endlessly with people who wanted one thing or another. And today was the worst of all. They had dragged people out of their dormitory bunks during the night, ordered them to get dressed, pack their things and hang their numbers around their necks. Then, at three in the morning, in the dark, with only torches and flares for illumination, they hounded them into the barracks courtyard, into the freezing cold. The confused children were screaming, the old men and women were groaning and moaning, sounds of weeping could be heard on all sides. And he, Richard Reisinger, together with the others, had to get them going, threaten them, herd them into groups. The troopers were waiting in the barracks courtyard, where they took over the guard duty.

He wore a funny peaked cap bordered in yellow, and his only weapon was a wooden truncheon. But even this clownish uniform created fear and made people avoid him or doff their hats respectfully to him: a uniform meant power. The power was conditional, virtually meaningless, because any SS man, however lowly in rank, could beat him up, smack him around or demote him to a job cleaning sewers. Even the troopers, though they had guns with bayonets, were puppets in the hands of the SS, who could do anything they wanted with them – they had already ordered a few troopers executed in the Small Fortress. But power, however conditional, however tenuous, still inspires fear. It gives rise to emptiness, it makes contacts with people impossible, it creates loneliness. And thus did Richard Reisinger live in the fortress town, a marked and godforsaken man, his only friends those with whom he carried out his work.

At six o'clock in the morning, in the dark and freezing cold, the transport set off on its journey. People burdened down with baggage trudged heavily through the snow, helping the children make their way as well. Every few minutes an old man or woman would fall by the wayside, pulled down by the weight of a heavy knapsack. The ghetto guards helped them to their feet and urged them to hurry. The procession trailed along slowly, spurred on by constant shouts, curses and threats. It took two hours for it to plod its way from the fortress town to the station, though the marker indicated only three kilometres. In their fatigue people forgot about weeping and lamenting. Only as they stood in the icy frost on the platform of the small station and saw the cattle trucks they were going to ride in did they begin to cry and lament again. Children, terrified by the despair of the adults, were shrieking, even though they didn't understand anything. It was necessary to stuff the people into the cattle trucks. Their feeble resistance was easily overcome because they had the mark of death on their brows already and didn't know how to defend themselves effectively. The gendarmes and ghetto guards crammed them into trucks in groups of fifty and then the trucks were sealed. And yet the suffering did not end there. The people in the cattle trucks as well as the people on the platform had to wait several hours before the train began to move in the direction of Dresden, destination unknown. Only then, finally, could the gendarmes march off to their dormitories and the ghetto guards return to the fortress town.

Richard Reisinger was frozen to the bone and looked forward to the warmth of the guardhouse. It was always warm there, even when it was freezing everywhere else, because the ghetto guards were able to get firewood for themselves. After sitting down on a stool and slowly beginning to thaw out, he began to think about his own fate. Things had gone so far that he had become an enemy of his own people, a driver of human cattle being sent by the murderers and robbers to the slaughterhouse. This was the last stop of his journey that had begun at the stone quarry. Now as he chewed a piece of dry, hard bread he had been saving and swallowed it down with the warm, unsweetened water they called tea, he had time for reflection. He understood that there was no other way out for him than the transport and death. He began to read a detective book and soon dozed off after the exertions of the night and day. He barely had time for a quick thought: nothing more could happen today because the transport had departed.

He woke up just as they brought the main meal into the guardhouse. The ghetto guard received increased rations and also enjoyed the great advantage of not having to queue up at the little window. That meant one potato in its skin or one dab of margarine more. They could eat in the warmth, comfortably, at a table. Some of them actually ate with forks and knives in memory of the old days. After eating Reisinger dozed off again; the members of the command that escorted the transport were given time off.

Around four in the afternoon the commander of the ghetto guards burst into the guardhouse, cast an eye on the sleeping men and gave Reisinger a shove. Reisinger stared at him uncomprehendingly. The commander paid no attention to him and awakened two other members of the guard in the same manner.

'Come with me,' he ordered sharply.

They staggered out, still warm and half asleep, but they came to their senses at once in the fresh air. They tried and failed to figure out what the commander might want with them, and why he had picked them out from all the others. He led them to the Magdeburg barracks. There in a large hall where roll call was sometimes held, they saw that twenty other ghetto guard members were already gathered. They didn't know anything either. They had been summoned from work. There were twenty-three members of the ghetto guard waiting there to hear what the commander was going to say.

The commander had been a high officer in the German Army during the First World War, not in the Austro-Hungarian Army, which the SS members scorned, and he had received several decorations for bravery. He observed military decorum, to which he easily added the habit of screaming he had picked up from his Nazi mentors. He addressed the ghetto guard bluntly: 'I need eleven people. All former soldiers step forward!'

There were only nine former soldiers, and so the commander picked two additional non-soldiers. Reisinger had been a corporal in the First Republic. The two people on either side of him breathed a sigh of relief: they hadn't been chosen.

The commander asked the eleven to come closer. The others stood behind them. He barked out: 'Are there any veterans of the First World War here?'

Only one of the eleven responded, but he had been drafted during the last weeks of war and never got to the front.

The commander looked at them scornfully. They all waited in suspense to hear what he would say next.

'Ten chosen men will assist at the execution tomorrow. They are to report to Untersturmführer Bergel tomorrow at nine o'clock at the moat of the Ustecky barracks. The others will be assigned special tasks.'

A wave passed through the rows of ghetto guards. What execution? Executions didn't take place in the ghetto. People were hanged or killed in the Small Fortress. They couldn't understand it. What did he mean?

The commander realised that he owed them an explanation. He spoke brusquely, as if snapping out orders during a military drill: 'Today at two o'clock in the afternoon the Jewish Council of Elders was called into the Command Office. The ghetto commandant swore them to secrecy on penalty of death and informed them that several residents of the ghetto would be executed by hanging tomorrow. He ordered a double gallows to be constructed in the moat of the Ustecky barracks and twenty-five coffins to be prepared. Nobody is to know of this event. Everything must be prepared by nine o'clock tomorrow. At three in the afternoon I was called into the Magdeburg barracks, where the Jewish Council of Elders was meeting. I received this information there and was instructed to procure ropes for binding the hands and feet, and two strong ropes for the hanging. And further, to pick ten men to supervise the execution along with myself. I am carrying out this order now and binding you to secrecy as well. I picked eleven men. The others will be assigned other jobs. So one of you may be released from the obligation of participating in the execution.'

The brusque words, delivered in military fashion, fell on the ears of the men. It took them a few moments to take in the horror that was about to happen. In the silent room you could hear the sighs of relief of those standing behind the eleven chosen ones. Those eleven stood as if riveted to the floor. They didn't want to believe the terrible assignment that was awaiting them. But they knew it was true. The news was so sudden that for a few moments they stood there numbly, unable to utter a single word, and yet they had to take a vote – one of them would be let off. Every one of them hoped to be that man; every one of them hoped to avoid this job, to forget he had ever heard about it. The one to be relieved of the duty to assist at the execution should be a weak person, one whose nerves couldn't stand such a terrible sight. So when they began to consider who it should be, they all turned their eyes to young Bauml, who was already shaking, obviously about to break down.

'Who will it be?' the commander asked sharply. 'You must decide quickly.'

Reisinger replied in the name of the others: 'We are recommending Bauml here, he's the youngest of us; he was never actually a soldier, but was simply drafted in May 1938.'

Perhaps he didn't have the right to speak for all ten,

perhaps any number of them were sorry not to be in Bauml's place. But nobody spoke up. And so Bauml stepped out of the line.

The commander gave further orders – to find ropes, to prepare twenty-five coffins, to erect the gallows. Those tasks were given to the others who didn't have to assist at the execution. But since it was necessary to preserve secrecy, how were they to avoid answering the inevitable questions of those who would be assigned these various jobs? Those assigned the job of weaving the rope out of hemp might be put off somehow, but what were they to tell the carpenters who were to construct the gallows and to set it up at the Ustecky barracks? They would have to let them in on the secret, at least partially, and force them to take a vow of secrecy also. They would have to draw them into the monstrous circle. The commander explained that the director of the technical division had been notified directly by the Council of Elders to arrange for the gallows to be designed and constructed and for the graves to be dug. The role of the participating guards would be to make sure that everything was ready by nine o'clock in the morning. That meant that the groups who received the orders from the director of the technical division would have to work the whole night.

Thus ended the pronouncement, and the ten who were to assist at the execution the next day were given time off. They were given permission to get some sleep – but how could they sleep? Nobody, not the commander of the ghetto guards or the Council of Elders, knew who was to be executed. Twenty-five coffins had been ordered, and so there would be twenty-five people executed. How long could such an execution last?

A great frost gripped the fortress town, and fog descended on it. The ghetto guards had gone out into the darkness to escort the transport on its final journey – and they were returning to their dormitories in the darkness to wait for the bitter morning.

SEVENTEEN

FRANTISEK SCHÖNBAUM set to work on the assignment given him by the director of the technical division. He knew that the messenger would not be a single minute late. To design a gallows that could be quickly constructed by carpenters was not such a difficult task. It was easier than the 'secret armchair', than the crazy kidney-shaped tables, than the chair on which one could recline but in no way sit. Of course, a gallows is not furniture, nor is it a cart for human carthorses: a gallows is destined for an execution. The director of the technical division didn't know who was going to be hanged, or perhaps he was pretending not to know. In any case, he ordered Schönbaum to design the gallows and told him that an execution would be held the next day at the Ustecky barracks. No more and no less.

Why did he have to be told that there would be an execution? It would have been enough to tell him to design a gallows, period. At least he could have found comfort in the thought that the gallows was only intended to scare people and would then be taken to the Small Fortress, where executions took place daily. But this way he had become a direct and conscious accomplice of the murderers. He was drawing so that people could be hanged. His own people. It might be a friend who had slept in a bunk directly above his own, someone he had shared packages with. The multi-layer bunks had also been constructed according to his design. Bunks, of course, are for sleeping, but when each person in the fortress town is allotted one-and-a-half square metres, then multi-layer bunks are the only answer.

But a gallows? This drawing would haunt him to his dying day, though he had nothing to do with the execution personally, though he knew nothing more than what the director of the technical division had told him about it.

The messenger did indeed arrive exactly one hour later, and Schönbaum handed him the drawing in a sealed envelope. Now he had nothing to do, because the director of the technical division hadn't assigned him any other job. But he didn't feel like leaving the warm little room to go out in the freezing cold or to the reeking dormitory, where there was hardly enough air to breathe. His mind wandered back to the plays he had once designed sets for, and the two actor-comedians who were always greeted with thunderous applause in those final days of the theatre, when they used to sing their song about the millions who go against the wind, a song that had become virtually a hymn at the time of Munich.

What he had designed might actually be considered a sculpture; indeed, the only sculpture permitted in the fortress town. It had a curious T shape. Of course, in the avant-garde French magazine called *Minotaur* he used to subscribe to, many abstract sculptures had that shape. Back then, when he used to go through its pages, it never occurred to him that he would become the first and only Terezin sculptor. His sculpture would be made of wood, like the old statues of saints. His statue would be a Pietà, and at the same time a symbol of the martyr's crown. But it would be erected for the benefit of those others, to be helpful to them in carrying out their murderous trade.

There was no escape for him now. All those who know the

secret and who take part in preparations for an execution of their own people are condemned in advance. Even if his role was insignificant, still he would pay for his crime. For those who work behind the barriers at Command Headquarters and who run the ghetto will want to hide their crimes and erase any record of them. This was the first time he regretted that the only thing he had accomplished in the world was to design meaningless furniture that future architects would ridicule when they came upon it in junk stores. But the gallows-sculpture he designed would undoubtedly live on in the memories of survivors. They wouldn't know who designed it, however, and that was good. Slowly his fear began to subside. At least he'd gain a little time, and who knew what might happen in the meantime. The Germans were losing on all fronts, they were dying of cold in the Soviet offensive. Maybe they'd be defeated soon and the fortress town would be liberated. Tomorrow he must find the latest reports from the front.

Richard Reisinger slept fitfully. He woke early in the morning – it was still dark. Everyone else was already up. He turned on the electric light, one twenty-five-watt bulb, though it was forbidden at that hour. At first everyone kept silent. Nobody wanted to talk about what was awaiting them. Finally someone couldn't hold back – fear forced him to speak. He longed to hear the words of others. But what words could console them? There was no consolation for them. They must be witnesses at an execution. Yet why did the murderers require them to watch as their victims perished? They wanted to draw them into their crime, they wanted to turn them and the Czech troopers into accomplices. Everyone fell silent again and seemed half asleep. All words were now useless. They were waiting for the commander's order to leave for the Ustecky barracks.

The commander of the ghetto guard was already up. His position in the ghetto administration was equal to that of a member of the Council of Elders. But although he had been an officer in the German branch of the Reich army up until the time he had been sent as a Jew on a transport to the East, his position was just as tenuous as that of the members of the Council of Elders. The ghetto guard could be dissolved at any moment, and then none of his decorations would save him from the transport, not even the Iron Cross, first degree. Of all the ghetto residents, only the commander knew what was happening in the East. He had been in the death camp himself until the Security Police pulled him out, sent him to the fortress town and assigned him his present position. But he would never tell a soul of his experiences in the death camp. Any careless word would cost him his life.

People were afraid of him, the whole ghetto was afraid of him, because he had been brought in from somewhere by the authorities, because he did not belong among the inhabitants of the fortress town, and because he had even more to do with Command Headquarters than the head of the Council of Elders did. He was thought to be a spy, although he wasn't. He had been forced to take on that role, and he took it on with all its consequences, because he had come from that place whence no one – except him – had ever returned.

At seven in the morning a messenger from the Magdeburg barracks burst into his room, generally called the Mansard, and handed him a sealed letter. The messenger asked him to sign for it in his delivery book and then ran off. The commander opened the letter. It contained a summons from the Council of Elders to come immediately to the Magdeburg barracks. From the early hours of the morning he had been waiting with his men to take part in the execution, waiting all dressed, shaved and washed – he could afford such luxuries because he received a special allotment of good soap.

He came upon the head of the Council of Elders and his deputy in a small room. Both were agitated and it took a few moments before they were capable of speaking. The head of the Council of Elders was a melancholy man, glum and always tired. His office lay upon him like a heavy weight. He was responsible for everything and obediently carried out the wishes of the SS. He was a Very Important Person in the ghetto, and many people licked his boots, hoping that he might save them from the transports. But at Command Headquarters he was a humble servant. On occasion they even beat him up when they felt their orders hadn't been carried out quickly enough. And yet he endured all the kicks and shoves, yet he fulfilled all their wishes: he expedited the transports to the East and established an eighty-hour work week that applied even to children over fourteen. He was an accomplice in all the deceptions blinding the eyes of neutral countries abroad. He didn't do it to save his own life. He had no doubt that he, too, was condemned to death. He had an idea of what was hiding behind the ghetto commandant's chance innuendoes. And still he believed it was possible to misdirect, to delude, to hoodwink. He believed it was necessary to give the appearance of following without question every order he received, even if it meant the death of tens of thousands, in order to have a chance to save the lives of children – children, the only hope of the future.

Now he had to arrange all the preliminaries to the murder that the SS chose to call an execution. He knew who was to be executed. Nine people had been chosen, men who had been arrested for small transgressions in the ghetto for which they had been found guilty by the ghetto court. It was a ridiculous court, another trick intended to demonstrate to the world the independence of the ghetto. In fact, if any of its inhabitants were caught committing a somewhat graver offence, they were taken off to the Small Fortress and never seen again. He thought he could make a pact with the devil, he thought he could give the devil a great deal in order to save at least something. He couldn't have known of the folder with the strictly designated deadlines. He couldn't have known that that very folder contained a resolution made at a secret conference which established that children, biologically the most valuable, must be exterminated above all others. It was the very folder the dying Reich Protector had been clutching in his hand, the folder that contained the plans on which the highest Reich police officer in Berlin was basing his latest orders.

The head of the Council of Elders could hardly speak. The news he had to give to the commander of the ghetto guard was terrible, unbelievable. Untersturmführer Bergel, completely drunk, had appeared at the Magdeburg barracks at six-thirty and summoned the head of the Council of Elders. His order, which the head now passed in turn to the commander of the ghetto guard, was as follows: 'You must find two criminal types by nine-thirty. They need hangmen.'

The commander looked uncomprehendingly at the Chief

Elder. 'Criminal types? That's ridiculous. Where would I find them? There aren't any here.'

'I'm sorry, but that's the Untersturmführer's order. And he received it from the commandant.'

'He can't ask me to do such a thing.'

The Chief Elder explained in a tired voice that it wasn't his fault, but a whim of the lunatics, and what was he to do? They began to consider how they might find a hangman among the ghetto residents. The residents were weak with hunger. There were neither rowdies nor criminals there. People submitted to the meaningless orders of their enemies. Time was passing – it was already eight-thirty and still they couldn't find a solution to their problem.

The Chief Elder said sharply, 'If you don't find a hangman and bring him in by the required time, the Untersturmführer will order you to be hangman yourself. Or he'll have you shot.'

The commander wanted to answer that he wasn't responsible for the ghetto and that the Untersturmführer was more likely to assign the role of hangman to the Chief Elder, but at that moment the building managers, who had been told to assemble here at eight-thirty, began to file into the room. The building managers were old and careworn, beaten down by constant quarrelling with people stuffed into the dormitories. They had no privileges other than the little rooms where they lived and worked. The residents of the buildings hated them because the managers had to enforce the rules, which they in turn received from the Council of Elders in the Magdeburg barracks. No one besides the managers even dared go there without a special pass, and that's why people vented their fury on the managers. At the Magdeburg barracks the managers were treated no better than anyone else. They were threatened with the transport if they didn't carry out their orders. They were caught in the middle.

The managers never expected that the Chief Elder would order them to be observers at an execution. Their job was to guard the residents of the buildings and keep them in line. Now they received orders to watch people being hanged. But the managers could not refuse or talk their way out of it. They were part of the ghetto administration and they always submitted to their superiors.

The Chief Elder added that it was also their responsibility to make sure that none of the inhabitants of the ghetto went outside into the streets or courtyards during the hours of the execution. The windows were to stay closed and no one was to go near them. This was not a difficult order, and the managers guaranteed it would be followed even in their absence. Every dormitory room had its own manager, who reported to the building manager. It would suffice to call together the room managers and tell them about the order. Heads bowed, the managers stumbled out of the Chief Elder's room. First they had been astonished. Now the burden that had been placed on them began to sink in. That was why their gait was so unsteady. Some of them actually stumbled on the threshold as if blinded.

The last one out of the door was the manager of the Sudeten barracks. He was almost outside when the commander of the ghetto guard grabbed him by the sleeve. 'You stay here!'

The manager was confused. He couldn't imagine what the commander wanted with him when all the other managers had been released. Neither the Chief Elder nor his deputy knew what was going on either.

The commander turned to the Chief Elder: 'I have an idea. The Sudeten barracks have the most people of all the buildings, and they also have the most butchers.'

'Butchers? Why butchers?' Then the light suddenly dawned. 'Yes, I see.'

The commander of the ghetto guards told the manager of the Sudeten barracks to take him to his building. They walked through the empty streets in the bitter cold. Here and there a trooper's bayonet appeared out of the fog. The troopers were patrolling the streets to make sure nobody went out. The troopers stopped them but immediately recognised them and didn't even ask to see their passes.

When the commander of the ghetto guards arrived in the Sudeten barracks with the building manager, he spoke to him again in a sharp, military tone. He understood that his order was unusual and hard to carry out. But he couldn't talk to the manager in a friendly manner to ask for advice. The manager was capable only of carrying out orders because horror had numbed his brain.

The commander barked out: 'Call together all the butchers in the Sudeten barracks.'

The manager asked: 'Where am I to call them together? They won't all fit in my room. The news would spread through the barracks and cause trouble.' Now that the manager had been given a direct order, he was capable of independent thought once again.

The commander answered, 'Isn't the guardhouse of the troopers and ghetto guards right behind this entrance here, just in front of the prison? The troopers know what's going on, we don't have to worry about them. We'll clear out the guardhouse and we can call together the butchers there.'

The commander went to the guardhouse and sent the

manager to summon the butchers. Everything went like clockwork. In a while eight butchers appeared. They didn't know what was going on and stood there in confusion. They knew something was afoot. It was an ordinary working day, yet nobody had been allowed to leave the building, even though it was long past the time work usually began. The troopers were patrolling the streets. That, too, was unusual, because they usually guarded the gates, while the ghetto duty was done by the ghetto guards. Nevertheless, the butchers didn't and couldn't have the smallest suspicion of what the manager and the commander of the guards wanted from them.

The commander looked them over very carefully. He gestured to one of them and asked, 'How old are you?'

The butcher answered, 'Sixteen.'

He picked another: 'And you?'

'Eighteen.'

'And what about that one in the corner?'

'Sixty.'

The commander dismissed them: 'You three can go.'

Five people were left waiting impatiently and anxiously, wondering what was going to happen. The commander drew himself up, struck a military attitude and addressed the butchers.

'Friends and kinsmen, I must tell you some sad news and at the same time turn to you with an urgent request. Several of our fellow residents have been sentenced to death by hanging. The judgement will be carried out at ten o'clock and two of you must do it. I am asking two of you to volunteer for the job and thus ease the distress of the others. According to the Untersturmführer's order, I was to find two criminal types, but where am I to find them? You butchers are the only ones who are suitable for this job.'

At first the butchers grew pale, and then they grew angry.

Kraus, a butcher from Horelic, yelled: 'Not on your life. Get some of your own rats to do it!'

And they all started in:

'I have two children.'

'I have children, too.'

Then, in the midst of all the noise, a man as big as a mountain out-shouted all of them: 'I'm a former trooper sergeant, but I wouldn't stoop as low as that.'

The butchers began to heap abuse on the commander: 'Get lost, you dirty spy. Find one of your friends to be a hangman!'

They turned and wanted to leave the guardhouse.

'If you don't do it, the whole Council of Elders will be shot, and I as well.'

One of the butchers began to chuckle. 'Dear, dear. But we wouldn't really mind.'

The commander roared at them: 'But you'll be shot, too!'

The butchers stood stock-still, as if struck by lightning. 'How come? It's not our business!'

The commander said quite calmly now, 'I'll denounce you.'

Trapped. They didn't doubt for a moment that the commander would denounce them. He'd want to pass the blame to someone else, even though it might not help him. They stood there in a state of shock, even the one who had shouted that he was a former trooper sergeant but wouldn't stoop so low.

'How should we do it?' asked one of the butchers. It was clear that nobody was going to volunteer.

'We'll draw lots,' the former sergeant suggested.

They wrote their names on pieces of paper and threw them into a hat belonging to one of them. The commander held the hat. The first butcher came up slowly to draw his lot. He hesitated a long time before he stretched out his hand.

Just then the door opened suddenly and a small, hunchbacked fellow with a wrinkled face and mean, malicious little eyes stepped into the room.

The commander did not manage to maintain his military attitude, because he was holding the hat. He could only scream: 'What are you doing here? Nobody's allowed in here! Didn't a trooper stop you?'

The hunchback smiled. He said in a soft, strangely refined voice: 'Pardon me, but I heard that you're looking for a hangman.'

He was silent for another minute.

'I am your hangman.'

EIGHTEEN

WHEN THE CALL CAME for Richard Reisinger and the other nine, it was to go directly to the Sudeten rather than the Ustecky barracks. The fortress town seemed to be sleeping. There wasn't a soul on the streets, just mist and frost and the occasional patrol who stopped them but as soon as they saw their uniforms asked no further questions. The ten members of the ghetto guard walked slowly, perhaps because the fog and snow kept them from a faster pace, but perhaps because they were afraid to arrive too early. They were supposed to arrive at nine-thirty exactly.

The commander was waiting for them together with a queer little hunchbacked person with long arms like a monkey's. Nearby stood a strong, muscular young man. It was one of the butchers chosen by the hangman as a helper. He stood aside from the two as if he didn't belong with them. The ten members of the ghetto guard joined the commander and the two unknown people.

They left the Sudeten barracks, led by the hunchback. A patrol stopped them on the street. They weren't interested in the guards or their commander, whom they knew, but in the two civilians.

The hunchback said sharply and loudly: 'Executioners.'

The troopers said not another word and quickly signalled to the patrol up ahead to ask no questions and let them pass. The shouts of the patrols from one to another resounded in the dead ghetto like a festive accompaniment.

One of the guards leaned over to Reisinger and whispered,

'I know that hunchback fellow. He's a hangman. I don't know where he lives, but he often comes to the ghetto. When he arrives he always gives out sweets to the children. The children are afraid of him and won't let him touch them, but they take his sweets. How can they resist when they haven't seen sweets for ages? The fellow used to be a morgue attendant and earned extra money by being the Prague hangman's helper.'

The commander of the ghetto guards found it unpleasant to have the hangman marching at the head of the procession. But he couldn't do anything about it, since the hunchback had appropriated the right for himself. The hunchback was in a talkative mood. He boasted that he was the permanent hangman at the Small Fortress, that at the completion of each execution he always got a bottle of rum, a salami and chewing tobacco. The commander was embarrassed by the hangman's boasting. How was it that he, a former officer in the German Army, had to listen to the babbling of a drunken hairy monkey like this? But he didn't dare shut him up.

They walked in this fashion all the way to the gallows, where the commander announced: 'Herr Untersturmführer, here are the volunteers!'

The SS man cried out loudly, 'Bravo!'

The group of ghetto guards, with the commander, the hangman and his helper, positioned themselves next to the gallows. The condemned men were not there yet.

As the members of the ghetto guard were arriving at the Sudeten barracks, fifteen troopers entered the very guardhouse where the butchers had drawn lots. Their job was to bring the nine condemned men out of the nearby prison and lead them to the gallows.

The prisoners had been sentenced for minor offences. Just about anyone in the ghetto might have been there in their place, with the exception of the officials at the Magdeburg barracks, who didn't need to break any of the countless rules. Any one of the ghetto residents would have taken a piece of wood from the timberyard for firewood if he had a chance.

Nobody considered stealing a few potatoes from the basement a real theft. Because people were hungry and cold, practically everyone was guilty of these infractions. One of the prisoners was guilty of not giving the required salute to an SS man. But if a hungry and exhausted person is heading home after a day of endless labour, he drags through the streets looking down at the ground to avoid stumbling. The punishment was mild: a week or fourteen days in prison. The ghetto court didn't even have the right to give longer sentences.

Some of the prisoners had just about completed their terms and were looking forward to being released soon. Some of them had only recently been sent there. They were helping to pass the time by exchanging stories of small everyday events in their lives. They were mostly young people who had had no great experiences yet, who were just beginning life's journey when the Nazis took over.

They were surprised when fifteen troopers burst into their cell and rushed at them as if they were criminals at large. They dragged them out in front of the guardhouse, pushed them together and marched them off somewhere at bayonet point. The nine former prisoners looked about in the fog, wondering where they were being taken. It hadn't been particularly warm in the prison, but the cold hadn't bothered them too much since the heat was always on in the guardhouse next door and some of it reached their cells. Now they were cold and they shivered. They couldn't imagine what the troopers wanted with them. If they were being taken to the transport, then the ghetto guards should have escorted them. Troopers? That could only mean that they were being taken to the Small Fortress. But why? They had been properly sentenced for small offences. What would the neighbouring Gestapo want with them?

The nine prisoners stumbled in the snow. In prison they had got out of the habit of walking. The troopers hurried them along. The execution must begin exactly on time because dignitaries were coming to see it and they liked promptness. If the troopers didn't get there on time, they would be punished. It was impossible to run in the snow – even the troopers were having trouble because their guns were in their way. Still, they got to the Ustecky barracks before the SS dignitaries appeared. The Jewish Council of Elders and the building managers were clustered together near the gallows, where they were supervised by the Untersturmführer, who had no particular authority to speak of. The commander of the ghetto guards stood next to them with his men. And directly beneath the gallows stood the hangman with long arms, testing the rope. His helper was looking down at the ground. The dignitaries had not arrived yet.

The nine prisoners attended by the fifteen troopers were herded into the moat. They saw the gallows, but they didn't understand what was happening. They couldn't be hanging them in broad daylight for offences that were completely insignificant! This was probably only a joke to scare them. Still, they were shivering; still, their hearts contracted with fear, because the gallows reached to the skies, a double monster in the shape of a T. They huddled together, for they were lost in the moat; they were alone among strangers who were looking at them with sympathy and horror as if they were already dead.

Now the SS dignitaries approached the gallows. First came the head of the Central Bureau, after him the magistrate from Kladno, though the Kladno district had no connections whatsoever with the fortress town. But it was known that the magistrate liked excitement. Behind the magistrate, strutting along in uniform with decorations, came the commandant of the ghetto, a disbarred lawyer and one of the faithful from Vienna. His career had begun with the Anschluss, and his present position was his reward for various services. At a respectful distance stood the last observer, the SS chauffeur. The dignitaries were animated, in a good mood. They had obviously just enjoyed a good breakfast with liqueurs at Command Headquarters. The commandant gestured to the Jewish Council of Elders to follow his group. And so the SS dignitaries and the Jewish Council of Elders, together with the building managers, stood at the edge of the moat. The nine victims waited below.

Richard Reisinger stood a little behind them with the commander and the other members of the ghetto guard. He was glad that they hadn't been ordered to look directly at the condemned men as the Council of Elders had been. The troopers departed; they weren't required to take part in the execution. And so the members of the Council of Elders, the building managers, ten of the ghetto guards with their commander and the SS dignitaries remained at the execution grounds. The hangman stood at the gallows and his assistant stood next to him. The nine prisoners huddled together in the moat. Only now did they notice that a common grave had been dug beside the gallows. Perhaps it was only there to scare them. Such things were known to have happened.

All at once the commandant of the ghetto stepped forward and read the verdict in a hard and incisive voice, looking at the prisoners as if they were loathsome insects: 'For defamation of the German Reich, by order of the Commander of the Security Police of Bohemia and Moravia, these Jews have been condemned to death by hanging.'

While murdering and pillaging throughout Europe, the Reich had lost tens of thousands. Now the Reich was dying of cold on the eastern front. And yet that Reich was still powerful, still convinced that it would conquer the world. It accused these unimportant, ordinary people of resisting or defaming it. It didn't say how – accusing them was enough. The theft of a half-rotten potato or a small piece of wood was called defamation of the Reich. Not saluting an SS officer or smuggling a letter out of the ghetto meant death.

The prisoners heard the verdict. They couldn't take in the idea that the crimes they had committed were so terrible that they would have to pay for them with their lives. They hadn't had a trial, they hadn't been sentenced by any court. The verdict was final, there was no appeal. Even if they had cried out their innocence there in the cold before the spectators and the SS dignitaries, it wouldn't have done them any good. Still, they kept hoping; still, they did not believe it. Only after the hangman came up to them and ordered them to strip to their shirts and underwear did they realise that it was true, that death was awaiting them, that this gallows was meant for them, and that their bodies would be buried in the prepared grave.

They looked around them, so that at least they could say farewell to the world in their last moments, but the fortress town was lifeless, covered with fog. They could see only the pale, sunken faces of the Elders, the building managers, the ghetto guards, and the aroused, grimacing faces of the SS men. One group looked at them with pain and horror, the other with excitement, in expectation of an interesting show to come. The hangman's face was expressionless. For him this was a job, difficult and tiring.

They wanted a last look at the sun and the blue sky, but the sky was enveloped in fog. They wanted at least to touch their native soil with their bound hands, but the ground was hard and frozen. They wanted to hear the sound of a human voice once again, but all around was silence. Not the smallest sound was to be heard from the fortress town. The world they were leaving was dead, insensible. And then the crows came flying. Never before had they been seen in the fortress town, for not a single animal or bird was to be found there. The crows lived in the high trees that formed an alley leading to the town gates. They accompanied the transports and prisoners' processions with their cries. The SS men shot at them and ordered their nests destroyed, but the crows lived on. Their number even seemed to be increasing. Now they appeared above the gallows and no one could chase them away. The SS men had only their revolvers, which were good for killing people but useless for killing crows. The crows flew above the execution grounds as if they, too, had come to be witnesses.

Perhaps it was the cry of the crows that awakened the prisoners' spirit. They were moved to courage. In the face of the murderers and in the face of the witnesses they must stand on the execution ground like warriors.

Only one of them cried out: 'I wasn't defaming the Reich. I was writing to my grandmother!'

He was eighteen years old and he wanted to live. The others quickly made him stop. They didn't want anyone to plead with murderers who knew no mercy and for whom every plea was merely a source of amusement.

'Be strong,' said the oldest. 'We must die with honour.'

They held themselves bravely, though the cold forced them to shiver. They tried to control their muscles, to keep the SS men from thinking they were shivering with fear and cowardice. And then a song came to their aid. One of the prisoners began it. It was a song from a famous play, a song that had become a consolation during the years of defeat, a song about the millions who would go against the wind.

They were only nine and they sang about millions. The SS men didn't know the song, and even if they had known it they wouldn't have minded their singing of it. They had power over life and death. They had determined that these people would die and it didn't matter to them if the condemned wished to go with a song. But the members of the Council of Elders knew it, the building managers and the ghetto guards knew it. Who could not know it, a song that had once been sung so often on the streets of Prague? The patrolling troopers on the streets of the fortress town heard it. The song penetrated chinks and crannies, and even the thickness of boarded windows that the residents of the ghetto had been forbidden to come near. It entered the dormitories and from one person to another it flew from barrack to barrack. For the scorned and rejected people already knew what was happening. Even though the penalty for revealing the secret was death, still the news spread from an unknown source, by invisible means.

The commandant of the ghetto waved his whip impatiently. He didn't want to freeze unnecessarily. The song ceased. They approached the gallows two by two. They were equal in death, and the rope that bound them to each other meant brotherhood. They stood there proudly, courageously. The hangman threw the rope around their necks. And then the first of the condemned cried out:

'You'll never win the war!'

The magistrate from Kladno gave a little start. The commandant of the ghetto frowned. The head of the Central Bureau smiled; perhaps he was thinking about the death camps. The second of the prisoners repeated: 'You'll never win the war!' Seven prisoners waited in the moat for their turns to come. They realised that they were an odd number and they didn't know who would be last. That one would have the worst fate, to be alone among the beasts of prey and mute witnesses. When two go to their deaths together they give each other courage, they die together in enforced brotherhood that has become true brotherhood. But that last one would have to watch the dying and deaths of the others, would have to look at their corpses with convulsively twisted green faces lying on the snow. They had to agree on who would be last, who would have the worst fate, or the hangman who bound the pairs together would make the decision.

The oldest of them said: 'Line up two by two. I'll stand behind you.'

They did not try to talk him out of it.

The pairs were bound together and the hangman led them away to the gallows. As he was hanging the last pair, the rope broke and one of the prisoners fell to the ground. When this happened the hangman called out a phrase he had learned from the Prague hangman: 'I beg to report that the judgement has been carried out according to the law.'

The commandant of the ghetto turned to him angrily: 'Shut up!' and he waved his whip: 'String him up!'

The prisoner was hanged again. But the dignitaries were no longer enjoying themselves. It wasn't pleasant to stand in the cold for so long, even though they were wearing fur jackets and high boots. The show was not as amusing as they had expected – nobody begged for mercy, and each one repeated the phrase the first one had called out: 'You'll never win the war!' There was such certainty in the voices of the prisoners as they said those words that the confident and arrogant sneers faded from the dignitaries' faces. They grew nervous and had to make an effort not to betray their feelings in front of the crowd of slaves witnessing the execution. Only the head of the Central Bureau remained calm. In the East he had seen so many killings carried out in so many various ways that this execution of nine people left him quite indifferent.

One of the hanged men gave several jerks. This disturbed the SS chauffeur. He pulled out his revolver and shot five bullets one after another into the dead body. The hangman smiled. What do these SS people know about executions? They hadn't even taught them that such things happen frequently, that these are the movements of a person from whom life has fled long before.

The shots diverted the SS dignitaries. They calmed the magistrate from Kladno somewhat, as well as the ghetto commandant. They were used to shootings. The execution had already lasted two hours and the SS people would have liked to leave, but they couldn't allow themselves to do so since there were witnesses here. Meanwhile, the witnesses were in far worse shape. They weren't dressed warmly and they were shivering with cold. They weren't able to move about, for they had been ordered to stand still. They were afraid of frostbite, because they were wearing ordinary shoes.

Richard Reisinger watched the execution along with the others. He paled and gasped with horror along with the others. He heard their song and repeated it soundlessly under his breath along with the others. He saw the way they hanged them, the way they died bravely, he heard the way each of them said, 'You'll never win the war!' Of course, they'd never win it, they couldn't win it. But all of those forced to watch the execution here would probably be dead before it was over. It would be awkward for the SS to allow such witnesses to stay alive. Nevertheless, the world would find out about this execution somehow. It wasn't possible to get rid of all the witnesses. Surely someone would remain to tell the tale.

The hangman dragged the last of the prisoners to the gallows. He was so frozen that he could no longer walk. He was alone – all the others were dead. As they left for the gallows they had waved to him with their bound hands in farewell and caressed him with their eyes. They knew his lot was the worst. He tried to call out, but his frozen mouth wouldn't emit a sound. And then in the complete silence a single word was suddenly heard and it resounded throughout the execution grounds: 'Stalingrad.' A word of victory and hope. The last prisoner walked to the gallows proudly with such a word. The crows cawed above the gallows and they seemed to be repeating the word, making it carry over the entire ghetto and the Small Fortress, too. The eyes of the Council of Elders, the building managers and the ghetto guards suddenly lit up. The faces of the SS dignitaries tightened into hateful grimaces. It even affected the head of the Central Bureau, because that word meant defeat, cold, hunger, dirt, captivity and death.

That was why the last prisoner could go calmly to his death, that was why the witnesses could reconcile themselves to their humiliation, and that was why, at least for a while, fear overcame the SS dignitaries.

The execution was over. The tired hangman was leaving with his helper. The nine dead bodies remained on the frozen ground. The commander of the ghetto guards told his ten men to throw the bodies without coffins into the common grave. Those twenty-five coffins made overnight by the carpentry workshop had been a cruel trick. When the grave was half filled the dignitaries departed. The Jewish Council of Elders and the building managers staggered back to the Magdeburg barracks to pray for the dead there. Only the ghetto guards remained on the execution grounds, to finish their work. Just then the troopers came back to the execution grounds, all of their own free will. They stood at the graveside beside the ghetto guards. The grave was already covered. At the graveside the sergeant-major of the troopers, their boss, called them to attention.

His second in command broke the dead silence: 'Let us honour the dead!'

Then the ten men of the ghetto guards left with their

captain, and the troopers with their sergeant-major. And when they looked up at the cruel and heartless sky, filled with black clouds, they saw that even the crows had returned to their homes. Perhaps they had left with the SS dignitaries.

They all looked back for the last time at the execution grounds. They were enveloped in fog. Only the gallows in the shape of a T reached to the skies, as if it would stand there for all eternity.

NINETEEN

THE TRANSPORTS ARRIVED at the fortress town and then departed again. But the SS men had a problem with the road to the station. They wanted everything to proceed smoothly and secretly, yet all sorts of things went wrong: people dragged along too slowly, old folks and children fell by the wayside, and the efforts of the troopers and ghetto guards to hurry them along didn't help. What's more, the station lay outside the fortress town, and though the transports arrived and departed at night, they ran into occasional witnesses – because of the conscription, many people had to work night shifts.

It wasn't possible to walk in the pitch dark; the blackout rules had to be ignored. Like will-o'-the-wisps, the glowing torches and flares wound their way along the roads. Like a procession of ghosts the transports moved along, accompanied by moans and cries. They had to walk past darkened cottages where sleeping people were awakened by the shouts of the guards and the weeping of children.

The SS men didn't like this. They preferred to do their dark deeds without witnesses.

They decided to build a special line from the station directly to the fortress town, so that the only witnesses besides the ghetto guards would be the troopers. They knew how to deal with them. After wiping out the Jews, they'd wipe out the troopers now guarding them.

The commandant of the ghetto ordered the Jewish Council of Elders to pick out engineers and workers – there were several railway engineers in the ghetto. One of them had actually built a railway in the South American jungle. They promised the workers a bonus of one potato each.

And so the construction began. The engineers drew up the plans and made calculations. The work was divided up into segments and work teams were established. Oddly enough, people worked quite cheerfully, though they surely realised that the special line was meant to make things easier for the SS. When a person holds a good tool in his hand, a pickaxe or a hoe, sometimes he forgets.

Above the town, where the only sounds once heard had been muffled footsteps, buzzing saws in the timberyard and the creaking wheels of funeral wagons dragged along by people, now the clinking of pickaxes and the clanging of railway tracks could be heard. The work groups started out at opposite ends, one from the station and the other from the fortress town. Finally they met in the middle.

One day the old locomotive – the one they used to call 'the coffee mill' – clattered right into the centre of town. The children all screamed joyfully, 'A choo-choo!' They thought it would take them home. But the grownups did not rejoice. They knew that now they'd be taken away on rails hammered in by their own hands. The whistle of the locomotive had the sound of a death knell to their ears.

The town was enclosed by battlements and gates which were guarded night and day. Forcibly extracted from the countryside and closed off from the world, the once sleepy garrison town had been turned into a massive prison. Nobody was allowed to look down from the ramparts. One time only – just before a visit of the Red Cross commission – they permitted small children to go for walks on the ramparts; the commission might notice that the children were too pale. After the commission's visit, the children were no longer allowed there, but long afterwards they continued to draw pictures of what they had seen outside: the enchanting countryside with its tall bluish foothills, green meadows and orchards (real apricots and peaches hung from the branches of trees and looked quite different from the fruit they had seen in picture books), roads with signs telling how many miles to the capital. Beyond the battlements people walked more freely and everything was different: children sat at tables set for dinner in rooms with curtains, waiting for their mothers to bring them their food. Or they played outside their little suburban houses; they went to school, they flew kites, they skated on ponds, they went sledding, in the summer they swam in the river and bought ice-cream, they rode on merry-go-rounds and played ball. Cars of all sorts went tearing along the roads, buses stopped at railway crossings, trams rolled out of stations, and aeroplanes flew over cities. Cats warmed themselves on windowsills, dogs barked beside their kennels, cows grazed in pastures, while horses drew carts along the roads. Here in the fortress town there were no animals. Even butterflies avoided it.

Only once did the children see live animals, emaciated, miserable sheep with singed wool. They were being herded through the town past the railway crossing where the SS authorities had their headquarters. It was evident that the sheep were exhausted, that they had come a long way. They had the same hopeless look in their eyes that people had as they placed their transport numbers around their necks.

The grownups avoided looking at the sheep; they were reminded of their own fate. The children heard that the sheep had come from a village that had been burned to the ground. The children knew nothing about the village and didn't remember its name. It must have been very far from the fortress town, because the sheep were so exhausted they could hardly move.

The children drew everything they saw. In their drawings the sheep resembled wooden sawhorses. But they drew the eyes more carefully.

The eyes were big and sad. Even though the town was carefully secured by battlements and guards, news of the world still managed to filter in somehow. It was passed along from mouth to mouth, filled in, distorted; sometimes it spoke of hope, sometimes it cried out in despair. How the news got into town nobody knew. To make it believable people said it came from the troopers.

Only a special few maintained a different connection with the world: a radio with transmitter and receiver that moved about from one chimney hiding place to another. It had been put together by skilled technicians out of various stolen components – they had even used part of a rubber heel. Those who guarded it in its small suitcase, the kind that is sold in chain stores, did not pass along any of the news they heard. Their purpose was to send word of the ghetto out into the world, and to listen for the signal bringing tidings of the end of the war.

But on occasion a few people from the outside world stole into the fortress town. They sewed on stars, and the troopers and ghetto guards allowed them to pass through the gate to meet their loved ones, if only for a moment. Some of these were caught, others got away. So it happened that a few managed to break through the iron circle and send greetings to friends and acquaintances, to bring in a little food and some books of poetry. These were exceptional beacons of light in the darkness and despair, small rays of hope. Songs and poems have been written about these people who managed to overcome all obstacles.

Meanwhile, the countryside surrounding the fortress town was silent. Barbed wire twisted through the meadows, with the blue hills in the background. The road-sign PRAGUE shone with the same yellow colour as the stars bearing the ignominious inscription in a foreign language.

Now, however, the special line brought a new element into town the SS men had not counted on: railway men.

The SS men knew how to handle the troopers. But railway men were a different story.

The trains went back and forth; they had to keep going, bringing weapons to the East and plundered goods back to the Reich. Without the trains the army couldn't fight and the robbers couldn't pillage. Once, they had thought they could manage without the railway. A fat marshal screamed about it on the radio, boasting of his Panzers' *Blitzkrieg*, which would roll across the Caucasus, ever farther and farther, all the way to the Ganges, where they would join the armies of the eastern predators. But the Panzers' glory ended in Stalingrad, and the army had to flee on foot in the Caucasus. Then the railway was all that was left. There were Dutch, Belgian, French, Norwegian, Bulgarian, Hungarian, Romanian, Yugoslavian railway trucks all mixed up together. And they needed people to make repairs in various shops and engine rooms, to throw switches, to drive the engines.

You couldn't just shoot railway men to create fear among them; you had to handle them carefully, especially at a time when the front stretched two thousand kilometres from the Reich and fuel was running low.

The Gestapo were well aware that the railway men were

enemies. The engineers who drove the trains were escorted by guards with drawn automatics. Still, trains collided, trains were derailed. Bridges and rails blew up in every occupied town. Lead seals disappeared from carriages, bills of lading were misplaced, and whole trucks full of ammunition and provisions were mysteriously lost on unused sidings or in out-of-the-way stations.

Thanks to the special line, a clever, tenacious and tough enemy found its way into the fortress town and with it letters, packages, newspapers and information. Now, in spite of the ramparts, gates and guards, they could no longer keep the fortress town so perfectly isolated.

In the centre of town they stuffed the living freight being shipped to the East into railway trucks: they unloaded goods for the SS men – food, wine, liquor and meat for their dogs, and they loaded furniture, ceramics and ornamental metal objects produced in the fortress town workshops. Also crates from the woodworking shop and split slabs of mica for the Wehrmacht armed forces.

The town lived in misery and hunger. People gasped for air in the multi-layered bunks of the overcrowded dormitories. The old were dying in the muck and dirt, and the helpless doctors didn't know what to do with them. Colonies of slaves went off to labour each day. The smoke from the crematoria filled the town with its fumes. In the *Appellplatz* prisoners stood in rain and wet snow from dawn to dusk, while the sick were carried away on stretchers to die to the sounds of noisy roll calls.

Behind the gate stood a new building where the SS men lived. They called it Friendship House. They decorated it with hammered metal sconces and ornamental screens. They would meet in a large room on the ground floor, where they would sit at tables covered with clean tablecloths and set with plates of Carlsbad porcelain. Wooden candelabra with burning candles hung from the ceiling. They ate and drank there and roared out their raucous songs. They drank to the health of the Leader and his Reich; they exchanged filthy anecdotes before collapsing on the floor in their own spittle.

The trains carried ammunition and new reserves to replace armies flattened by Soviet tanks and shattered by Soviet guns. The trains carried their suffocating and dying human freight to the East, where they were unloaded on to platforms in the extermination camps and herded with sticks into gas chambers.

Richard Reisinger was often on duty at the special-line station. From the day he had to witness the execution, his job was ever more hateful to him. But were he to quit he'd immediately find himself among those being sent to the East. He was thinking about running away – some people had tried it – but he had seen them brought back all bloody and beaten up, to be displayed in the *Appellplatz* before being taken off to the Small Fortress.

One day he was standing by the train with the old locomotive and the battered cattle trucks from all countries of Europe. The railway men were resting, looking around them at the queer streets with houses marked with letters, plaster cracked and falling off, at the broken-down courtyards and wooden animal sheds that now contained people. The train was surrounded by ghetto guards, troopers and SS men. They were waiting for a transport.

The SS men and the troopers guarded the outer circle. Only the ghetto guards stood directly next to the train. The day was just beginning, and darkness still lay on the town. The ghetto was sleeping. Soon the procession of the condemned would appear, bowed down under the weight of their baggage. Suddenly, in the semi-darkness, someone crept out from under a railway carriage directly in front of Reisinger. Reisinger couldn't make out the man's face clearly, but from his uniform it was evident that he was a railway man.

He looked at Reisinger for a while, and he seemed particularly interested in his yellow belt and cap. Then he said slowly and quietly, 'You wouldn't know Reisinger, Richard Reisinger?'

'That's me. What do you want with me?'

'I've got regards for you from someone called Franta. He's sending you this.'

It was a box of Victoria cigarettes. As the cigarettes changed hands, the railway man's movement was imperceptible in the half-darkness.

As long as the transport didn't arrive and as long as it remained dark, they were able to talk together. The railway man told him about some Finnish huts built for the Wehrmacht that were supposed to be taken to the East but had mysteriously found their way to the Vranany station. With a fake bill of consignment it would be quite possible to get them to the fortress town if only there was someone to receive them.

Reisinger promised to inquire – maybe it could be arranged. Wood for crates arrived regularly at the timberyard. Neatly numbered sections of huts with ceilings of deck wood could easily vanish there, to be transformed into wood slivers, chips and slats. This was possible to arrange, for confusion was mounting in the midst of the perfect organisation.

They agreed to meet again. Reisinger had to work carefully, but he had an acquaintance in the timberyard. And so it happened that when the train finally arrived with a shipment for the fortress town, sections of Finnish huts managed to get in as well. From there they were sent to the timber yard and quickly processed. The wood was distributed to the dormitories in small bundles, and loaded into stoves, fireplaces, tin barrels. The children's houses received the biggest load. The warmth brought colour to cheeks. It heated the soup made of bread crusts. It helped nurses sterilise hypodermic needles and doctors examine undressed patients.

A circle was completed that had started somewhere at a shunting station where a bill of consignment seemed to be lost; then a chain of signalmen, brakemen and dispatchers moved the train to a blind siding at Vranany so that it would end in the fortress town and give a little warmth.

It was a small nothing in the overall economic picture of the Reich, where they squandered millions, where they destroyed, slaughtered, burned, and then plundered, amassed and used up again.

But this small nothing signified a helping hand and solidarity with all people who uphold freedom and sacrifice their lives, solidarity with the Soviet Army, which swooped down upon the half-million-strong horde of arrogant marauders with all their decorations and crosses and medals in Stalingrad and drove them out to die like rats.

This small nothing overcame Richard Reisinger's irresoluteness. Now that he had decided to fight, he had something to sacrifice his life for.

The wood had been burned long ago, yet the trains kept arriving and leaving from the fortress town. Occasionally

Reisinger ran into the railway man who had smuggled in the wood, and some friends of his as well. They rarely had a chance to speak: either the troopers were too near or the SS men were paying too close attention.

Then one day Reisinger said to the railway man, 'I'd like to get out of here, but I don't know how to go about it.' He told him he'd been thinking about it a long time, and that he hoped to climb over the battlements and walk along the highway to Prague.

The railway man knew a better and simpler way: they'd hide him in the brakeman's hut and get him a uniform. Then he could simply leave from the station. Nobody would notice an extra railway man, because there were always so many of them hanging around. After that, Franta would take care of everything.

One day a member of the ghetto guards disappeared. They searched for him long and hard, but they didn't find him. They tore apart the entire countryside, they asked their neighbours in the Small Fortress for help. But the trail grew cold. Nobody knew what had become of number BA 450.

In the end they dissolved the ghetto guard and sent all its members on a transport to the East. They left the commander of the ghetto guard in the fortress town for a while longer. Perhaps they thought they might need him again.

TWENTY

THE TRANSPORTS LEFT for the fortress town and for the East. Thousands of people went on them. Weighed down with baggage, numbers hanging from their necks, they walked through the gates of the Radio Mart and past the SS man on guard there. They were never to return. They were detained for as long as a week in makeshift huts and then they departed at night in sealed cattle trucks. Passers-by had to notice the SS man standing arrogantly on guard; they had to notice the procession of the condemned, burdened with bundles, wearing yellow stars.

One day the transports ceased. The supply had been used up.

In the offices of the Jewish Community new faces appeared. New workers arrived, ones whose life expectancies had been extended by the Central Bureau because they were related by marriage to people classified as Aryans.

The departing ones bore a grudge against the new arrivals: they had stolen their jobs, they believed; it was the new arrivals' fault that they, the departing ones, were forced to go off into the unknown. Unwillingly they handed over their daily schedules of affairs, filled with petty and meaningless activities, meaningless because there was only a tiny number of people left. Yet they boasted about their work as if it were incredibly important, as if it required extreme skill and experience.

The meaningless affairs passed into new hands, and so

did the stolen property in the warehouses, where those from the Reich would come to pick out requisitioned goods. And because they also stole many other things, it sometimes happened that the warehouse manager ended up with nothing but the bill of consignment.

Of all the original workers at the Collection Agency, finally only eleven remained. These were indispensable because they helped the Central Bureau steal and store property. Among them was someone who searched for jewellery hidden in pawnshops or safes. Another was an antique dealer who specialised in paintings and knew how to estimate their value. Yet another was good at tracking down foreign currency and secret bank accounts. All eleven had become the robbers' helpers – that was why they remained in town with their families. The twelfth was Dr Rabinovich. He had nothing to do with stolen property. He was a scholar. The head of the Central Bureau had charged him with creating a monument to the triumph of the Reich, a museum of the extinct race, and promised him the same protection as the other eleven.

Dr Rabinovich was not happy. His new co-workers didn't care about religion and most of them didn't even belong to a congregation. They didn't treat the religious objects that continued to come in from out of town with respect and they considered their work in the museum to be just another job. They weren't as zealous as their predecessors, but they conducted themselves with greater self-confidence: they weren't afraid of him, Rabinovich. They didn't seem impressed with the fact that the head of the Central Bureau himself often called him. Rather, they seemed to scorn his role. Their lives were secure, at least for a while, and that gave them the strength to avoid meaningless work. They didn't bow to him, nor did they ask him to intercede for them. Secretly they laughed at him, some of them even openly. He was unable to yell at them and threaten them with the transport as he had their predecessors. They weren't lazy, indeed they were glad to be able to work. But they didn't extend themselves.

He was obliged to work with these new people now. Only twelve of the original people were left, and he was one of them. They had been saved, and perhaps they would survive the war together with these new ones. The head of the Central Bureau continued to summon him to his office, but he had been in a bad mood recently. The Reich was losing on all fronts, and that equanimity he had always boasted about was beginning to go. He no longer went to the theatre wearing all his decorations. He no longer interested himself in music – indeed, lately it seemed to annoy him. He frantically devoured the various strategic studies forecasting staggering victories of the Reich in the nearest future, which he believed and didn't believe. For doubts were beginning to assail him in spite of everything. He was irritable, bad-tempered and rude to his staff. The city where his mother lived hadn't been spared the bombing after all. The old white-haired lady had not been killed, thank God, but her villa was destroyed. All the valuable keepsakes were now ashes and dust. Even that exquisite figurine of *The Judgement of Paris* fell victim to a bomb. Now there was only the one original left, in the Meissen museum.

He had never been one to drink, but now he began. He drank alone, so his staff wouldn't see him, carefully choosing the wines and liqueurs from the warehouse. People assigned to the Jewish Community created a little hideout for him with rugs, armchairs and a special cabinet for bottles and a radio. It was actually a nicely furnished room, though it was underground. He took refuge there, to listen to foreign broadcasts and to drink. Once drunk, he'd find a German station, turn it up to top volume, and listen to noisy patriotic songs about airmen who were always victorious, about the homeland where everything would be beautiful when the victors returned. And yet the airmen were victorious only in the patriotic songs. Bombs were falling on the homeland. The cities were piles of rubble. After these patriotic songs he would sometimes hear a cajoling, gentle voice exhorting his countrymen to hold back the savage hordes, promising that the Reich had secret weapons it would use to conquer the enemy. At those times he'd pull out his revolver and shoot wildly into the air – anything to avoid hearing that voice he knew so well. He knew that the voice came on only when it was necessary to cover up defeats.

Nevertheless, he'd appear in his office every morning in a clean uniform with decorations, clean-shaven and fresh as a daisy, or so it seemed. He'd shout at his staff, tell them to work faster. The operation in the Protectorate was almost over. There were about three thousand people left who were protected by marriage to Aryans. He hadn't got the nod from the highest police officer of the Reich about them yet, but he had no doubt that their time would come. And finally there were these twelve here. He no longer needed them. All the Jewish property was already stolen and stored in warehouses; gaining the property of those protected by marriage was an unlikely prospect, as they had hidden it, or what remained of it, with various relatives long ago. Now he could send the twelve off to the East, while the chimneys of the crematoria were still smoking. The war might be lost, but his task in the Protectorate was virtually completed.

But he told those twelve nothing. Let them work to the last moment. Indeed, he spoke to them more kindly than he did to his own staff. He must allay their fears, lull them, until it was time to strike.

Slowly Dr Rabinovich grew reconciled to his new helpers, and grumbled at them only when he saw them handling the sacred articles as if they were ordinary goods. Even now the shipments continued to come in, to be entered in a ledger, given over to teams of skilled workers and stored in warehouses. The new workers soon learned the ingenious and rather simple system. But they didn't try to work quickly. Production was decreasing, but in no way dangerously.

The head of the Central Bureau, however, seemed to be losing interest in the museum lately. Whenever Rabinovich tried to submit his accounts, the head of the Central Bureau just waved his hand. These days he often talked to Rabinovich about the Holy Writ, about the Talmud and the Cabala. He posed cunning questions touching on certain passages in the Talmud that might appear to be judgements against Christianity. He didn't really care about Christianity – he had left the church long ago, as all members of the SS were ordered to do. But he liked to show off his knowledge. He took pleasure in embarrassing the 'learned Jew'. Rabinovich answered the questions humbly and evasively – he didn't know the purpose of the questions and whether they contained some trap for him. But the head of the Central Bureau was apparently only enjoying himself, because he dismissed Rabinovich graciously. He even patted him on the shoulder. Of course, he never offered him his hand, even when he was in a good mood.

After dismissing Rabinovich he smiled maliciously. They were ready to strike. The net was drawn so tightly that none of the twelve suspected a thing. Otherwise those who had helped in the robbery might try to hide some secret records of the transfer of assets achieved by torture, records of the jewels and gold, of currency in the hands of those who were considering escape abroad if the Reich was possibly to collapse. But not a single trace of the thefts must remain – that was his major concern. That was why the journey of these twelve must be short and swift.

In the Rabinovich household, life proceeded as if nothing had changed, as if so many tens of thousands hadn't gone into the unknown. Although his sons weren't allowed to go to school, he was able to tutor them himself in the evenings. Life went on, grey and colourless. It was a waiting game, a battle against time. Few people with stars appeared on the street these days.

One evening they were sitting at the table eating potato pancakes fried in margarine and drinking rose-hip tea. Suddenly there was a loud banging at the door. That was strange. They had a doorbell, after all, and nobody came visiting at such a late hour. Rabinovich opened the door. There stood two SS men with pistols who screamed at him to pack his things, up to fifty kilograms in weight, and to be ready in precisely one hour, or else. A van would come for them and they mustn't be one minute late. The SS men brandished their pistols and slammed the door behind them.

Rabinovich's wife began to cry. So this was the end. What about all the promises the head of the Central Bureau had made to him? Was this his reward for faithful service? Rabinovich consoled her. They couldn't be calling them for the transport, because they were sending a van for them. They were probably going to take them to the fortress town, where he'd have various privileges again. The head of the Central Bureau must have decided that the Rabinovich family would be better off there. Who knew what bad things were about to happen in the main city? In the ghetto he would belong with the prominent ones who weren't sent to the East.

'How can we pack up all our things in an hour?'

Once again Rabinovich calmed her down. They could take only the most important things, in any event, so an hour would suffice. And if a van was waiting for them in front of the house they wouldn't have to drag around their heavy baggage. All the while he suspected that a worse fate awaited them. A night summons never meant anything favourable, and the deadline of an hour meant that the SS men were in a hurry. If they were doing things quickly, that was always ominous.

But maybe they were just playing tricks. They loved the kind of trick that terrified people. And besides, the head of the Central Bureau had promised him protection. But could he believe him? Not long ago they'd suddenly arrested a certain manufacturer and inventor and sent him and his entire family away, even though he had been designated an 'honorary Aryan'. They had emptied out his apartment with lightning swiftness that time, and the things they didn't want they sent to the museum. He himself saw the family albums and read the letters from the new authorities with whom the family had maintained friendly contact until the last moment. But the manufacturer owned stocks, gold and jewels, and that sealed his fate. Rabinovich, however, had no assets whatsoever. There was nothing to plunder in his poor apartment.

Precisely one hour later, Rabinovich and his family walked

down the steps. The other tenants watched them through opened doors. Outside, the van was waiting, covered with a canvas roof. It looked a bit too big for his family and their baggage. The chauffeur in an SS uniform stood next to the van and motioned them to climb the plank into the back. When they got inside they saw several other people huddled there in the midst of their baggage. The van filled up as the chauffeur stopped in various streets. More and more people with baggage kept entering. When the van was filled to bursting, the chauffeur started abruptly and began to pick up speed. As the van hurtled along, the baggage bumped against the travellers and the children cried with fear.

Although it was too dark to distinguish their faces Rabinovich knew at once who they were: the very eleven who had remained after all the rest had gone. And he was the twelfth. They were all terrified and no one spoke a word. The noise of the engine would have made talking impossible in any case. He knew they were as protected as he was, but he had scorned these fellow workers because they served Mammon, because they helped track down stocks and shares, gold, jewels and valuable paintings. Now he was riding in the same vehicle with them, now he was forced to travel with them to an unknown destination.

Night had fallen by the time the van reached the station at the outskirts of town. All the transports to the fortress town as well as to the East left from this same station. Nobody knew to which trains the trucks of the transport would be attached along the way, not even the railway men. At the platform stood six SS men. As was their custom, they screamed, '*Los, schnell!*' at the people getting out of the van and pushed them along, together with the children and baggage, towards the long freight train. An old dilapidated passenger carriage with high steps leading to it was attached to the train. They had to scramble up the steps with all their baggage, urged on by the SS men and their whips. The windows of the car were boarded up and it was dark inside. The SS men closed the door behind them and stood guard outside. A long period of waiting began. They lost track of time – perhaps it was already morning.

It wasn't until they were inside the train that the people began to talk to one another. They complained about the broken promises of protection. They told about various big shots, generals and magistrates to whom they had delivered valuables and who had spoken to them so graciously, so cordially. They exchanged names of people from secret offices whose task had been the evacuation of Czechs. They had all been in touch with such important people. Surely these people wouldn't abandon them after they had been provided with so many valuables, surely they would save them at the last moment; surely a fancy limousine would appear any minute now and a general would step out, all covered with medals and decorations, and say, 'This person performed good services for the Reich. I demand that he and his entire family be released.' The SS guards wouldn't dare disobey such a command, for this person's rank would be so high that even the head of the Central Bureau would be unable to stand up to him.

These were the fairy tales they told each other in the boarded-up railway carriage in the midst of their crying children. Yet it was clear to them all that they had been sacrificed, that no one would stand up for them. They could only hope that their journey would end in the fortress town and not in the East. But even that hope was faint.

Only now did they realise that they were too deeply implicated in the robberies, that those who had received money, gold and precious things by means of their help must get rid of them now, in order to use their stolen riches in peace.

Rabinovich listened to these conversations and felt bitter that he had to travel with people whose acts were so obviously wicked. But didn't he belong in their category as well? Though he hadn't provided his masters with gold and jewels, still he had helped them. At their command he had gathered together the confiscated sacred articles and created a museum for the amusement of the enemy. He had entertained visitors arriving from the murderers' main city. He had violated the most important religious commandments and committed the worst sins. Now he must pay the price, for he had blown the ram's horn to amuse the Reich minister. He had allowed himself to be used in identifying a statue, he had committed the sin of false idolatry by re-creating a Seder in the museum. He had desecrated everything he touched, he had violated virtually all the commandments in order to save his family. And because sins must be paid for in this world, his punishment had caught up with him. The words of the prayers would no longer help him, the consolations of the Psalms would no longer work. His tribe would be wiped out and nobody would be left to say the prayer for the dead in his memory. But perhaps God would have mercy on him, for he had not sinned with any evil intent.

Suddenly they heard the door screech, and it was as if their impossible dreams were about to be fulfilled. The door to the carriage opened abruptly. Which of them would be freed at the eleventh hour? Which of them had so powerful a protector coming to his aid? They couldn't see what was happening outside, since the windows were boarded. Then the door opened and they all saw two Czech troopers enter the train with a man in chains. No, it wasn't a general coming to intercede for any one of them. It was a prisoner who seemed to be coming to join them directly from prison, because he had no baggage with him. The troopers unchained him under the watchful eye of an SS man and then left without a word. The door was slammed shut again. Another noise was heard outside – they must be sealing up the car again. Daylight was beginning to come in through the cracks of the window boards, allowing them to make out the features of the prisoner.

He introduced himself at once and rather cheerfully to the company: 'My name's Otto Pokorny and they brought me here straight from prison. I was caught for having false papers. Of course, I was doing something else also, but they never found out about that.'

None of the others answered him, none of the others introduced himself. The helpers of robbers felt they were too lofty to speak to a common criminal. Dr Rabinovich, who didn't even want to speak to the others, looked at the new man scornfully. As if those bankers' flunkies weren't bad enough, to throw in a person like this!

But Pokorny was undaunted by their silence. 'You can't imagine what it was like, six months of solitary, just going to Bredovska for hearings and sitting there in a bunker. I never heard a single word the whole time, only people yelling. So talk to me, for goodness' sake, tell me who you are and where we're going!'

For a while nobody answered. Then one of the eleven began to speak. He explained what important positions they had all had, and how they had been protected, and that they were sending them away only now, to the fortress town, no doubt, where they would have important work to do.

He suddenly paused, for he realised that this one was also going with them. If such a person was being sent with them, then they must be going to the East, for there'd be no place for such a person in the fortress town. They'd never have released him from prison if they hadn't been preparing a worse fate for him. And that same fate must be awaiting them as well. But perhaps they were going to the ghetto, after all. They'd drop them off there and send Pokorny to the East by the next transport.

Otto Pokorny didn't notice the pause and began to ask questions: What was the news from the front? What were the chances that the Germans would lose the war soon? Then everyone began to speak, except Rabinovich. They told Pokorny about German losses on the eastern front, about Italy's capitulation, about the destruction of German cities. The news was encouraging. They gave the news eagerly, providing details and anecdotes. It was as if they had become aware of Pokorny's presence only then and were accepting him as part of their group.

In prison Pokorny had received only rotten vegetables and watery soup for meals and his stomach was contracting with hunger. Now that the car was sealed, they all began to eat ravenously. They didn't have to be afraid that someone might burst in. They had plenty of food with them and warm clothing. They even had cigarettes. He would have liked to ask them for a piece of bread, but he was sure they wouldn't share it with him; the food was for themselves and their children.

The waiting went on endlessly. But now there was enough

light in the car. One of them looked at his watch, which they hadn't taken from him in their haste, and said that it was ten o'clock. At eleven the train began to move.

They moved along slowly, but couldn't figure out in what direction. All they could hear was the clacking of the buffers. Perhaps they were rolling through fields where people were working, or passing by factories where people were standing at machines. Perhaps they were going by little towns where women were standing in queues with their shopping baskets, or roadside taverns where farmers were idling at the bar drinking bitter beer. They didn't know where they were going and they were afraid to touch the window boards. Their escorts were travelling in a better carriage somewhere, maybe the very next one, and looking out of the window.

The freight train came to a stop at the end of a line far from a station. They stood there for a long time and could hear carriages being uncoupled: their carriage and that of their escorts were probably being attached to another train. Again an endless wait. Outside, they could hear the voices of railway men – they were still in their native country.

It was almost evening when the new train began to move. It was a goods train again – they could tell by the clacking of the buffers. It moved along as slowly as the previous one. At night they remained standing on a side line somewhere. They could feel the two carriages being uncoupled. All night their carriage stood at an unknown station. They were unable to sleep, because it was almost impossible to breathe in their boarded-up car. A little air came in through the cracks and they took turns standing near them and lifting the children towards them.

The night passed thus in uncertainty. The former helpers

of robbers had long since lost their self-importance. Now they were friendly to Pokorny – one of them even gave him a slice of bread. The worst thing was the lack of water. Nobody had thought to bring a thermos. There had been a small reserve of water in the lavatory, but that was soon exhausted. The children cried, 'Drink! Water!' That was when those who had continued to have the highest hopes finally understood that they had been sold down the river and that only the smallest speck of hope remained. That tiny snippet of hope was the fortress town. Earlier they had been afraid of it. The very thought of going there had been enough to evoke dread and fear of the transports. Now they dreamed of it as of the Promised Land, where they would meet their friends and relatives, where they would be among their own people and would share the same fate with them. They no longer dreamed of enjoying higher privileges. They would be happy with any work whatsoever.

In the morning their carriage began to move again. Their thirst was becoming unbearable. But even worse was the uncertainty about where they were being taken. None of them dared try to widen the crack in the window boards and look out. Only Pokorny was willing to give it a try. Nothing daunted him. He had come from prison. He knew his fate was sealed, he knew he had nothing to lose. He offered to find out where they were. It was the right moment – the SS guards were still asleep. Surely they had been fortifying themselves with liquor at some tavern during the night.

If the SS men were to discover that someone was looking out through a crack they would punish everyone, not just the offender. That was their method of punishment. All were tormented by the lack of air and by thirst. They watched with passive approval as Pokorny set to work.

With a borrowed knife he managed to widen a crack. Everyone waited impatiently to hear what he could see.

'A field,' Pokorny announced. 'Just a field and a village in the distance. It's impossible to guess where we actually are. Meadows,' he continued as the train made its way through the countryside, 'a pond with willows, plains, mountains in the distance.'

He spoke as if he were broadcasting news, slowly and distinctly. But people weren't satisfied.

'Are we in Germany?' one of them asked.

'No,' answered Pokorny without turning, continuing to peer through the crack, 'fields and meadows and ponds like these are found only in Bohemia.'

They were disappointed. They had been travelling so long and they still hadn't arrived at the fortress town. They wouldn't be able to endure it, they would choke on the bad air, they would die of thirst. Yet their train must be going somewhere! Perhaps they were just going around and around, perhaps their captors were waiting for them to suffocate.

'Nothing,' continued Pokorny, 'just fields, meadows, gardens and villages.'

Suddenly he cried out. 'A transmitter,' and he jumped away from the crack. He thought he had heard a voice in the adjacent carriage.

A transmitter. There were only two in Bohemia. One was on the way to the fortress town. Yes, everything was going to be all right, they were going in the right direction. Another little snippet of hope had appeared. Soon they'd be in the fortress town and their suffering would end. Someone would take care of them there and give them something to drink.

They rejoiced in a steel structure standing in the middle of a field. Earlier they had hated everything that served those others. They weren't allowed to have radios at home, but they had to listen to the loudspeakers attached to street lamps broadcasting news of victories, boat sinkings, executions. The news was always followed by the same raucous patriotic songs. Lately the loudspeakers had been talking about the savage hordes and the strength of the Reich, and the patriotic songs were even noisier – clearly they were trying to dispel fear. People avoided those particular lamp-posts, but they couldn't help hearing the ear-piercing voices.

The transmitter was a good sign. They weren't in a foreign country yet. They were still home.

The train continued its journey the whole day. They should have been in the fortress town long ago. Pokorny didn't dare look out. Their supplies of food were running low, but they weren't hungry. They just wanted to drink. They didn't speak; even the children were quiet.

When at last the train stopped during the night, they sensed they were in a foreign country. The door of the carriage opened abruptly, the blue light of a torch gleamed, an SS man handed them a canteen of water. A drop like that was to suffice for them all! They gave a little drink to the children, and the others were barely able to wet their lips. Their thirst was even more terrible after that. Their carriage and that of the SS men were once again uncoupled. They were standing far from a station. Even when Pokorny looked through the crack he could only see outlines of freight cars. But he had travelled about the world often before the war and he had a way of figuring out the names of towns almost by smell.

'Dresden,' he said. 'I'm sure it's Dresden.'

Now they knew they were in a foreign country. They might have hoped they were being sent to a work camp, but none of them besides Pokorny was capable of heavy labour. So they were probably being taken to the East. Now they were overcome with terror, though they were exhausted and weak with thirst.

During the whole journey, day and night, Rabinovich kept silent, repeating prayers to himself, though they would be of no avail to him as a blasphemer. He paid no attention to the talk of the others, he didn't even take in his sons' cries or his wife's moans. He sat on his bench as if he were already dead, as if they had put a shroud over him and were preparing his coffin.

But he gave a start when he heard the word 'Dresden'. He was the only one in the carriage who knew what the word 'East' really meant. Hadn't the head of the Central Bureau often spoken about people going up the chimney in smoke those times he was in a good mood, those times he used to pat him on the back and say, 'Good boy,' as if he were a dog?

They were going to their deaths, it was clear, even he, even his family. Nobody could save them any longer. Everything had been planned and figured out long before. How the head of the Central Bureau must be laughing now! That's why he had been so kind to him the last time he had met him. All the others sitting in this car, and he as well, had made a pact with the devil, and now the devil had come for their lives. Only one of them, that thirteenth one the troopers had brought in in chains, only he had nothing in common with the devil; he was fighting against him, in fact. That man was one of the legendary thirty-six Just

Men and he would share their fate with them. It was good that a Just Man would be in their midst. He would speak for them at the hour of their death.

TWENTY-ONE

THE COUNTRY INSULTINGLY called the Protectorate was a small country with small joys and pleasures. Because people had to go on living, because they were closed in on all sides, restricted, conscripted, arrested and killed according to the whims of their conquerors, people looked for small comforts.

Trips by bike or train to nearby places replaced travel abroad. Rides on little sightseeing boats evoked memories of ocean liners.

The steamboat had been rented by one of the ministries, and Jan Krulis worked for the Historic Preservation Department under its jurisdiction. He was able to meet his contact inconspicuously on the boat. Nobody noticed their casual conversation in the midst of the din, the commotion and the blaring music.

They set sail early in the morning; the city was just waking up. They shoved off from a little wooden bridge. The river was quiet, meandering around the islands, splashing at the weirs, playing over the boating pools as if the invaders with fifes and drums and horsetails didn't exist. It laughed, it was timeless, and it had a woman's name. People tamed it with floodgates, locks, weirs and bridges. It changed its face a thousand times.

The boat crossed the river to drift towards the first lock, at the end of which rose a statue of a lovely slender young girl. She was meant to represent the river surrounded by its tributaries. It was a portrait of the river in her youth, twisting through meadows, wandering past high cliffs and deep woods, mirroring castles as she flowed, filling and turning mill wheels. Statues made by foreign hands stood on the stone bridge that spanned her, unfriendly ones, put there by previous invaders. From below they seemed even more grotesque, more convoluted. Then she encountered other statues at the newer bridges, statues that spoke of hope, statues celebrating the end of bondage. They sported wings, as if they wanted to fly for victory's sake. On yet another bridge stood several substantial statues with solid limbs that seemed to be growing out of the ground, firmly rooted in pedestals one at each end of the bridge.

Divided into two parts, the city looked out at the river from old palaces and from new houses decorated with little turrets and bay windows, from warehouses, tenement houses and little cottages that had once been part of a village. At a narrow inlet the boat touched the green banks of a big park. Now it was just about to leave the city.

The people on the boat felt happy and contented. Life in the bureaus they worked for was grey, full of fear and anxiety. Although the bureaus had proud names, they were typing pools, do-nothing offices. The new masters seemed to keep them there out of whim. On the boat, people could float through the city and they didn't have to listen to commands in a foreign language. Everything seemed the same as it had ever been – the smoke from bad coal rising from the chimney, the regular vibrations of the engines, the waves radiating to the shore and then beating against the banks, the roofed bow for those who liked shade and benches at the stern for those who preferred sun. The boat's slow passage was calming; when the engines were turned off in the locks, the music sounded even louder. The countryside they passed was familiar to everyone; one man on board could actually name every little hill and identify practically every cottage.

During their break, as the musicians rested with half litres of weak and bitter beer, volunteers went around selling raffle tickets. The raffle was a big deal – one could win a toothbrush, a wooden doll or a metal ashtray.

Krulis's contact had bad news. The organisation had been exposed, its cover blown. People connected to it, even remotely, had to be warned quickly. The two spoke together quietly. Nobody heard them, thanks to an amateur singer who was singing 'Crinoline' as they spoke. She was obliged to repeat the refrain of that popular song several times, and then to sing an encore, another well-known song: 'Cricket the Musician'. Neither 'Crinoline' nor 'Cricket' had anything to do with the life people were leading, but these songs were still better than the raucous patriotic songs accompanying the news broadcasts from the Leader's headquarters.

Krulis's companion wanted to get off inconspicuously at the first stop – the game park and castle – to try to make arrangements and save whomever he could as quickly as possible.

Everyone disembarked, glad to be able to walk around a bit and look at the castle. Krulis took out a piece of bread and skim cheese and lay down in the grass. The castle didn't interest him. He knew it from the old days.

Barges loaded with goods sailed down the river, heading for the Reich. Every few minutes sirens went off, but they were harmless, familiar sirens; their sound didn't alarm anybody. Everything was peaceful and friendly; it was as if the river and its surroundings knew nothing about the war. People in the park were laughing, exchanging funny stories, singing. It was a perfectly ordinary outing. Yet a heavy shadow loomed over the people's merriment. They had created that carefree world as a defence.

They were defending themselves against death, each in his own way. The invaders rejoiced in death. They celebrated it in their patriotic songs. It was their best friend. But those who had fallen under their rule wanted to live.

Jan Krulis looked out at the countryside. Meadows and fields stretched into the distance. Smoke rose from cottage chimneys. The river, flowing gently and peacefully, belonged to this countryside. It hadn't yet joined the larger river that would rush through ravines to a foreign land. It still carried the water of its own tributaries with women's names, filled with goodness and kindness.

As he lay there above the river, he reflected on his fate. He knew that one of these days death would find him, too. It would come to him in the guise of men wearing trench coats and green tufted hats. Then the countryside would dim and take on the darkness of a bunker. It would die, but just for him. Its hills and mountains, its fields and meadows, its forests and rivers would live on. Let them burn it to the ground, let them ravish its fields and transform its meadows into swamps. Grass would still grow out of the ashes, the earth would absorb the water, and people would plough its fields once again. They could never conquer it.

Adela and Greta. Once he had made the decision to fight, he shouldn't have taken on that responsibility. What would happen to Adela and Greta when they arrested him? They couldn't stay too long at the Javureks', and even if they could, who would bring them food? He'd already made another arrangement, and had told the Javureks about the contact, but now that the organisation's cover was blown, the contact was blown as well. Who knows, he might have been followed in recent days. If he had been, then of course they would know about the Javureks.

People were returning to the boat and Krulis went back with them. He'd stay on the boat until they reached the vineyard town stop and then he'd decide. His friend had recommended that he slip away from the day trippers there, get on a train and return to Prague. It would be easy to do – many people who weren't interested in the raffle and didn't want to waste too much time on the long voyage home would surely be doing the same thing. He wasn't connected with any group and nobody would notice his absence.

But did it make sense to go back by train? If they were after him, he might gain a few hours that way before they arrested him. But he still had to return to his apartment to try to destroy any evidence they might find. He could hope that they weren't on to him yet and weren't waiting for him at his apartment. Then he could quickly try to change his name and address. He decided to go back by boat. It might actually be less dangerous, because at railway stations there were often searches for travellers who were smuggling provisions. But who would bother with trippers returning to the city?

They landed at the shore and climbed a steep path all the way up to the castle, surrounded by gardens and parks.

They had ordered a modest lunch for their group at the castle restaurant – they could pay with their food coupons. They would even be allowed wine, but of course only two glasses. But when they arrived at the restaurant they were sorry they hadn't chosen some ordinary restaurant in town. There in the glassed-in terrace offering views of the river and the whole countryside were *they*: the whole terrace was theirs. They ate and drank, ordering vintage wines and rare foods, for no rules applied to them and they had as many coupons as they wanted. They sat there all worked up with alcohol, some in uniforms and others in plain clothes. Surely they hadn't come by boat or train but in their own cars. Among them was a single Czech, but he spoke German. The trippers recognised him. He was a well-known comedian who sang scurrilous songs on the radio about Jews who were moving out, who were not allowed to ride the buses: about columnists who'd crow when the Reich was victorious but who would crawl on their knees afterwards. They must have taken him along as a clown, the after-dinner entertainment. Meanwhile, he sang their rowdy and sentimental songs along with them, making sure that his voice rang out, that it wasn't lost in the drunken din.

The waiters quickly led the trippers to a special dining room off to the side. The distinguished guests mustn't be disturbed, the subhumans had no right to stare at them. From the room assigned to them they could see neither the river nor the city; their windows looked out on a courtyard. They could hear the cries of the revellers out on the terrace only faintly. The waiters passed out watery soup, meat rissoles with old potatoes and, for dessert, a pudding made without milk. That was their lunch – they didn't need too many coupons for it.

After lunch Krulis sat down on a bench overlooking the river. After a short while, an older man sat down next to him, obviously wanting to talk. Finally he took the plunge.

'Are you from Prague?' he asked.

He didn't wait for an answer, but continued: 'This used

to be a nice town, a rich one. The local people hardly knew what to do with their money. And now we're just a hop and a skip from the border. So that means they can get here from that Reich of theirs very easily, and get to the capital too. They booze here and stuff their faces and we're supposed to look at them. Well, it's probably the same in Prague, but it's not so obvious there, right?'

Krulis was silent. He could no longer look peacefully at the countryside. And maybe this was the shadow following him. No, the man didn't look the type. He just felt like talking and nobody could overhear from here.

'Aren't you afraid?' Krulis asked him.

'Oh, I know people, I just have to take one look. I'm a dowser, you see. I've discovered all the wells around here. The thing about water, you know, is you have to be truthful to find it. Water knows only the truth. That's what a person learns from water. In some places the water is very deep, because it's hiding from human deceitfulness. Water is clean and people make it dirty. This river used to be clean, and look what they've done to it. Water doesn't want to rise to the surface and be among people. I have to come with the rod and persuade it. People in this part of the country need water a lot. Everything grows here. I tell it the truth, that it is time for it to come out and be helpful, even though it means getting dirty, because people need to eat. The water listens to what I tell it, and it comes out. But now my conscience is bothering me, because I've also looked for it in the part of the country that now belongs to the Reich. So thanks to me the water has to help those thieves. But water knows the truth and one of these days it'll show them.'

'Thank you,' Krulis said in parting. 'You are so right about the water. I've got to go now.'

'Good luck. We'll get them, everything will turn out well. They're already on the run, and they'll have to get out of here, too.'

The trippers returned to the boat in groups. Krulis won a pair of cuff links in the raffle.

They sailed against the current for quite a while. Dusk was falling quietly. People dozed off and lovers embraced. Finally the boat landed. The trippers got off carefully and crossed the little bridge to the shore. They were happy to be home, happy to have enjoyed a nice day. It was already dark, and only the river glistened. But when Krulis got off, the light of blue torches suddenly glared in his eyes.

Two men in trench coats stepped up, one in front of him and one behind him. Their guns were obviously drawn although Krulis couldn't see them.

'Come with us,' they barked in a foreign language.

There had certainly been a spy on the boat.

TWENTY-TWO

IN THE MIDDLE OF THE NIGHT someone banged loudly at the Javureks' door. You could hear the sound all through the building. People came running out of apartments in their night clothes. But the Javureks didn't open their door. First they quickly took care of Adela and Greta. They roused the sleepy little girls out of bed, rushed them into the cubbyhole, threw their things in after them, and then placed the cupboard in front of the cubby entrance. In the midst of the din created by the night visitors, nobody could hear what was going on in the apartment.

As soon as Mr Javurek opened his door, everything happened quickly. Adela and Greta heard the stamping of heavy boots, the hubbub and clatter, the yelling in a foreign language. Then they heard the door of the apartment bang shut and the lock click, and it was quiet again. Adela and Greta were left alone in the cubbyhole, with the cupboard blocking the entrance. They knew they mustn't stay in the apartment, because you-know-who would come again to search through everything and confiscate anything of any value. They must get out of the apartment that very night, before it was too late.

First they must move the cupboard – that would be hard work. But if they both leaned against it they would surely manage to do it. They also knew how to unlock the apartment, for they knew the drawer where the extra key was kept. They'd wait until the house quieted down. The neighbours would wonder at the smallest sound coming out of the apartment. They might think that an animal had been left behind, a dog or a cat, and they'd call in a locksmith.

They sat in the dark for a long time, waiting for people to go back to bed and to stop trying to figure out why the Javureks had been arrested. Finally it seemed to them that everything had calmed down. People would sleep heavily after so much excitement. Carefully they nudged the cupboard away, afraid of every small sound. When they managed to get out into the kitchen they listened for a while – was everything quiet? Only then did they turn on the light. They could turn on the light because the windows were completely blacked out and not a single ray of light would escape. Mr Javurek was an expert at this – he blacked out the windows for all the other tenants as well.

Now that they could see, they began to get dressed and they discussed what they should take with them. They couldn't take too much, and it had to be food. They didn't know where to go and who in the city might take them in during the night. But if they had a little food with them, that would definitely be better. Last week Uncle Jan had brought them a little jar of lard and they would take some of the Javureks' bread – it would go to waste in any event. Adela had a little knapsack. They placed the food in it. Now they only had to make their way out of the building.

They found the key to the apartment in the drawer and the house key hanging on a hook next to the keys to the basement and the attic. They must lock the apartment quietly – that would be easy. Mr Javurek had oiled the lock not long ago. It wouldn't squeak. They'd have more trouble with the big house key. That one was hard to open. But once they were out in the dark nobody could catch them.

And they wouldn't have to lock the house behind them – people would think you-know-who left it because they were in such a hurry.

They went down the stairs carefully, step by step. And at the front door a surprise was waiting for them: someone had forgotten to lock the door. Now everything was very easy. They slipped out of the door so quietly that not the tiniest sound could be heard.

It was no longer completely dark. They could distinguish the outlines of buildings, as they walked along the pavement. Without realising it, they headed for the centre of town, towards their parents' apartment. It was a long walk. Finally they crossed a bridge and found themselves in a street they knew very well. But they couldn't return to their old apartment – new tenants were living there now, they knew that. Fatigue began to overcome them. They sat down in the little park just across from their old apartment. They had played in that little park all their lives, they knew every bush in it. It reminded them of home. They sat there huddled together and they shivered with cold. Suddenly a figure loomed over them – a policeman! They wanted to run away, but their feet would not obey them.

The policeman looked them over carefully. They were obviously not runaways, they were too neat and well dressed for that. He figured they had come to town by train, had lost their way, and now couldn't find the house they had been sent to. The railway station wasn't far from there.

He questioned them gently at first: 'Where are you from, little girls? What are your names and where do you live?'

Adela and Greta were silent. A policeman was a terrifying person. Everybody had warned them about policemen.

'What's the matter – don't you know how to talk? You're old enough to know better. Hurry up, then, you're from the country, right, and your mother and father sent you here to visit your aunt. And you've lost your way. Isn't that right?'

Adela and Greta were still silent.

The policeman didn't know what to do with them. He yelled at them sharply: 'Come with me.'

Adela and Greta stood up meekly and followed, one on each side. He took them to the police station. There all the policemen questioned them, but Adela and Greta continued to be as silent as the grave.

'Let them sleep here and the sergeant can speak with them in the morning,' decided the policeman who had found them.

They took them to a dirty, repulsive cell with bunks and threw them some reeking blankets. Adela and Greta didn't mind – they had been through so much already.

In the morning a policeman took them to the sergeant, who began to question them. Adela and Greta continued to be silent.

'Maybe they're deaf and dumb,' said the policeman.

The sergeant slammed his revolver down on the table so suddenly that Adela and Greta couldn't see it coming. They jumped.

'No, they're not,' said the sergeant. 'Something else is going on here. Look through their knapsack. Maybe we'll find something there.'

The policeman took out the jar of lard, the hunk of bread and two keys.

'What apartment are these keys for?'

Adela and Greta kept silent.

'We're not going to torture children here,' said the sergeant, ending the interrogation.

'I know who they are. They're little Jews who ran away from the transport or from some hiding place. This isn't our business. Give them something to eat and take them to the station at Josefovska Street. They're authorised to deal with such things there. You're off duty now, so let Sochor take them there.'

The police station at Josefovska was a branch of the Gestapo dealing with Jewish affairs. That's where they brought people who were then handed over to the Gestapo. The policemen there were brutal, obedient to their masters, and corpulent because they received special rations.

The children were held at the station until it was almost noon. No one was allowed to question them – that was the Gestapo's job. The policemen jeered at them, using bad language, words the children had never heard in their lives. Then they assigned a policeman to take them to the Gestapo, and pushed them out of the door roughly. The policeman walked especially fast, in order to torment them. He saw that they were dead tired.

Adela and Greta knew where they were taking them. Gestapo was a terrible word.

They had to stand in the waiting room for a long time with their faces to the wall. They weren't allowed to sit on the bench. The guard paid no attention to them.

'They're going to ask who was hiding us, and there's the death penalty for that,' whispered Adela. She knew a great deal already. 'You mustn't answer when they ask you.'

'But what if they beat me?'

'You have to stand it! We'll each sing a different song to ourselves. Which one do you want?'

'I'll take "Andulka the Goose Girl".'

'Then I'll take "The lime tree was burning".'

The guard heard their voices and snapped at them: 'Shut up. You're not in Hebrew school here!'

Adela and Greta fell silent again. They looked at the white wall. They were terribly tired.

Finally they were called into the office of the investigating officer for Jewish affairs. He had little work to do these days, because almost all the Jews had been deported from the city in the transports.

Interrogating children was ridiculous, but that wasn't the point. They'd be handed over to the Central Bureau in any case. They'd deal with them there. But first he must get them to tell the address of the people who had been hiding them – that was the important thing. They couldn't have escaped from a transport, because there hadn't been any transports for quite a long time. A ridiculous job, but an easy one. They would surely talk the moment he began to terrorise them.

He addressed them quietly at first. There was no need to scare them right from the start. 'Well, what are your names?'

They were silent.

'Will you answer or not?'

They understood that now they must speak.

They answered respectfully, 'Adela and Greta Roubicek.'

'Where are your parents?'

'Nowhere,' answered Adela. 'They died.'

'And where do you live?'

'Nowhere,' claimed Adela.

The Gestapo man began to grow angry. The interrogation would not be as easy as he had imagined. He turned to Greta.

'Why are you standing there like a dummy? Tell me where you live.'

'Nowhere,' answered Greta as well.

The Gestapo man was beginning to lose his temper. 'I'll get it out of you, you little Jew girls. Hurry up and tell me where you were hiding.'

'In the forest,' said Adela.

'In the forest,' repeated Greta like an echo.

Now the Gestapo man began screaming: 'What apartment are those keys on the table from? Answer quickly: name, district, street!'

'We don't know.' Adela shook her head.

'I'll get it out of your thick skulls!' The Gestapo man threatened them with his outstretched hand, which was holding the keys.

'You'd better tell me who was hiding you: name and address. Who helped you? Who got you food, and where did they get it?' He turned to the older one, to Adela.

'Nobody,' said Adela. 'We were hiding in the forest. We ate mushrooms, blueberries, raspberries and strawberries, and things like that.'

'Shut your mouth, you Jewish whore!' shrieked the Gestapo man, and with a swift movement he struck her in the temple with the keys which he still held in his hand. The blood ran down Adela's face. 'Are you going to talk? What apartment are those keys from? Who gave you the lard and bread?'

'I don't know.' Adela's voice quavered. The tears mixed together with the blood.

> The lime tree was burning and burning
> And 'neath it the maiden was turning . . .

'Now you! Come over here!' The Gestapo man dragged Greta over. 'Maybe you'll do better.'

'I don't remember anything,' said Greta. 'I've lost my memory.'

The hand with the keys struck Greta in the teeth. Blood ran from her gums. The Gestapo man had knocked out an incisor.

> Andulka, wake up, it's day.
> Your geese are all running away . . .

Now she wouldn't even be able to speak properly.

The next blow only grazed Adela; the Gestapo man's hand slipped.

'Where were you hiding?'

'In the forest,' said Adela.

Greta repeated after her with difficulty: 'In the forest,' and the blood ran from her mouth.

> The sparks were falling over her,
> The young men wept and cried for her.

Greta forced herself to sing another verse.

> The geese are all eating the hay.
> Come quickly, chase them away.

They're making a nice mess of my office, thought the Gestapo man. I should have questioned them in the bunker.

He controlled his fury. Now he dealt with them coldly. He had to get the addresses out of the children. He calculated each blow with the keys in such a way as to produce the maximum amount of pain, in order to break Adela and Greta.

'In the forest,' said Adela, and Greta repeated after her, 'In the forest.'

> Why are you weeping and crying for me?
> There are other girls just like me,
> I'm not the only one, don't you see,
> The world is full of girls just like me.

After Adela, Greta chimed in with her chosen song:

> I would go to chase them away
> But what would my master say?
> I am afraid he will shout
> To hear that I let them out.

Again the Gestapo man lost his temper. He beat them savagely with the keys.

The little girls were almost unconscious, but still they sang 'Andulka the Goose Girl' and 'The lime tree was burning'. These were songs they had learned when they still went to school. Now they used them to defend themselves.

'The addresses!' yelled the Gestapo man.

But there were no addresses. Only pain, blood and darkness. They fainted. The Gestapo man struck them with the keys and kicked them with his boots.

The Soviet Army rolled out of the East from the plains of Stalingrad, from Gumrak and Pitomnik, from Rostov and the Don basin, from Kharkov and Kiev and Velikiye Luki with tanks, Panzers, rocket launchers, artillery. Unstoppable, it advanced, and it broke, crushed and ground the once proud Wehrmacht, all dressed in its finery and armed by the whole of Europe, into the snow. The murderous army fled to the West with its crew of troopers, generals in fancy uniforms, airmen without aeroplanes, tank drivers without tanks, and along the way they still slaughtered, they still burned down villages, blew up factories, mines and fortifications. They left behind only blood, decay and scorched earth, discarding their plunder of rugs, icons and furs.

And at their heels marched the Soviet Army, bringing freedom first to its own people and then to other nations. It crossed the boundaries and continued to fight its way through. It routed the newly mobilised regiments called back from the western front. It crushed the Leader's Elite Guard, who were desperately trying to hold the line, because only now did they realise they would have to pay for their criminal deeds. The army rolled forward steadily to the West, greeted by laughter and flowers in the liberated lands. Then they entered the land whose Leader kept promising victory, even at the last moment.

Cities turned to ashes. One hundred thousand big guns thundered out day and night in the capital city of the Reich. They destroyed houses, they blew up long-darkened street lights. The victorious Soviet Army made its way through the ruins, breaking down the furious resistance. It reached the concrete bunker, the last hiding place of the bloody madman. The waters of the river flooded the underground passageways, and tens of thousands died within, the wounded, women, children. The flag with the hammer and sickle flew from the ruins of the Reichstag, and the flags once accompanied by fifes and drums and horsetails now fell to the dust at the feet of the victors. They lay in the dirt and mud and mire of the thousand-year Reich. The proud statues that lined the Alley of Triumph collapsed and their broken limbs lay on the ground. The Arch of Triumph caved in. The people who survived crept by the fallen, gaping heads and looked down at the ground. But the ground was a desert of stone. Nothing grew on it. It was dead under its cover of dust and rubble.

The bloodstained keys remained on the table. The keys were mute. Even the blood couldn't make them speak. Adela and Greta lay on the ground. Their lips still seemed to be moving.

'In the forest,' Adela was saying.

'In the forest,' Greta was repeating.

Nearby, just a few steps away, murmured the forest. Trees were growing out of seedlings, casting roots in the ground, holding fast against storms, against whirlwinds, against thunder and lightning. Insects fell upon the trees and conquered them. But blackberry brambles and blueberries began to sprout at their bases. Pine needles fertilised the ground so that life would spring up even after their death. When the fire overcame them, they twisted and turned, their ashes fell to the ground, and the forest grew out of the ashes even more radiantly green. Everything flourished in the forest – mushrooms, raspberries, strawberries, blueberries and blackberries, shade and moisture and even warmth that came when its trees were felled and split into firewood and the countryside was redolent with its smoke.

The trees kept growing, victorious and deathless. They held firm, they served, and when they were forced to die they died standing up. They weren't engraved on memory in cold stone, to threaten or remind. They were the life that overpowers death.

‘In the forest,’ whispered Adela and Greta, dying. They were there in the forest at the hour of death.